JEN TRINH

Crushing on You

This novel is entirely a work of fiction. The names, characters and incidents portrayed in it are the work of the author's imagination. Any resemblance to actual persons, living or dead, events or localities is entirely coincidental.

First edition

Cover art by Jia Liu

This book was professionally typeset on Reedsy. Find out more at reedsy.com

Contents

Dedication

This book is dedicated to all of the friends out there who make relationships possible...

...to my parents and my family, for their relentless love and support...

...and to my husband, the greatest bub of all time (GBOAT).

Preface

You guys…

There's some graphic sex in this book.

It's a lady in the streets, freak in the sheets.

I know it might be kinda shocking, given the beautifully illustrated cover, but that's one of the great things about self-publishing—you don't have to compromise on your vision!

You can have a cute and pretty cover instead of a photo-realistic image of two people in a hot and heavy embrace.

You can write about an intimate moment between two people's lives, and not have to censor either character's thoughts, or use euphemism where it doesn't make sense to.

You can write with medium-good style (forgive me, it's my first time!), but still get a touching story out there.

Yes, there is sex. There's flirtatious foreplay and wordplay, and maybe some things that you won't understand until you get older (put this book down, child!). But there's a lot more than that, too.

This book is about all of the gritty details in people's lives that shape who they are, and the relationships that they share. But it's also fun and frivolous in the way that romance novels often are, with characters who are a *bit* unrealistically attractive, and perhaps slightly over-primed for happy endings.

It's probably not going to win any literary awards, and that's fine—I'm proud of it anyway. And even though it's not perfect, I know that I will get better at it with time.

This book draws a lot from my own personal experience, but please don't be fooled—it's not about me, nor is it about you, nor any of my family members or friends. It's a story that I completely made up in my head, after decades of reading and reading and reading.

And feeling.

And learning.

And growing.

This is my first book, and I'm so thrilled that you've picked it up.

I hope you're thrilled, too!

A few additional notes:

This book is written from the first-person perspective of each of the two main characters, Anna and Ian. I alternate between their chapters, so for narrative continuity, there are a few times when events that occur concurrently are addressed out of order (i.e., something that happened in a previous chapter is addressed later by the other character in their next chapter).

There's a decent amount of climbing in the book, especially in the second half. I tried to explain most of the terms, but if you aren't a climber (yet), you might want to look online for a climbing terminology guide.

There's also a lot of music in the book. I wanted to give readers a closer connection to Anna's character, so check out the Crushing on You companion playlist on Spotify. You can find it through my website (jentrinhwrites.com).

Prologue

-Anna-

From the first few seconds of a song, I can usually tell if it's going to be a *groover* or a *hoover*.

Hoovers are simple. They suck. Three seconds in and I press the skip button.

But *groovers*...no matter how fast or slow the song is, groovers make me want to dance. *Need* to dance. They put me under a spell, force my body to sway, and turn my head into a slow wobbling vase on the pedestal of my neck. My eyes drift closed and my body becomes one giant sound vessel, quivering with anticipation for the next note and the next. And when the song ends and I awaken from my trance, I'm a woman possessed, rabid with music, and I can't rest until I've passed the feeling on to someone else.

I need to infect you with my earworms.

And that, my dear hosts, is why I blog about music and create playlists. Why it's my dream to become a music journalist.

So you can imagine how stupid psyched I was when I'd learned that a small music news site had actually read one of my pieces, and (holy shit!) that they even wanted to *buy* it. Or how incredibly rich I felt when that money actually hit the bank.

I was $80 closer to realizing my dream.

BOOYAH! *Take that*, parents! *Suck it*, step-dad! Anna Tang's gonna make it on her own!

To celebrate, my boyfriend Asher took me to a ritzy sushi restaurant in Williamsburg. We'd just demolished a huge seven course meal (with sake pairing!), featuring a delicate matsutake mushroom broth, a sweet and savory unagi omelet, and a rainbow of raw fish slices that melted like butter on our tongues. I barely had room for dessert, molten black honey mochi with roasted matcha ice cream...but of course I ate it. It was *ice cream*.

All in all, it probably cost a fortune, way more than what I'd been paid for my piece, but we were celebrating the *significance* of my accomplishment, not its fair market value. Besides, Asher came from money—he wouldn't care.

Tall and lean, with wavy chestnut hair and expressive brown eyes, he was cute and approachable, like the boy next door. He acted like a boy sometimes, too, like just then when he sat back in his chair and belched, long and loud. I wrinkled my nose.

"*Excuse me.*" He lightly beat his chest and emitted a series of smaller burps. "Wow, I'm *so full*. Do you want the rest of my ice cream?"

My eyes lit up at the sight of the large spoon of ice cream still on his dessert plate. The mind was willing, but the flesh...ah, screw it. Stomachs were elastic for a reason, and that reason was dessert. I *ahhh*-ed and he slipped the spoon into my mouth, business end first.

"Bathroom, be right back." He leaned down to kiss my

2

temple before taking off towards the restroom.

On his way there, he nodded at a handsome older Chinese woman who was walking towards me. Everything about her screamed well-off Asian mom: the dark blue wool cardigan and black silk pants, short permed hair, and of course, oversized designer handbag. My eyes nearly slid past her, but snagged when *her* eyes widened, openly staring at me as she walked by. I didn't recognize her (thank goodness! Not family!), so I flashed her a polite smile before glancing around at the other patrons and licking the last of the ice cream off the spoon.

The restaurant was cozy and stylish, softly illuminated with flickering candles and pale yellow lanterns, the live flames faintly reflecting off the dark wooden furniture and matching wall panels. A large, fully-stocked bar occupied nearly half of the restaurant, and was surrounded by a gaggle of women, all of whom were decked out in little black dresses and flashy penis jewelry. In their midst stood a very drunk and very loud bride-to-be, complete with sash and tiara.

Behind me was the older Chinese woman's family. I tried not to listen to their conversation, but it was hard to ignore them when Asher wasn't there to distract me from their loud Mandarin. Besides, they were clearly talking about *me*.

"That Chinese girl behind you is very pretty," said the older woman. "She has a very good face."

"*Shhh, Ma,* what if she can understand you?" whispered her son.

"Then let her. She knows she's pretty, this isn't news to her." I smiled. *Damn straight.*

"*Ma,* please. Just eat more sushi. *Ba,* you too."

"Eh, it's too salty. I just want dessert," said the father.

3

"*Ba*, you shouldn't eat so many sweets. You already had two donuts today. Too much sugar is bad for you."

The dad scoffed. "A little extra is okay sometimes." I silently agreed with him and placed the sparkling clean ice cream spoon back down on Asher's plate.

The mom continued, "You should talk to her. She might make a good wife for you." I quietly snickered. Whoever he was, there was no way I'd be good, or a wife, to him.

"*Ma!* Stop that. *Ba.* Here, just eat..." Geez, especially when he was such a *nag*.

Asher rematerialized and sat back down, grinning, his long legs bouncing up and down beneath the table. "So, did you enjoy the meal?"

"Yeah, it was delicious. Thanks for bringing me here." I gave him my 10/10 post-food smile.

He pushed the empty plates aside and reached for my hand across the table, his legs still jackhammering underneath. "Anna...we've been together for three years now."

Oh shit. Mentions of romantic history or longevity always made my skin prickle. Those types of conversations usually didn't end well. "Yeah, it's been fun," I said, my face and tone carefully neutral.

"I...I've really enjoyed our time together, and I think we make a great couple. I mean, we both love music and dancing, both love having a good time. Whenever I look down from the stage and see you dancing there, I just...it always means a lot, to see how much you enjoy my music." He smiled sweetly, though his hands were slick with sweat.

I relaxed a little and smiled back. Music was my element. "It's easy to enjoy! Your band's music is fantastic." His electronic music band, Spice Dust, was actually pretty good.

I'd met Asher at one of their shows, where I'd been dancing in front of the stage, trying my damndest to seduce him. I'd succeeded, of course.

He squeezed my hand and finally stopped bouncing his legs. "Anna, I'm really glad that I found you, and I hope...ah..."

In one sudden motion, he stood up and got down on one knee in front of me, knocking over his chair and announcing the spectacle to the entire restaurant. He snapped open a blue velvet box to reveal a delicate, rose gold ring, twinkling with an assortment of little white diamonds. "Will you marry me?"

I froze, hands outstretched but too late to stop him. Had I heard him correctly? There was no way that I had. I'd told him dozens of times throughout our time together that I didn't want a family, didn't like being dependent or depended on, that there was no point in my getting married. It was an antiquated practice, and it hadn't worked out well for my mom nor anyone else in my family.

Yet somehow, here we were.

Dozens of pairs of eyes turned our way, and the restaurant fell quiet, awaiting my answer along with Asher. The only sounds were the bachelorette party loudly *awwing* and the older Chinese woman muttering, "He's not even half as handsome as you." Her son quietly shushed her again.

With a tight little smile, I whispered, "Stop joking around and get up. People are looking at us." Surely he was joking, right?

But his crestfallen expression...*oh no.*

"Anna...I'm serious."

Bile burned my throat, and I regretted every last bite of food from our meal. I tried to pull him up by his arms, but he wouldn't budge. "Get up, Asher," I whispered fiercely.

His eyes hardened, but he calmly pressed on. "Answer the question."

I shook my head and blinked away the moisture in my eyes. "Don't—I can't—*please just get up*," I begged.

The disappointment...no, the *devastation*...on his face. I turned away, unable to stand it. Without another word, he snapped the box shut, stood up, and walked out of the restaurant.

The girls in the bachelorette party all booed.

Numb and cold, I stared down at my empty plate, trying to process what had just happened. Conversation resumed, slow and uneasy, as I put my head in my hands and tuned out everything but my thoughts.

Why had he forced my hand that way? We'd been totally fine together as we were. We didn't need to get married. He fucking *knew* how I felt about marriage, and yet...why? Did he think that I was just playing hard to get? That I didn't know what I actually wanted? I'd told him, clear as day, that I was never going to get married. Yet somehow, after three years of dating, he hadn't listened.

And we lived together, so now...now I had to go home and face him, in private, assuming he'd gone straight home. *Fuck.*

I stood up to go.

Out of nowhere, the waitress appeared with the server book, her face carefully blank. "How was your dinner this evening?" she asked, placing the book on the table and beginning to clear away our plates.

FUCK. Asher had said that dinner was his treat. He'd been the one to pick the place, and *I* certainly couldn't afford it, not on my meager office admin salary. I grabbed the book and checked the bill. $267.43. That didn't even include tip. My poor, abused, low-limit credit card would almost certainly get declined for that amount.

"Ah...it was good." I reached into my purse, made a show of rummaging around, then gave her my credit card anyway. "I'm going to the bathroom, be right back." I needed to call Asher and tell him to get back here and pay.

The waitress sniffed and frowned, likely discerning hints of cheap nylon dress with afternotes of thrift store heels from my person. She took my card between her forefinger and thumb as if it were contaminated, then dropped it into the server book. I wasn't fooling anybody.

As she walked away, I escaped in the other direction, towards the bathroom. I hurried into an empty stall and nearly dropped my phone into the toilet in my rush to call Asher. *Breathe.* The phone rang and rang, but he didn't pick up. I tried twice more, until my call went straight to voicemail.

What to do what to do what to do?

I rubbed my temples, the beginnings of a massive headache brewing. Had he deliberately saddled me with the bill? To demonstrate how dependent I was on him? I snarled. *How fucking dare he?*

I sat down on the toilet and held my head, pulling on the roots of my hair, willing myself to just breathe, keep breathing, keep breathing...until several minutes later, when my head was finally clear.

Well. It was simple. I just had to explain to the waitress what the situation was. Maybe she'd hold on to my phone or ID as collateral while I looked for Asher. I had no family, and my only New York friends were *his* friends, all of whom were casual music show buddies, at best. It had to be Asher.

But what would happen when I found him? Would he even

care anymore? Was it over between us? And beyond being romantic partners, he was my best friend in New York. He wouldn't just throw that away, would he?

If our tumultuous history were any indication, he *would* still care, and I'd figure out some way to manage things between us. I always did, because I had to.

But a rejected proposal seemed like a much bigger issue than late rent or accidental flirting, and there was no way that I was budging on this. I was not getting married.

Breathe. We'd find a solution, somehow.

I smoothed my hair and my dress, unlocked the bathroom stall, and walked out, back towards the table. I repeated my carefully crafted excuses over and over to myself, preparing to face that snob-goblin waitress. But the words evaporated when I saw that the table was clean and empty, with nothing other than the red rectangle of my credit card in the center. There was no shameful credit card slip with DECLINED printed at the top waiting for me.

The waitress reappeared with a clean set of plates and flatware and began setting the table, not looking my way.

"Did you run the card?" I asked her.

She fiddled with the alignment of a fork for a moment before turning my way. "Ah, *no*. The family sitting behind you offered to pay for your table." Her tight-lipped smile didn't even meet her *nose*. "Have a good night, *miss*." She resumed setting the table, so she *missed* my eye roll at her extra emphasis.

But...*whoa*. I thoughtfully gazed at the empty table where the older Chinese woman and her family had sat. What had induced them to pick up my check? Had the mother wanted to ingratiate her son with me? If so, why hadn't they stayed and waited for an introduction? I definitely wouldn't have been interested in him, but I would have thanked them, at least.

*Or...*I gritted my teeth. Had they done it because they'd pitied me? Like the waitress, could they somehow detect that I couldn't afford the meal? That I was dependent on the man I'd just rejected, and had no one else to turn to?

Either way, they were gone, and I could neither ask them nor thank them.

With one last passing glance at their table, I picked up my credit card and headed home to face Asher.

Chapter 1

-Anna-

Four months later

Who the hell was calling me at 1am? I blearily reached under my pillow and pulled out my phone, which had been buzzing incessantly for the past two minutes. The name on the screen, *Cassie Green*, surprised me because:

1. I hadn't spoken to Cassie in years;
2. She knew from our four years as college roommates that she should never call me this late. I'm bad when I'm hangry, but I'm especially bad when I'm *slangry*.

I swiped the screen and slipped the phone under my face. "*Ugh*, Cass, why are you calling me so late?" The words were nearly unintelligible through my mega-yawn. I considered greeting her with the usual, *hi, how are you, we haven't spoken in forever*...but not now. Not at 1am on a Monday.

"*Girl*, you have *not* responded to my wedding invite. Are you coming? Yes? Good."

"Wait, what? What wedding invite?" I frowned, trying and

failing to recall an invitation. I didn't remember receiving anything from Cassie, other than her annual Christmas cards.

"The Christmas card! It had all the details about the wedding on it. Did you get it?" *What?*

"One sec." Groaning, I rolled onto my belly and switched on my bedside lamp. I yanked open the drawer with all of my sentimental crap in it, then flailed my hand around until I found the card in question.

On one side, Cassie and her boyfriend of five years, Michael, wore matching Santa outfits, though he didn't have an impractically large diamond on his finger like Cassie did. They were both holding onto their black german shepherd, Frankie, who wore a festive green elf hat, and all three wore giant goofy grins on their faces.

I flipped the card over and read the following:

Wishing you a happy holiday season and a beautiful new year.
Much love from the Green and MacDermott household!
By the way, here's your fortune for next year:
September 20, 2019
The Vineheartery
Marin County, California
4pm - 10pm
YOU'RE COMING

I snorted. "That's not a real invite, Cass. But that's nice that you're getting married." I couldn't quite bring myself to congratulate her. Marriage was a terrifying bullet that I myself had dodged just months ago.

"Yes! In two months! *And you're coming.* That's it." Her tone brooked no objection.

"Cassie, that's not how—none of this—is this a prank call?" My tired brain could *not even.*

"You wish! I'll email you the official RSVP form, but I wanted your verbal commitment. Your *word.* Can I count on you to be there?"

"No. Bye." I prepared to hang up and go back to bed. I'd call her back with regrets and excuses at a sane hour.

"*Please*, Nana," she charmingly wheedled, using her personal nickname for me. "I haven't seen you since college and this is the perfect excuse to get our old crew back together. You didn't come to Jessa's or Lisa's weddings this year, so you *have to* come to this one."

Ah, a change in tactics. She was pulling out all the stops, trying her best to confuse and guilt me into attending her wedding. The late call was likely part of it. I lived in New York and she lived in San Francisco, so with the time difference, she'd called me right after I'd fallen asleep, when I was groggiest and my defenses were low. *Wily woman.*

"Yes, but—"

"It would be *so so fun.* Like, when will we ever be together like this again?"

"Sure, but I—"

"So you're coming? Nana, you haven't even *met* Michael yet. We've been together for FIVE YEARS and you've never come to visit. Have you ever even BEEN to San Francisco?"

"Cassie, no, I have—"

"Then you're coming. You *have to.* Oh my god, I'm so excited, I'm going to tell the girls! *Love you!*" She hung up, deaf to my protests. I knew that she wasn't really that dense, but she was so good at playing it, and I did love her. My life had completely fallen apart in college, and if Cassie hadn't been there for me every step of the way, things would've ended up so much worse than they had. I didn't want to let her down on what she considered to be her *Big Day*. And luckily, I did have a few days of vacation available, as well as a tiny bit of savings.

But *weddings*. Ugh.

Marriage is a trap, and weddings, the ultimate bait, so cleverly crafted by the well-oiled marriage machine. After all, there's no escaping the propaganda—weddings are *all about the photos*. There are very few other non-business occasions for which you'd be expected to pay literally thousands of dollars for a photographer. But really, you're just paying your taxes and doing your patriotic duty, because Uncle Sam (and everyone else in your family) wants *you* to get married. Keep calm and marry on.

And don't think that guests are passive participants, either. As a guest, it's *your* duty to get into that photobooth, take photos of yourself looking as hot and attractive as you'll ever get, then spread the images on social media. Look, weddings are fun! Marriage is great! I want one of those!

All. Fake. News.

Even the games they played at weddings, like catching the bouquet or garter, were like sending chain letters out into the crowd, spreading the curse of marriage. Hurrah! You're next!

No thanks. I'm good.

To be clear, it wasn't *relationships* that I railed against. Just marriage. I readily acknowledged that human beings need physical intimacy and social interaction to survive. But relationships were not meant to last forever. People are individuals, with their own dreams and wishes, and it's impossible to always want the same things as someone else.

Better to just pair up when it suits, and go our separate ways when it doesn't.

So I'd RSVP'ed *NO* to almost every wedding that I'd ever been invited to. I'd be a hypocrite not to. Besides, in addition to perpetuating false dreams, weddings are lame, formulaic, and lastly, *expensive*, and I'd rather just travel for the sake of traveling.

But for Cassie, that beautiful, charming dictator...I would deal. Just this once.

I fell asleep again not long after, but my dreams were invaded by fascist brides who drove giant, sparkly-white wedding cake tanks, all shooting bouquets at me.

* * *

Two months later, on the Friday night before the wedding, I boarded the plane and found my aisle seat, shoved my bag into the overhead compartment, and quickly got settled in. The plane was old, one of the ones that didn't have any seatback screens or device holders, and the seat leather was well-worn, with little cracks and tufts of fluff here and there. A middle-aged woman with short auburn hair was resting in the window seat, eyes closed, already snoring lightly. The middle seat was empty, and as people filed in and continued to pass me by, my hopes increased that it would stay that way. I put my earphones in and smiled.

But soon, there was a slight commotion towards the front of the plane. Someone (probably a guy, based on the jeans and deep voice) was carrying a large black duffel bag in front of him, awkwardly brushing against everyone who was seated in an aisle seat. He muttered, "Sorry," as he went, unable to see in front of him, until he reached my row and stopped. *Damn.*

I'd just put my bag up there, so I knew that there was no way in hell that his bag was going to fit. But he threw the bag into the remaining space anyway and began to push, rocking back and forth as he adjusted the suitcases around it and forced the bag in deep enough for the compartment to close. As he pushed, his hips repeatedly brushed against my shoulder. I leaned away from him, trying to keep his crotch out of my face, but he shifted his weight forward to be able to push the bag in deeper, and therefore pushed his crotch deeper into my field of view. I turned my face away, refusing to look. *What a dick.*

With one last big shove, the duffel slid into place, and he finally closed the compartment. Then he glanced down at me, and I scowled up at him.

"Hey, really sorry about that. I'm in E." He pointed at the empty seat beside me, an apologetic smile on his face. My scowl deepened as I took in his appearance: chiseled, bearded jaw, nice tan, black side-swept hair, plain gray tee and dark jeans. Jeans that I was now all too familiar with. I continued scowling as I stood up and into the aisle, allowing him to slip by me and into the middle seat.

While he'd been thrusting his crotch into my face, I hadn't been able to focus on much else. But as he passed me by, I caught a hint of his cologne: subtle and masculine, a little bit spicy...and very delicious. Even though he looked like a New York tech bro (*so* not my type!), I discreetly flared my nostrils and inhaled. *Mmm.*

He threw his hoodie onto the seat and his backpack under the seat in front of him, then awkwardly tried to situate himself. He was tall and leggy, probably around six feet, so

15

his knees pushed up against the seat in front. I slipped back into my own seat and reached for my seatbelt, which he was now holding.

"That's mine." I took the buckle from him, fingers brushing his.

"Oh, sorry." He felt around and beneath him until he found his own seat belt and clicked it into place. Finally settled in, he leaned back and let out a sigh. For a moment, he just sat there and looked about, tapping his fingers on the armrests, each *tap-tap-tap* vibrating up along my own arm, which was pressed against his. He was manspreading, using more than his share of both armrests, and he had fairly broad shoulders, so it wasn't like he was just *touching* the armrests—his warm, meaty arms spilled over them. I could see that our window neighbor had her hands in her lap and was leaning further into the window than before, ceding extra territory to our male neighbor. Guess she wasn't as asleep as I'd thought she was. Meanwhile, I didn't plan on budging. I'd paid for my space, and I was going to use it.

Besides, my thin silk blouse was virtually nonexistent against the cold blasts of air coming from all sides of the plane, and my sweater was buried in my bag in the overhead compartment, which he'd just crammed his own oversized bag into. I did not want to deal with removing *his* bag, rummaging in *my* bag, and then throwing it all back in there and trying to close the compartment again. So while I was annoyed that he was encroaching on my space, I secretly welcomed the feeling of his arm against mine, and greedily absorbed as much warmth from him as I could.

Two quick cracks of his neck was all it took to skim his eyes over me, but his face revealed none of his thoughts. He just

16

turned to look out the window, his fingers continuing their steady beat on the armrest. Finally, he reached under the seat in front of him and pulled out a book from his backpack, and began to read.

I closed my eyes and tried to ignore him, though I could still smell him and feel his arm flex against mine with every page turn. As we taxied to the runway, my focus narrowed to the music that I was listening to, a new song from one of my favorite bands, The Llama People. The lyrics:

The steady rhythm of our piston,
Smooth and lubricated,
Internally combusting in my head,
Revving me up with each mile marker...

The thought of performing road head on my neighbor came unbidden, and my eyes snapped open to dispel the visual. I hadn't even gotten a good look at him and now my sex-starved brain was already inserting him into fantasies? Stupid brain. It'd been six months since I'd last gotten laid, but I could tell that Crotch Guy was not my type. *Definitely not.*

Crotch Guy turned another page, and I felt his arm shift again. I pretended to look out the window at the rain and used my peripheral vision to glance his way, just to confirm how not-my-type he was.

He was probably close to my age, but it was hard to tell. I'd been mistaken for anywhere from 20 to 35, and the same could be said about him. I was surprised at how well he was built—lean and long, with tan, muscular arms. His t-shirt hugged his chest, and I bit my lip as I studied the outline of his shapely pecs. I was definitely more of a pecs girl than an ass girl, and I could not deny the appeal of his. And underneath, there was no sign of a paunch; just the opposite.

A neatly trimmed beard darkened his chin and jaw, which he thoughtfully rubbed as he read. I peeked at the book. It was some thick fantasy or sci-fi looking book by Something or Other Liu.

Yup. No thanks.

I leaned my head back and closed my eyes again, satisfied with my findings, as the plane took off and left JFK behind.

Chapter 2

-Ian-

She'd been checking me out. I could tell because I'd been secretly checking *her* out. But after looking-not-looking my way, she closed her eyes and withdrew into whatever she was listening to (The Llama People, according to her phone). Guess she wasn't impressed.

My back was still sore from the previous night's climbing session, so I took a moment to roll my neck and shoulders, which felt amazing, but more importantly offered me the opportunity to casually glance at my aisle-seat companion. Her long, wavy black hair transitioned to a deep teal on the ends, and her thick eyeliner and cute sapphire nose stud contrasted starkly with her creamy white skin. My eyes followed the deep v-neck of her flimsy pink blouse, which revealed her modest, but still very appealing cleavage...and also revealed how cold she was. *Ahem.* Goosebumps peppered her forearm, which was rigid on her half of the armrest where it firmly pushed against my own.

She looked like she could use a hoodie, and luckily, there was one just sitting in my lap. Perhaps unluckily, her eyes were closed and her earphones were blaring music in the universal *do not disturb* sign. So I didn't bother her—I could take a hint.

But when she shivered a moment later, visibly uncomfortable, I took action.

I lightly tapped her hand, which immediately earned me an annoyed scowl. She removed an earbud to hear me say, "Hey, I know this is kind of forward, but you look cold. Do you want to borrow this?" I held up my warm, gray, Stumpstash-branded hoodie.

Her nose twitched and she scowled even harder, as if I were offering her a live squid instead of an article of clothing. But after a moment, she ran her hands up and down her arms and answered, "Yeah, thanks. It *is* really cold on this stupid plane." I nodded and handed her the hoodie, which she quickly slipped around her shoulders and zipped up to her chin. It looked good on her, better than it looked on me.

She shot me an appreciative smile. "Thank you. This is much better."

"Sure. I hope you've got warmer clothes in your bag. People always think it's warm in California, but it's almost always chilly in SF."

"Oh." She frowned, then asked, "Really? Even in...ah..." Her brow furrowed in thought, "Marin County?"

"Oh yeah, definitely. It's nice during the day sometimes, but evenings can get pretty cold. Is that where you're headed?"

Pouting slightly, she nodded. "Yeah. For a wedding."

"Oh...huh. Not Cassie and Michael's, by any chance?" I asked, hopeful. How many weddings could there have been in Marin County that weekend?

Her eyes widened. "Uhhh, *actually*, I am." She paused her music and took out her other earphone, giving me her full attention. "I'm Anna, nice to meet you. How do you know them?"

I snapped my book shut and shook her offered hand, which was long-fingered and creamy soft. Shame that she wasn't a climber. "I'm Ian, I'm a colleague of Cassie's. We both work at Stumpstash, but I'm based in the New York office and she's in the SF office. What about you?"

"I was her college roommate."

"Well, nice to me—wait, you're her college roommate?" I rubbed my chin, recalling what Cassie had told me about her college roomie.

"Yeah, why?"

I chuckled, the details clicking into place. "She told me about you."

Her eyes narrowed, clearly suspicious, but she playfully asked, "What'd she say?" When I only chuckled again, she casually flipped her hair behind her shoulder and said,"C'mon, you can't just say that and then not tell me."

"Well...she told me that you love music. That you write about it and create awesome playlists. That you live in New York." I leaned towards her across the armrest, then whispered conspiratorially, "And that you don't date Asian guys."

She stiffened beside me, then exhaled slowly. Didn't back away, just coolly met my eyes. "Is that so? And why was she telling you that about me?"

I hoped that I hadn't just gotten Cassie in trouble. Cassie and I'd been a couple of beers in when she'd started telling me about Anna, and her filters usually disintegrated after just one.

Leaning in slightly further, I caught a hint of her rose-scented hair as I said, "She was telling me that you and I would

21

be perfect together, if it weren't for your *No Asians* rule."

She arched an eyebrow at me, her eyes flicking down to my lips, then back up. "She said that? *Perfect* together?"

My lips curled into my most charming smile. "She did. Ask her."

She searched my face, no doubt taking in my rugged good looks. But then she grimaced and turned away. "You're definitely not my type."

I barked a laugh and leaned back, retreating from her space. "Uh huh. So what *is* your type?"

She crossed her arms and legs, giving me an appraising look. "I like guys who are creative, confident, and know what they want."

I'm confident and know what I want. Out loud, I teased, "And Asian guys aren't like that?"

Wrong thing to say. Her eyes flashed and her arms tightened over her chest. "I don't have to defend my personal preferences to you."

I held my hands up in a placating gesture. "Hey, no need to. I was just curious." When she rolled her eyes, I added, "Not that I'm hitting on you."

"Sure. Right." She rolled her eyes again.

"Suit yourself." With a small shrug, I sat back and resumed reading my book.

Silence ensued, for a few blissful moments. I successfully read four sentences before she continued, "Look, you seem like a nice guy, and you're friends with Cassie, so you can't be that bad. But you're definitely, 100% *not my type*."

I frowned at her and lowered the book to my lap. I'd already gotten the picture—she didn't have to keep repeating herself. But if she wasn't done, then neither was I. "Because I'm Asian?

Because *you're* Asian?"

She pursed her lips and looked away. "I'm not having this conversation with you."

I rolled my eyes and sat back again, annoyed. She was the one who had continued talking to *me*, trying to put *me* down.

I'd certainly met her type before—women who refused to date Asian guys for any number of ridiculous reasons. I'd been perfectly nice to her, a total gentleman so far...at least until we started talking about why she insisted on being racist. What really confused me was the intensity in her eyes, the way she refused to back away from me, and the subtle flare of her nostrils each time I came near, a slight inhalation. She was clearly as affected by me as I was by her. There was *something* between us. Yet she still held onto whatever small-minded, misguided beliefs prevented her from just viewing me as an individual. She still referred to me as "not her type," as if she could exclude an entire portion of the population just based on, what, how slanted their eyes were? That pissed me off.

"I'm not a fob, you know. Not that there's anything wrong with being fresh off the boat."

She pursed her lips and doggedly stared into the aisle.

"What, it's not fobbiness that turns you off? Is it—"

She tipped her head back and groaned. *"Ugh*, I'm an *American,* okay? I want to live for myself, not the..." Her hands waved in my general direction. *"...Asian American* dream."

I snorted. "Wow, really? You're calling me the Asian American dream?"

"Well aren't you?" She listed my qualifications on her fingers. "You work at Stumpstash, a fintech company, so you're probably making a fortune. You probably did well in school. You're dressed like a typical tech bro. Everything about you spells safe, bland, *mama's boy*." Contempt bled from her eyes.

I tittered. "Y'know, a lot of what you just described could be said of half the guys on this plane. Not just me, not just Asian guys. Besides, what's wrong with being smart and making money? Or heaven forbid, loving your mom?"

She sighed and threw her hands up in the air, exasperated. "I'm just not into guys like you. Period."

The dead horse was already tenderized...yet still, she persisted. "Hey, I—"

"Excuse me." Our window seat neighbor cleared her throat and made eye contact with me, then with Anna. "Is he bothering you?" She switched her gaze back to me and did her best Bad Cop impression.

Anna shot her a grateful look. "*Yes*. But it's okay, we're done talking." Bad Cop nodded slowly and leaned back against the window, closing her eyes. The tense line of her shoulders suggested that she was ready to pounce again if I persisted, though.

Anna leaned in and whispered, "Just drop it. You wouldn't understand."

I studied her face: the sapphire nose piercing, the teal-colored hair, the thick eyeliner. The proud, disdainful expression, as if she knew everything about everything, myself included. The whole of her look screamed *cool, rebellious, sexy, independent*...but perhaps a bit too loudly. It hid the fact that she was also *defensive, judgmental,* and *pretty damn fickle.*

So I leaned in closer, triumphantly noting my effect on her—her shallow intake of breath, her wary eyes glinting with something *more*. She didn't lean away, just let me trace my fingers along her ear and brush her hair aside, then whisper against her cheek, "Good thing you're not *my* type."

It took her a moment to register what I'd said. Then she stiffened—she hadn't been expecting *that*. With one last smirk, I turned back to my book. She shook her head and looked away without responding, but I gleefully noted that she squirmed a little in her seat.

Chapter 3

-Anna-

What an *ass*. Screw him and his stupid good-looking face. And his deep, sexy voice.

Good thing you're not my type.

Oh yeah? Then what was with all that leaning-in-and-breathing-on-me bullshit? I bit my lip and squirmed in my seat, bitterly noting that his comment had elicited an unwanted physiological response in the form of moisture between my legs. While his words had spelled rejection, his *tone* had suggested an invitation. The caress of his whisper, his tantalizing scent...urgh, whatever. I clearly just needed to get laid soon, and not by him.

I briefly glanced his way, noting the straight line of his nose, the masculine hand that rubbed the neatly trimmed hairs on his chin. His double-lidded eyes. Hmph.

I really didn't date Asian guys. Why would I, when they almost always presumed to know everything about me, just because *I* was Asian? They usually had judgmental families who would never accept nor understand me, my past, or my future. And of course, they were boring goody-goodies who only liked to play video games and watch movies.

Not. My. Type.

Obviously, there were exceptions to rules. Maybe he wasn't what I thought he was—a cocky, presumptuous, bland alpha-male wannabe. But I didn't care to find out, regardless of whether or not Cassie thought we'd be *perfect together.* I'd have to have a few words with her about that later.

I took out my notebook and jotted down some notes while listening to the rough playlist that I had prepared earlier in the week. I tried to release a new playlist every two weeks and it was almost time for the next. As usual, I was struggling to finish this one. I liked the individual songs that I'd chosen, but didn't have an angle, something tying them together that I could write about.

Try as I might, the brainstorm wouldn't gather. With how scattered and agitated I was by Ian's words, it was barely a light brain-drizzle...and the steady shifting of his arm against mine, one page turn per minute, was a constant disruption.

He couldn't possibly understand my reasons for rejecting him and guys just like him. And it wasn't worth my time to explain anything to him anyway, not with his giant ego in the way. Besides, the coward wouldn't even look at me anymore. Every so often, I cast a furtive glance over at him, but he didn't seem to reciprocate. The fact that he could focus and I could not annoyed me even further, and soon I was tapping *my* fingers on the armrest. I forced myself to stop.

At one point, he rubbed his bare arms and crossed them over his chest. He was probably cold—after all, I was wearing his hoodie and the plane still felt like a walk-in fridge. I didn't really want to talk to him again, but the hoodie did belong to him, and *I* wasn't a jerk. With a quick tap on the arm, I said,

"Hey. Do you want your hoodie back?" I held the zipper in my hand, poised to unzip and return it to him.

He glanced up, surprised. "No, it's fine, you're probably colder than I am. Just keep it for now."

I began to unzip. "You should just take it—"

"Hey, don't worry about it. I'm not that cold."

He reached into his backpack and pulled out what looked like a small resistance band with holes. He slipped it onto his fingers and extended them, then contracted, extended, contracted, extended, repeating the motion over and over. The muscles in his forearm flexed with each repetition.

I was grateful that he hadn't asked me to return the hoodie, and even more grateful that he hadn't taken my talking to him as an invitation to continue talking to me. He just silently focused on opening and closing his fingers with the resistance band and reading his book.

Sigh. Maybe he wasn't a huge ass. Just kind of one.

I tried to return to my music, but found my gaze sliding back to his sinewy forearms and his thick, callused fingers as they continually stretched against the elastic band. It was oddly hypnotic. I imagined his fingers—

That way madness lies.

I sighed again. The hand exercises were objectively lame. Even so, I decided to be polite. He was Cassie's friend, and I didn't want to have things be weird between us this weekend. So I took out my earphones and asked, "What's with the finger exercises?"

He glanced up again, eyebrows raised, then slowly answered, "I injured my finger not too long ago. It helps with rehab and preventing further injury."

"How'd you injure it?"

"I was climbing and went for kind of a burly move. I lunged for a two-finger pocket and something felt like it popped. It doesn't seem to be that bad now, but I don't want to take any chances."

I winced at the word *popped* and compulsively flexed my fingers. "What's a two-finger pocket?" I decided not to ask him what *burly* meant, though I could guess. I'd already interrogated him enough.

He stuck his middle and pointer fingers up and mimed shoving them into a narrow cavity. My eyes narrowed at the sexual gesture. "It's like...a hole that you can stick your fingers into," he explained, deadpan. He cleared his throat, vaguely embarrassed. *As he should be.*

I couldn't help it. I chuckled. "I see." Then I braced myself, sure that he would use that gesture, that opening, to say awful, sexist things to me.

He kept on with the finger exercises. "You know, I'm actually going climbing with Cassie and a few other wedding guests on Sunday morning, if you want to come."

My brain latched onto his last few words, but my hackles dropped as I took in his innocuous meaning. I hesitated, toying with the laces of his hoodie before responding, "Maybe. I've never done it before, and it looks really hard. I might suck at it." I cringed at my own words. Somehow, *I* was the one with my mind stuck in the gutter.

"It's always hard the first time," he said, a twinkle in his eyes. My ears burned with embarrassment. "But you'll pick it up quickly. You've got a great build for it."

My body simmered slightly as he eyed me up and down, but abruptly cooled when he added, "Your hands are pretty big and your arms are long. Your ape index must be pretty high."

29

I scowled. I was not proud of my orangutan proportions. "I don't know about that. But thanks for the invite. Maybe I'll take you up on it." I honestly wanted to say yes. I'd always wanted to try climbing. Cassie was an avid climber, and her photos on social media were so badass and inspiring. Plus, the rock gym that I walked past each day on my commute had giant warehouse doors that were usually open, and I regularly peeked in at all of the fit, happy people on the walls. I wanted to be one of them.

But climbing was *expensive*. With student loans and New York rent to pay, and a job that didn't cover much of either, climbing wasn't in my budget.

Then again, I was on vacation—a little extra expense couldn't hurt. And maybe it wouldn't be so bad to go with the group, because then I'd get to hang out with Cassie for longer. I doubted that I'd get to see much of her at the actual wedding.

He reached into his back pocket and pulled out his wallet, then handed me a business card. "Here. We're going to the Granitarium on Sunday at 10am. Just call or text if you can't find us or have any questions."

We both knew that I could've just called Cassie, but I accepted the card anyway. *Ian Gao, Technical Lead at Stumpstash.* His cell phone number and email were printed next to a picture of his smiling face. I put it in my back pocket.

"Thanks." With one last, brief smile, I slipped my earphones back in and pointedly returned to my music. My work was done, our cautious truce complete. He soon returned to his finger exercises and his book.

The rest of the flight passed relatively uneventfully. There were a few bouts of turbulence, and at one point I woke up to find myself drooling a bit on his shoulder (I'd jerked awake and hit my head on his), but not too long after, we landed. I went to unzip the hoodie and return it, but Ian held up his hand.

"You can return it tomorrow at the wedding. I just checked the weather and it looks like it's pretty chilly tonight. And anyway, I have a jacket in my duffel."

Thank goodness. The hoodie was so warm and comfortable, and I hadn't been ready to return it yet. I clutched my hands against my chest and smiled gratefully at him. "Thanks, Ian, I really appreciate it. I'll definitely give it to you tomorrow."

"Sure thing." He paused and thoughtfully rubbed his chin. I'd never dated a guy with a beard before. What would it feel like—

"Actually, are you by any chance staying in one of the rooms that Cassie reserved? At the Windbreak Hotel?"

"Ahh, yeah, I am." I warily met his eyes. *Please don't be a creep.* "Why?"

"Do you want to ride with me? I'm going to stay on for work after the wedding, so I'm renting a car and charging it to my company."

"Oh. Yeah, I'd love a free ride." Score! Public transit would have taken over an hour, and a cab or rideshare would have cost way too much. I congratulated my past self for her forward thinking in patching things up with Ian.

We waited for the slow tide of people to clear the plane, then grabbed our stuff and walked to the rental car area. I browsed the latest music news in the parking lot while he went into the rental office and dealt with the paperwork. Soon he walked out with an attendant and gestured for me to follow. He'd rented a sleek red Tesla Model S, the first I'd ever been in.

The retractable door handles surprised me, but I eventually got the passenger door open and slipped inside. I closed my eyes and luxuriated in the front seat, stretching my legs and kicking off my tight shoes.

Ian finished up with the rental car attendant and got into the driver's seat. "You look like you're ready to pass out," he said, turning the car on. He seemed perfectly at ease with the controls as he adjusted the settings to his liking. Maybe he drove one at home (though who the heck drove in New York?).

"Yeah, it's been a long week," I yawned.

"Yeah? Tell me about it." We pulled out of the lot and merged into traffic, heading towards the city.

"Well...I work as an office admin at a law firm, and they've got a really big sexual assault case right now for some hotshot rich dude. I can't talk details, but I can tell you that I've definitely been considering quitting because of it. I don't want to work for lawyers who defend douchebags like this guy." The case pissed me off more than I let on. I didn't like rich guys, douchebags, or even lawyers, really. Probably not a great job for me.

Ian glanced at me sidelong. "Sounds like it'd be tough to work at a law firm in general. There are plenty of douchebags who need attorneys."

"Yeah. It's really not ideal. But I haven't found a better job yet, and the commute isn't bad, at least." I stretched and yawned again. "Also, I've got a playlist due on Monday and I'm not sure what to do with it."

"Do with it, how? Like what songs to put in?"

"Kind of. I've found a bunch of songs that I've really enjoyed over the past few weeks, but I need to arrange and connect them in a meaningful way. That's my schtick."

"Do you want to put it on? I'd love to hear it."

I hesitated. "I dunno...it's not really ready for listening."

"I know nothing about music. I definitely wouldn't be one to judge. But I'd love to listen to The Alpaca Humans or whatever you were listening to on the plane, to see what they're like. Maybe telling me about the music will help you with the playlist."

I smiled, sure that he'd deliberately botched the name. "Fine. Listen to each song and let me know what you think. I'll tell you about each one after it's over." I connected my phone to the car via bluetooth and soon the first notes of the first song began to play. On cue, my head began to bob. Definitely a groover.

He didn't react, just kept his eyes on the road, a slight furrowing of his brow the only indication that he was listening. But after roughly a minute, he finally nodded and said, "Mmmm, I see. Yes."

"What, what are you thinking?"

His eyes flicked towards my face, then back to the road. "Sassy horse disco."

I burst out laughing, impressed and delighted. At 120 beats per minute, with syncopated wood blocks, a saxophone synth, and a funky bassline...I nodded in agreement. Sassy horse disco.

He was filled with similar revelations about the other songs, too. Here's what I wrote down for the six songs that we got through:

1. Sassy horse disco
2. Deep space bossa nova

3. Morning climbing gym music, or music to drink coffee and read the news to
4. Bird seduction / forest orgy
5. Music to snap your fingers and do the grapevine to while trying to pick up the ladies
6. Evening climbing music, walking around at night when you can't sleep

He seemed to be a sucker for songs with electronic pianos and dreamy synths, in large part because of his gym. Like one of Pavlov's dogs, hearing those sounds made him excited and ready to climb.

Despite the silly images that he painted, the dynamic direction of his thoughts helped me view each song in a new light, and I found myself trying new combinations and hunting for old samples. By the end of the drive, I knew what the theme was going to be: *Second Impressions*. I silently thanked Ian for the help.

Though I was excited about our progress on the playlist, by the time we arrived at the hotel, I was wrung out from the long day of traveling and ready for bed. I blearily checked in beside him, and was somehow unsurprised to find out that our rooms were right next to each other. We took the elevator up and walked down the hallway together until we paused in front of our respective doors. "Here," I said, unzipping his hoodie and handing it back to him. The air-conditioned hallway was cold, but I knew that a warm shower and a bed were just steps away. I yawned, then added, "Thanks again for the hoodie and the ride. Goodnight."

I opened the door and stepped inside as I heard his echoed, "Goodnight."

After shutting the door with a small click, I leaned against it and sleepily reflected on our interactions that evening. We'd gotten off on the wrong foot, but after correcting course, he'd been attentive, curious, and playful. Our conversation had an easy flow, and I actually kind of enjoyed talking to him. And though I'd swear to my death that I wasn't attracted to him, I couldn't deny that he was quite the masculine presence, which was definitely not something I was used to noticing.

He had potential. As a friend.

Chapter 4

-Ian-

Once inside my room, I raised the hoodie to my face, inhaling her scent and warming my nose with her residual heat. Soft and floral, with hints of something herbal. Maybe rosemary?

I tossed the hoodie onto the bed and chuckled, reflecting on the evening's events. She'd make the world's worst poker player, what with the way her eyes lit up whenever she talked about music, or the death rays she'd shot at me during our heated exchange. She'd been so lively, her feeling so infectious, and it had been a long time since I'd felt so much easy chemistry with someone.

I looked forward to getting to know each other better that weekend. Maybe I'd ask her out when we got back to New York. It'd been a few months since I'd last gone on a date, and I was looking forward to getting back into the game, especially if it was with someone like her.

She seemed...different.

All the women I'd dated before shared three qualities: they were sweet, pretty, and highly educated. They'd also all been really into me. But there was always some other adjective that I didn't find out about until later: possessive, awkward, manipulative, bland, etc. So while my parents wanted me to get married relatively soon, and I wasn't opposed to the idea, I just seemed to have terrible luck. It'd been a rough couple of years, and I'd gotten tired of trying.

But Anna intrigued me more than any other woman had in a long time. Once she'd let her guard down, we'd had a great time talking to each other. She was definitely smart and pretty, *beautiful* even, although I wasn't so sure about sweet. Even so, I was drawn to her passion and her fiery spirit, things that I'd never really thought to look for in a partner before.

The only problem was that she seemed to take her "No Asian Guys" rule seriously. It was pretty off-putting that she was so closed-minded about it, but I wanted to give her the benefit of the doubt. Maybe she'd had terrible experiences with other Asian guys in the past. But I knew that she wouldn't have a terrible experience with *me*. I just had to figure out how to get her to give me a chance.

I drifted off to sleep that night to pleasant fantasies of how I would do just that.

* * *

The morning passed by quickly. I woke up early, went to the gym for an hour, showered, and went downstairs to the hotel cafe to grab a light breakfast. Hoping to get some work done, I'd brought my laptop down with me. Anna was there, too, hiding in a corner with her earphones in, carefully avoiding eye contact with everyone. She briefly looked up and waved at me as I passed, though.

After picking up a croissant and a cup of black coffee, I sat down at a high-top table by a window. I cracked my neck and fingers, opened up my laptop, and began chipping away at my huge backlog of work.

30 minutes later, as I was deep in some python, someone tapped on my shoulder.

"Hey. Mind if I sit and work with you?" Anna had come over with her laptop and a half-empty mug of coffee. She was looking pretty cute in her navy blue sweater and white shorts, her hair pulled back in a high ponytail.

"Not at all," I said. I usually preferred to work alone and undistracted, but I would've rather gotten nothing done that day while talking to Anna than plow through all of the code reviews that I'd planned on doing.

"How'd you sleep last night?" I asked, moving my stuff from the seat next to me so that she could sit down.

"Like a log. I was so jet-lagged. It's only a three-hour difference, but I was so tired. Still am." She jumped into the high chair, her ponytail swishing back and forth, bouncy and energetic and in direct contradiction to her words.

"Well, you *look* like you got you enough beauty sleep." I winked, feeling slightly cheesy...but hey, my wooing her had to start somewhere, and girls liked cheese, right?

She rolled her eyes and said, "Uh huh. So listen, I wanted to run an idea by you. About the playlist last night."

"Sure, go ahead."

She opened up her laptop and handed me an earphone, then walked me through her rearrangement of the tracks, given her idea for the playlist theme and title, *Second Impressions*. The first few tracks were old classics from the 70s and 80s, followed by some newer songs that had sampled or referenced lyrics or sounds from the first few. But the newer songs sounded entirely different, evoking seduction instead of joy, or dreaminess instead of funkiness. The samples were stretched, sped up, cut, or modified—still recognizable to the discerning ear, but used in completely unique ways.

"That's really thoughtful and insightful of you. I wouldn't have even caught those samples if you hadn't pointed them out."

"Thanks! That's what I'm going for." She sipped her coffee, smiling slightly into her mug, then added, "I wanted to thank you for letting me bounce some ideas off of you last night. It really helped to talk it through with you."

"Of course, anytime. Do I get a mention in your blog post?" I joked.

"Mmm, I'll think about it." Eyes playful, she turned to her laptop and began typing.

I turned to my own laptop and stared at the code on the screen, scanning for any potential issues. Occasionally, I looked up at Anna and caught her frowning or rubbing her smooth, supple neck in thought. As a result, I frequently found myself reviewing the same section of code two or three times. At one point, we both looked up and locked eyes.

"What are you working on?" she asked, quickly shifting her gaze back down to her screen.

"Code reviews." I turned the laptop around so that she could see the brightly colored lines of code. "Making sure my team's code quality is up to snuff." I spun it back around to face me and frowned as the text blurred together slightly. Staring at a screen all day sucked.

"Do you have to review *everyone's* code?"

"Not everyone's, just the most important pieces." I sighed. "It's pretty boring right now, though." As usual. I popped the last of the forgotten croissant into my mouth.

Anna's eyes widened when her stomach rumbled in response. She slowly placed a hand on her belly, her face sheepish.

"Uh...do you want to grab lunch?" I asked, suppressing a smile and closing my laptop.

"*Yeah*, that might be a good idea. What do you want to eat?" She gently shut her laptop, too.

I considered. *What was in the area?* Ah! "How do you feel about Ethiopian?"

"I've actually never had it before."

I rubbed my hands together. "Oh, then we're popping that cherry, right now."

She smiled and rolled her eyes yet again. "Sure, whatever."

* * *

We put our stuff away in our rooms, then walked to the Ethiopian place that was four blocks away. It was one of my favorite restaurants, and I was glad to have an excuse to stop by during that trip. There was just something so carnally satisfying about eating with your hands and using the sourdough injera to mop up the delicious, spicy juices from the stewed meat and vegetables. Anna was in for a treat.

The waitress seated us at the last available table, then brusquely handed us menus to look at. Ethiopian jazz played in the background, and the air was heavy with the scent of meat, butter, and berbere. My mouth watered—*I* was in for a treat.

After a minute of browsing, Anna deferred to me, putting down her menu and craning her head to look at the colorful arrays of dishes on the other tables. I hadn't even glanced at the menu, having already planned on ordering my two favorites, the kitfo and the veggie combo.

"I can't believe you've never had Ethiopian food. You're going to love it." I rubbed my hands together, excited to see her reaction to one of my favorite cuisines.

"I hope so. I don't get to eat out much." She sipped her water.

"In New York? That's like half of what there is to do there."

"Yeah, but I mostly eat the same things. A lot of pizza. I once challenged myself to try every pizza joint in New York."

"How far did you get?"

She scrunched up her face in thought. "Mmmm, over 40? Then I lost count."

"Wow. That's pretty impressive that you even got that far. What's your favorite place?"

"I have several favorite places. But what I realized throughout my pizza journey is that I like Sicilian pizza the best. No matter where it's from, if they make Sicilian, it's good."

I laughed at the image of her going on a pizza journey, then filed away that tidbit about Sicilian being her favorite. No doubt it would help in my conquest.

We discussed the merits of various pizza places and how New York pizza differed from anywhere else's pizza (it's got to be the water!) until our Ethiopian feast arrived.

Anna's eyes went wide at the huge platter of food. "Uhhh, I hope you're going to eat most of this. I have a really tight dress that I need to be able to fit into tonight."

I looked forward to seeing it. "Hmm, yeah, that might be a problem. Ethiopian food tends to result in food babies. Twins, at least."

I demonstrated how to use the injera to eat. She followed suit and ripped off a piece of injera, swiped it into the mound of shiro wot, then brought the tiny wrap to her mouth. Her eyes drifted closed as she slowly chewed, savoring the flavor and letting out a small moan of pleasure. The shiro wot dripped down onto her fingers, and I wanted to take each one into my mouth and lick them clean.

"Oh my god," she said, mouth still full. "That is *so good*. Holy shit." One by one, she slowly sucked on her own fingers, each one slipping out of her mouth with a slick little *pop*.

Wow. If she was that erotic with Ethiopian food, what would she be like with sausages? Eclairs? *In bed?* I discreetly adjusted my pants under the table, then shook my head, frowning at myself. There was a sumptuous feast before me—I should focus on *that*.

We ate in silence for a little while, punctuated only by the occasional groan whenever Anna tried something new. It was more than sensual; it was nice. I'd forgotten how it felt to just sit and enjoy delicious food together with someone, especially someone as enthusiastic as she was. Experiencing every new flavor and mouthfeel with her, through her, somehow made it taste even better.

After a particularly long, throaty sigh (she'd finally tried the *kitfo*, the marinated raw beef), she asked, "So are there good Ethiopian places in New York?"

"Yeah, definitely. But I think the ones in the Bay Area are better."

She licked her lips and hummed with pleasure after trying the atakilt wot, which consisted of stewed carrots, potatoes, and cabbage. "I wish I could cook like this. Or like, Indian food. All those spices...it must be so complicated."

42

I picked up a slice of stewed potato and popped it into my mouth. "It's actually not that hard."

She stared. "You know how to make Indian food?"

I tried not to look too smug as I said, "I make it all the time. And Ethiopian. You just need to buy the ingredients at a good market. There are several in the Bay Area."

She nodded slowly and gave me a *Not Bad* face. "So you cook a lot?"

"Yeah, I love cooking. It's a nice creative outlet, and I find it really relaxing and satisfying to make my own food." I hesitated, then said, "You know, you're welcome to come over for dinner anytime. I love cooking for other people. The only people who really eat my food though are my parents, and they're not exactly impartial critics."

She smiled, lips and teeth stained red from the kitfo. "I'd love to."

I chuckled. Did she consider that a date? I did.

* * *

We came close to finishing all of the food, but in the end, there was just way too much of it. I offered to pay, but for some reason, Anna vehemently protested. So we ended up splitting the bill, which hadn't been very much anyway. And from the satisfied look on her face, it was clear that she was going to be a lifelong fan. I was glad to have been the one to introduce it to her.

We got back to the hotel and went into our respective rooms. Luckily, we had a little over an hour for the food to settle and to get dressed. I breezed through and approved a few more merge requests, then put on my new bespoke cobalt suit, pale pink tie, and brown leather shoes. My mom had insisted that I buy a new suit when she'd splashed soy sauce (accidentally? *Unclear.*) onto my old light gray suit at my cousin Lianyang's wedding, but I was glad for it—I looked *good*. I restyled my hair to give it a tad more volume, then spritzed myself with a tiny extra bit of cologne. Satisfied, I went downstairs and lined up with several other wedding guests who were waiting for the shuttle to the venue, which was about a 30 minute drive north.

From where I stood in line, I saw that there were a couple of Stumpstashers from the SF office standing near the front. That was no surprise, as Cassie seemed to be friends with everyone at work. I turned to look behind me at the rest of the line and—

Damn.

Anna was walking towards me, and she was absolutely stunning.

She wore a rose pink satin gown that hugged her curves in all the right places, with a long slit that stopped high up on her hip. A simple black belt emphasized her slim waist, no food babies in sight. The pale pink of the dress complemented her teal-colored hair, which she'd elegantly coiffed, with curled tendrils artfully slipping out and framing her face and neck. Her black stilettos accentuated her shapely ankles, the added height completely inverting her high ape index and making her legs look miles long.

Double damn.

After eyeing her up and down, I knew that I'd have more material for my fantasies that evening. That is, if I didn't succeed in getting the real woman into my bed. I usually waited until at least the fifth date to seduce a woman, not the zeroth, but that dress...I shook my head.

She saw me and gave me a once-over of her own as she walked up. "Not bad. We even match." She traced a finger down my pink tie, stopping at least a full foot above where I wished she'd touch me.

Before I could respond, someone said my name. Another group of Stumpstashers drew closer, ones from the New York office. We exchanged greetings and introductions, *hey, this is so-and-so, how are you*...though what I really wanted to say was, *hey guys, go away, stop cockblocking me.*

"So is this your date?" asked Emily, one of the product managers at Stumpstash. "She honestly seems too cool for you."

"*Thanks*, Emily. No, she's Cassie's college roommate. We met on the flight last night." I introduced Anna all around. By the way their eyes leisurely roved over her, the three guys, Tom, Rich, and Tony, were all charmed. I cracked my knuckles while Emily and another product manager, Prisha, both welcomed her warmly.

"So you're also from New York?" asked Tom. *Tom*, who had nose hairs visibly protruding from his nostrils. He was standing too close to her, leaning down and in to talk. I didn't like that one bit, but could do nothing about it as Rich started asking me about how my project at work was going.

"Is the backend ready for the new UI?" he asked. Rich and I didn't like each other. I don't know why he tried to talk to me. Maybe he could tell that I wanted to talk to Anna and was trying to piss me off. It was working.

"Not yet. We..." I watched from the corner of my eye as Tom and Anna chatted. She looked up at him coquettishly and slapped his arm, laughing at something he'd said. Really,

Tom? I frowned, then turned away and focused on answering Rich's question.

"We had to deal with some security issues." I explained the issues in excruciating detail until Rich hurriedly wished me luck and turned to talk to Prisha.

By the time I turned around again, Tom was talking to Emily and Anna was gone. Hmph.

After a few minutes, the shuttle arrived and we all shuffled on board, our group filling up the rows in the back. I eventually saw Anna take a seat in the front, surrounded by what I assumed were some of her college acquaintances, based on their polite chatter.

I spent the next 30 minutes staring at the back of her head, the gorgeous slope of her neck and shoulders, only periodically turning away when one of my coworkers addressed me directly. They talked about sports, new shows, the latest restaurants and bars in New York, and occasionally, work gossip. *Small talk.* I didn't have much to add to the conversation. If this was Anna's experience of people in tech, no wonder she assumed that I was bland.

I glanced out the window as the shuttle pulled into a paved parking area. Everyone began *ooh*-ing and *ah*-ing at the sight, and even I had to whistle. Cassie and Michael (or their parents) had spared no expense—the venue was absolutely breathtaking. The entrance to the high-ceilinged barn was decorated from top to bottom with pale blooms, succulents, and ivy. Trellises with grapevines and delicate white lace lined the path to the outdoor ceremony, then continued further on to the reception area. Golden vineyards stretched for as far as the eye could see, charming and rustic in the afternoon sun.

We all swiveled our heads to take in the views as we got

off the shuttle and slowly filed towards where the outdoor ceremony was to take place. I noticed Anna ahead of me, her heels periodically sinking into the dirt, causing her to jerk her feet up in order to get the shoes out, then tiptoe on the balls of her shoes like a T-Rex.

I left my group and caught up to her, taking her arm and looping it through mine. "Seems like you could use a hand."

She got me a grateful look. "Thanks. I thought I was about to get really cozy with these trellises."

I laughed and placed my hand over hers. "You'd fit right in, so pretty and pink like the flowers."

"Uh huh." She smiled wryly and shook her head. *No eye roll?* Progress!

"What? You are. You look like a thousand bucks."

"A *thousand*? Don't you mean a million?"

"If you weren't walking like a drunk runway model, maybe."

Her shoulders shook with quiet laughter. Then she casually placed her other hand over mine and looked up at me through her curled lashes. "You know, you shouldn't waste your breath flirting with me. You're never getting into my panties." The flirtatious look she gave me suggested otherwise.

Hmm. Was it the Ethiopian food? My bespoke suit? Whatever it was that did the trick, she'd somehow started to come around. I smiled and rubbed my thumb along her fingers.

"Never?"

"Never."

"Good thing you're not wearing any right now," I guessed.

She stopped walking and gaped at me. "How would you know?"

I laughed. "Your dress doesn't leave much to the imagination, especially with that thigh slit."

She frowned at me, then shook her head and continued walking. "Whatever," she muttered. "You know what I mean."

Not breaking stride, I shifted towards her and lifted her hand. She watched me closely, her face difficult to read, as I pressed a lingering kiss to her knuckles. "I can't help flirting with you," I told her. "You look absolutely stunning."

She stopped walking once more and scanned my face, something flickering in her eyes at what she found. Whatever it was, she soon turned and continued ahead without responding, pulling me along with her.

People turned their heads as I escorted her to the ceremony area—she looked that good. So I didn't mind that we'd ended up standing near the back together, as nearly all of the seats were filled by the time that we'd arrived.

The ceremony itself was fairly standard. Cassie, in a huge white princess gown, was escorted down the aisle by her father, a large man with a cartoonishly happy face. Michael stood at the makeshift altar, tall, lean, and bearded, beads of sweat dripping down his forehead. The ring bearer, their dog Frankie, wore a bowtie collar with the rings looped through it. He'd trotted up the aisle admirably, and Michael's best man rewarded him at the end with a small treat.

A couple of their friends did readings (two poems by e e cummings), then the bride and groom exchanged vows. They promised the usual to each other, were pronounced husband and wife, and sealed it with a PG-13 kiss while we all looked on and cheered.

No more than fifteen minutes after we'd arrived, the ceremony was complete, and we were asked to head on to the reception area.

I turned to Anna and offered her my arm again, but she was already walking away, once more stepping on the balls of her shoes.

"Hey, I'm going to talk to my friends." With one last unreadable look, Anna turned away and waved excitedly at two women, one of whom was Cassie's maid of honor. Soon they were all screeching with joy, jumping up and down and hugging and talking over one another. I left them to it.

I made my way to the seating chart and checked for my name and Anna's. We weren't sitting at the same table, not even close. I'd been seated with the Stumpstashers, and she'd been seated with what I assumed was the college crew. Shame.

Not looking to mingle, I picked up my place card and headed to the bar for a drink.

Chapter 5

-Anna-

I wasn't used to talking to big groups of people anymore, but I grabbed a glass of wine and threw myself into the task, feigning enthusiasm. I had to, in order to get my mind off of Ian…

…his tantalizing cologne…

…his firm bicep and rough hands…

…his soft, warm lips against my knuckle.

That last one had really surprised me. The kiss was an old-timey gesture, one that I would have laughed at had someone else been on the receiving end. Instead, I'd found myself melting, my brain turned to mush, dripping and pooling down between my legs. An utterly illogical response.

It must not have been completely illogical, though, given the number of heads that turned as we walked into the ceremony space.

I didn't like where things were going. The things he did to me. *Those* types of feelings were not supposed to come from *that* type of guy. Acting on them would surely bring disaster.

I actively avoided him for the rest of the evening.

For dinner, I was seated at a table with Jessa and Lisa and their new husbands, Jake and Prashant, as well as some of our other college friends. I thought that they'd be sore at me for missing their weddings, but right off the bat, we were giggling and joking, just like in the old days. Each inside joke and playful exchange filled me with bubbles of warmth, and I silently thanked Cassie for strong-arming me into coming.

The whole wedding was really sweet, and I was grudgingly affected. Not that I would ever admit it to anyone, but I started tearing up during the ceremony. Despite my cynicism about the institution of marriage, I could see how genuinely pleased Cassie was. This was *not* Fake News. They way they looked at each other, the same way that Frankie looked at both of them...I was so happy for her, so glad that she had found someone who loved her just as deeply as she loved him. Plus, the speeches from Cassie's mom and Michael's dad were hilarious, and Jessa gave a heartwarming speech about how Cassie had brought together all of our friends. She'd even given a shout-out to each person in our crew who had come to the wedding, and I was glad once again that I was there, especially when Cassie came over to our table after the speech to take a silly selfie with us.

That was one aspect of weddings that I could get behind—bringing old friends back together. In their company, I laughed and cheered and enjoyed myself way more than I'd ever thought possible at a wedding.

After the speeches came the first dance. For the first minute or so, Cassie and Michael did the usual slow sway, back and forth and side to side. But partway through, the DJ cut over to an upbeat pop song, and Cassie tore off the bottom of her dress, tossed the fabric to Jessa, and broke out into some disco moves with Michael. It was impeccably executed, fun and entertaining and true to Cassie's style, and as soon as the song ended, the audience erupted in cheers and applause.

Right after, the DJ invited everyone to join them, opening up the dance floor. The music was top 40, and while it wasn't my usual cup of tea, I didn't mind getting up to bounce around with Jessa and Lisa and our old college buddies. It felt a little like we were at a frat party again, especially with the open bar, which I found myself taking advantage of more than once.

Maybe weddings weren't *so* bad.

But then the DJ announced that it was time for the bouquet toss. I planted myself in my seat, refusing to budge, despite the fact that Jessa and Lisa were both chanting my name. I ignored them and turned to look at Cassie, whom I was annoyed to find staring at me and waving me over, exaggeratedly mouthing *Come on!* I hid my face behind my hand and stared at the table, mortified. Then Jessa and Lisa chanted louder, and soon my entire table was encouraging me to go.

Finally, the DJ announced, "Looks like there's a pretty young lady over there who should join in. Let's get her to come up, everyone!"

And then *everyone* was chanting my name.

Fuuuuuuuuuuuck.

I threw my hands up in exasperation and everyone clapped and cheered as I walked over to the dance floor, to where the bouquet toss was happening.

I vowed not to catch the bouquet, even if it hit me in the face.

There were maybe ten of us single ladies, a couple of whom were just young girls who were running and jumping around, excited to participate in the festivities. I noticed Ian then, sitting at the table just behind where I was standing. He'd turned his chair out to face the dance floor (undoubtedly to better see me be humiliated), and he gave me a thumbs up when he saw me looking his way. I stuck my tongue out at him and turned around to face Cassie.

Cassie peered out at the crowd on the dance floor and purposefully made eye contact with me. She then turned around, peeking over her shoulder to see where I was, and very obviously tried to toss the bouquet in my direction. Her aim was pretty good, and it looked like it might actually hit me, so I took a step back, thinking to dodge it...but then I looked down, too late, as one of the little girls bowled straight into me, trying to catch the bouquet in earnest. I took a few stumbling steps back to try to catch myself, then squawked and fell gracelessly into someone's lap.

I could guess whose it was, based on the location and the familiar scent. Hands lightly cupped my hips, his solid chest pressed against my back, warm breath on my neck. "You okay?" he asked, his voice husky against my ear. I arched my back slightly at the sound.

"Fine." I struggled to sit up, placing my hands on his knees and sliding back to push myself up. As I did so, my ass encountered something...hard. *Oh!* My body, ever the betrayer, wanted to sink into him and press his growing erection up against me where I needed it most. I wanted his warmth and his soothing scent to envelop me, his hot hands to touch me all over. Instead, I jumped up and off of his lap. Rather, I tried to, then fell back down and encountered the *considerable* evidence of his arousal again. Ian's hands, still on my hips, did very little to help, and his silent laughter rumbled against my back. I had to reach behind me and push *hard* off of his chest in order to stand. Finally on my feet, I smoothed my dress, turned around, glared at him, and stalked back to my seat. A deep laugh followed me, and I growled at the answering clench low in my belly.

The DJ just had to make it worse: "I hope the gentleman tips her well after *that* lap dance." And then *everyone* was cracking up. Except me.

FUUUUUUUUUUUUUCK.

I sat down and took a deep breath, willing my heartbeat to slow. It was harder than I thought it would be, for two reasons:

I still felt eyes on me after what was one of the most humiliating moments of my life so far;

Every cell in my body was prickling with a burning desire. For Ian.

The first, I could do nothing about, other than to keep a low profile for the rest of the night. I sat down in my seat, took out my phone, and pretended to stare at it. *Nothing to see here, people*.

The second, I tackled with cold, hard logic. My body's reaction to him had been only natural. As I'd mentioned previously, it'd been six months since I'd last gotten laid. It was unfortunate, but...I was thirsty. And I was primed for romance, given the excessively romantic setting. Plus, I'd had a few drinks, which never failed to make me horny, and in my somewhat buzzed state of mind, I had to admit that I found him at least a *tiny* bit attractive. Alcohol was known to make even the most unattractive of people slightly more appealing. I glanced sidelong at his broad shoulders and long, muscular limbs, packaged all too neatly in his crisp, cobalt suit. *Fine*, maybe he was more than a bit attractive. But I didn't want to deal with all of the baggage that undoubtedly came with a Guy Like Him. I was sure that there were just mountains of it. *Not my type.*

I tamped down on my desire and tried not to think about him *or* his sizable bulge.

After the bouquet toss was the garter toss. I noticed that Ian chose not to get up for it (and wasn't heckled by his friends or the DJ about it! Stupid double standards), but merely clapped politely as his colleague Tom caught the garter. For some reason, Tom glanced my way. *Uh, no thanks.*

Chain letters sent and future marriage victims selected, the DJ played a classic couple's song, and Jessa and Lisa got up to dance with their husbands. Alone at the table, I took out my phone and checked my messages for the umpteenth time.

"Care to dance?" I looked up and found Ian, eyes already dancing with amusement, holding out his hand to me.

"You mean, beyond the *lap dance* that I just gave you? No thanks." I turned back to my phone and tapped and swiped at random.

"C'mon. Just this song." He leaned closer and whispered, "Besides, if you don't dance with me, I'm pretty sure Tom is going to come over and ask you, and he's got two left feet. And possibly a cold."

I glanced up and saw that Tom was indeed staring at me. He pushed his thick glasses up and rubbed his nose on his sleeve, as if preparing to come say hi. *Ugh.* He had a bowl cut, for goodness sake.

"*Fine.*" I took Ian's hand and he led me out to the dance floor, my pulse beating rapidly in my neck. Probably from the alcohol.

Ian pulled me close, his hands on my lower back. Not sure

of the best place to put my own hands, I tentatively placed them on his shoulders. We swayed like that for a bit, my eyes hovering somewhere near his Adam's apple, not daring to look further up. But then Ian surprised me by stepping out to the beat, taking my hands and spinning me around until my back was to his chest and my arms were crossed in front of me. We swayed like that for a couple of beats, his breath caressing my neck while I desperately fought the urge to lean into him. Then he spun me out again, uncrossing my arms, and pulled me close once more, my hands landing neatly on his chest.

"Huh. You're actually a pretty good dancer." I was genuinely impressed with how smoothly and easily he'd handled my body. Our eyes met, and something fluttered deep in my chest at the keen look in his eyes. I dropped my gaze back to his Adam's apple.

"It's easy when you've got a good partner," he said, turning his head to press lightly into mine. His breath tickled my hair and gently warmed my scalp. He was so *hot* and—

I swallowed. *Just keep talking.* "So do you go dancing a lot?"

"Ha, no. One of my exes was really into it and she made me learn some moves. Dancing's okay, but it's not really my thing."

I tsked and ignored the twinge in my chest at the thought of Ian holding another woman close, dancing with her like he was with me. "That's a shame. I love dancing. It's so fun to get absorbed in the music, to just let go and see where the beat takes you. Maybe you just haven't found the right music to dance to, yet."

"Maybe. Isn't that your job? To tell me what I should listen to?" His tone was teasing, but something told me that he was only half-joking.

"I guess. But I feel like the act of discovering new music is half the fun. If I just told you to listen to stuff, would you actually like it?"

He shrugged slightly. "I like most music."

I shot him a skeptical look. He'd clearly never really *listened* to music before. "*Ok*...so you don't really care for music or dancing. What *is* your thing?"

He stepped through and spun me out again, brought me back in and switched hands to spin me out to the other side, then switched hands behind his back once more until we were face-to-face again. I grinned at him. For someone who didn't really listen to music, he sure seemed able to *feel* it.

Finally, he answered, "I wouldn't say that I don't care for those things, but I definitely don't go out of my way to experience them. I do really enjoy cooking and climbing, though."

"I see. So what is it about cooking or climbing that you love so much?" The song had changed to yet another classic couples ballad. Although I'd only promised him one dance, I noticed that Tom was still watching us. I ignored him and pulled closer to Ian, whose hand shifted lower, shifting my awareness of him lower, too.

"For cooking, it's enjoying the fruits of my labor, and being able to share what I make with loved ones. For climbing, it's getting stronger, both mentally and physically."

"Mentally?" The physical part was obvious, but mentally? I wasn't buying it.

"Yeah. It's scary on the wall sometimes, so part of the mental challenge is overcoming that fear. But also, climbing's just hard. When people encounter enough setbacks, or fail enough times, it can be easy to get discouraged. It's really important to have a growth mindset and believe that you can always get better, always improve."

Ah. I shook my head. "That's a nice thought, but people definitely have limits. You can't just keep getting better at things." I bitterly thought of my stagnant music writing career. After selling one piece several months ago, I hadn't sold any since.

He smiled wryly. "Not with that attitude."

"Uh huh." I adjusted my hands so that they were comfortably clasped behind his neck. His rough calluses caught on the fabric of my dress as he smoothed his hands over my hips and pulled me even tighter against him, gently crushing my breasts against his hard chest.

The close contact between our bodies...his clean, masculine scent...the warm fuzzies from the alcohol...conditions were *very* bad, and I was liable to make a mistake tonight. I tried to smother the growing warmth between my legs.

"You know, I was right," he said.

"What?"

He lowered his head so that we were cheek to cheek, then whispered into my ear, "You're not wearing any panties." His hands gently squeezed my hips.

The warmth exploded into a searing inferno. I knew that I should step away from him and douse the flames, but the reckless, perverse part of me wanted to play this game with him...to tease him back.

"I'm not wearing a bra, either," I whispered, slipping my fingers into his hair. "Doesn't mean anything. You're still not getting laid tonight." Although the way things were going, I wasn't so sure.

He smiled against my ear, then slid his hands lower to rest on top of my ass, fingers lightly pressing. I reveled in the sensation, both wanting to slap his hands away and willing him to go lower.

Before he could respond, the song switched over to an upbeat dance track, and couples time was over. We slowly broke apart, the distance tempering the heat between us ever so slightly. I quietly thanked the DJ for doing something *helpful* for once that evening.

"Do you want to grab a drink?" he asked, offering me his arm. After a moment's hesitation, I took it, curling my hand once more around his hard bicep as we walked off the dance floor.

"My face is probably red and puffy, so you know I've already had enough." *His* face, I noticed, was still as tan and attractive as ever. The wine goggles were working a bit too effectively.

"I guess you look a bit flushed, but it's cute," he said. *Liar.* No one looked good with Asian glow.

"What I really want is to get out of these heels." My feet had gone from *fine* to *tormented* over the course of our dancing, but at least the pain helped distract me from the lust.

He craned his head and glanced around, then said, "There's a terrace out there with some grass. Might be nice to walk on."

Oooh. Cool grass on bare feet sounded lovely, and some fresh air might help put out the raging California wildfire between us. "Yes, please."

He opened the door and led me out onto the terrace, where we were greeted by the steady chirping of crickets and a huge, low full moon. It was somewhat windy and chilly, though, which may have explained why no one else was around.

Without my asking, Ian took off his suit jacket and placed it around my shoulders. I gratefully pulled his jacket closed around me and sat down on a wooden bench. He sat down beside me, his legs straddling the bench to face me, when he suddenly reached down to pick up my left foot.

"What are you doing?" I asked, cocking an eyebrow at him.

His eyes met mine, and my heart pounded at the answer that I saw there. With nimble fingers, he undid the clasp on my shoe, tracing my ankle with the rough pad of his thumb as he gently lifted the shoe from my foot. Awareness zipped like lightning down the rest of my leg, and I longed for his fingers to wander higher.

Then he put my shoe behind him on the bench and began massaging my foot.

He rubbed his thumb up and down along my arch. I clenched, each stroke of his thumb seemingly mirrored deeper within. I nearly moaned at the sensation, but instead, I shifted my weight so that I was leaning backwards on my hands, making it easier for me to watch him work.

He gently rolled my ankle, then briefly massaged my lower calf, followed by the ridge above my heel.

With each warm caress, each stroke of his hands...my defenses eroded.

So what if he wasn't my type? We could have a little fling, right? It didn't have to be a long-term romance. We were at a wedding, a temporary gathering, so I'd probably never see him again after this. And it'd been way too long since I'd last had sex. I just wanted to have fun tonight.

Ian looked like he'd be a *lot* of fun.

Besides, I didn't want to let these stirrings for him turn into feelings. I wanted to own my lust for what it was, and nothing more.

There was no point in denying what was happening between us.

So I took charge. "Clearly, you think you can just foot rub your way into my panties."

He gave me a flirtatious smile, still slowly massaging me with his strong hands. "So it's working?"

I smiled coyly at him. "No."

He raised an eyebrow. "Guess I'll have to try harder." He kneaded the ball of my foot between his two thumbs and I nearly arched my back in pleasure.

After a few more seconds, he lowered my foot down to the grass and picked up my right foot, then repeated the series of motions. *Mmm.*

I'd never had my feet used in foreplay before. Maybe I had a foot fetish that I didn't know about.

Or maybe it was just Ian.

"Is that all you've got?" I asked when he placed my foot back down. My feet felt much better, but now other parts of me were aching to be touched.

In answer, he lifted my legs onto his lap and slid down the bench towards me, eyes intent on my face, lips slightly parted. And before I could land another teasing barb, he'd slipped his fingers into my hair, leaned in close, and kissed me.

My body tensed instinctively, but as he kissed me softly and sweetly, his breath warm with whiskey and autumn spices, I parted my lips and allowed his tongue to brush against mine...tentatively at first, then questing slightly deeper, teasing and taunting, continuing our playful banter from before without words.

But when he slipped his arms around me and pulled me

further onto his lap, our kisses grew bolder, hotter…from playful to *desperate*.

My whole body lit up with desire.

My hands greedily grasped his tie and held onto him, unrelenting, demanding *more*. The satin dress was torture against my bare skin, sliding up and down as I wriggled against him, seeking more friction, more contact, more *him*. And while Ian had talked a big game about seducing me earlier, after a few moments, it was clear that he was content to just make out on the bench. He was playing the long game, then, the aggravating man.

I wasn't. I didn't want a slow tide of affection to build, or for him to chip away at my defenses—I wanted him to just fuck me and move on.

I took his hand from my hip and brought it to my breast. He followed my lead and gently fondled me, then caressed my nipple through the thin material. I gasped softly into his neck and raked my fingers through his hair.

I was very, embarrassingly wet. I hoped that it wouldn't seep through my dress.

His own arousal was hard and insistent against my thigh. I lowered my hand and pressed my fingers against his considerable length until he pulled away from me, panting. "Did you want to go somewhere more private?" he rasped.

"Yes," I said breathlessly. Though I was still reeling from his kisses, and though I'd *wanted* him to go further, I made a mental note that he had asked me for *permission* to go somewhere more private. Point for Ian.

He grabbed my shoes and unceremoniously scooped me up. I laughed, exhilarated. Instead of going inside like I thought he was going to, he stepped out over the terrace railing and down to the gravel below. It was only a one foot drop, but I gasped in surprise anyway. He carried me around the side of the building and back to the front entrance, where he took a right at the entryway and then turned into the gender neutral bathroom. He set me down on the counter, then turned around and locked the door.

The bathroom was clean and spacious, with beautiful dark wooden paneling on the walls and a gray ceramic floor. The counter that he'd set me on was slightly damp, and I was sitting between a pile of napkins and a giant bouquet of pale pink and lavender blooms that lightly perfumed the air.

As far as places to have sex went, this wasn't half bad.

Behind me was a large mirror with two warm yellow lamps on either side. In the dark, illuminated only by the moon, our coupling hadn't seemed so real...but in the soft golden glow of the bathroom light, I could see Ian's face in full, and it reminded me of what I had vowed to myself years ago. I hesitated.

Ian seemed to sense my hesitation, and he took his time in picking up where we'd left off. He tentatively reached out with his fingertips and traced my lower lip, swollen and sensitive from his kisses, then leaned in slowly, giving me time to push him away if I wanted to. I didn't. Our lips met, and his tongue gently caressed mine, leisurely stoking up the flame and rebuilding the fire.

His considerate gestures only further affirmed my decision to let him seduce me. He was a good guy, caring and kind, not the douchey tech bro that I had originally assumed him to be. He deserved a night of fun, too. Nothing more.

His fingers traced their way down my arms as he slipped his jacket off from around my shoulders. I melted into him and opened my legs to let him stand closer, pulling him to me with his tie once more. He lay me back against the mirror, still thoroughly ravishing my mouth with his, and his hands sought my breasts, teasing my nipples until they were tight and chafing against the satin. I mewled needily, rubbing myself against his erection until he broke our kiss and lowered his lips to my heated neck, trailing kisses down to my collarbone. *Fuck, it felt so good.*

He lowered his head further and sucked my nipple *through* the satin dress, leaving behind an obscene wet spot. I arched my back in ecstasy and sighed with pleasure as he switched to the other.

My dress was going to be a sordid mess by the end of the night. I giggled at the thought.

His eyes met mine as he slowly pulled away and lowered his head. He traced his hand up my thigh, then pushed the satin aside and lifted my knees, pulling my legs apart to expose my glistening wet pussy.

Fuck. Was he about to do what my ex had refused to do? And the guy before him?

He got down on one knee and planted a sweet, tantalizing kiss, right where it was wettest. I moaned so loudly that people could surely hear it over the music.

Now I was *truly* glad that I'd decided to let Ian have his way with me.

He dipped his tongue into me and I arched my back again, craving more contact. He kept his eyes on my face the whole time, watching my every expression as he swirled his tongue inside me, round and round. I fucking *loved* it, and I cried his name to let him know. Then he pulled my clit into his mouth and sucked, his facial hair grinding against the sensitive skin of my inner thighs. I slipped my fingers into his hair and held on for dear life. *Oh my god.*

I'd only ever had one guy go down on me before, and he'd clearly had no idea what he was doing. And he'd certainly had no facial hair.

Ian had a fucking *PhD* in this. It was. So. Fucking. Good.

But I was well-past ready for him. And Ian, aggravating man that he was, continued at his leisurely pace, slowly exploring me instead of breaking and entering like I needed him to.

I didn't want his slow worship. That led to feelings, and feelings were useless to me.

I needed him to just fuck me and get out of my life. If I could just scratch that itch, just break that seal between us, I was sure it would go away.

Instead, even as he seduced me, he tried to win me over. *How annoying.*

"Ian," I moaned. *"Please.* Fuck me."

He lazily ran his tongue up and down my wet folds, as if he had all the time in the world. I slipped my fingers deeper into his hair, grinding myself against his mouth, closing my eyes and reveling in the sensation. Then I pushed his head away.

"Hurry up," I begged.

Instead of immediately getting up and sticking it into me, he met my eyes again, casually licked two fingers and slipped them into my...two-finger pocket. I gasped at the sensation, the emptiness inside me only partially relieved. His fingers were so deliciously rough, the friction softened and perfected by the intense moisture that my body was producing. He crooked his fingers inside of me and stroked me closer to oblivion. His tongue went back to circling my clit, and the combination was almost too much. If he kept going, I knew

I'd come completely undone.

But only one thing could truly break the spell between us.

"Ian, fuck, I want you *inside of me!*" My voice was so annoying and whiny, but I couldn't take it anymore.

With one last flick of his tongue, he withdrew his fingers and stood up, then pulled his wallet out, from which he produced a condom packet. I eyed the very visible bulge in his pants, straining against the perfect cut of his pants.

Finally!

His phone rang. I tensed.

Our eyes met, and I frowned. *Don't you dare.* He reached into his pocket and must've silenced it because the ringing soon stopped. I slowly relaxed again and watched him put the condom packet on the counter, then unbuckle his belt. He unbuttoned his pants—

The phone rang again. We both froze.

"Sorry. I should check who it is." He reached into his pants pocket and pulled out the phone. When he saw who it was, he sighed. "Hold that thought."

I scowled, frustrated. Who could be calling on a Saturday night worth interrupting *this?*

He lewdly licked his fingers clean and winked at me, then answered the phone in Chinese. "Wei? Ma?" He unlocked the door and stepped outside, closing the door behind him.

What. The. Fuck. *It was his mom?* He was going to ruin his chances with me to talk to his *mom?*

The lustful fog lifted, swept away by cold, hard reality, and I hurried to obliterate any evidence of that night's terrible mistake.

Chapter 6

-Ian-

I probably shouldn't have picked up the phone. I knew that I could call my mom back later, and that there might not be a later with Anna. She was so close, literally begging for me to finish her off. My mom couldn't have picked a worse time to call.

But my mother had severe anxiety, though she'd never admit that anxiety was a real illness and would rather suffer than go to a psychiatrist or take medicine for it. And lately, it'd been worse, much worse. She had trouble sleeping, partly because of the anxiety, partly because of the chemo and the steroids that were part of her breast cancer treatment. I'd told her that she could call me whenever, wherever, but even then, she usually didn't call me unless it was particularly bad.

So I picked up the call.

"*Wei? Ma?*" As I closed the bathroom door behind me, I caught a glimpse of Anna's incredulous face. *Uh oh*.

"Sorry to call you so late, Ian," my mom said in Mandarin. "I couldn't sleep."

"It's okay, *Ma*. You can call me anytime. How was your day?

Did you have chemo today?" I decided to talk to my mom for just a couple of minutes. I didn't want to rush her or make her feel like she couldn't call me, but I knew that Anna wouldn't wait forever.

"Yes. I felt so nauseous. I couldn't eat at all today. Your *Ba* tried to make braised pork for me but he burned it again, which only made me *more* nauseous."

I chuckled. I definitely hadn't gotten my cooking skills from my dad. "That's *Ba* for you. But you have to try to eat, *Ma*. If you can't sleep, maybe you should eat something now?" Guilt and hope warred in my chest at the prospect of ending the call so quickly.

"I will, I will. But I haven't heard from you in a few days. Where are you?"

"*Ma*, I'm at my friend Cassie's wedding, remember? I told you about it last week." At the reminder of how my mom's memory had become increasingly spotty, hope glimmered and died, leaving only guilt. My mom deserved better.

She grunted. "How's the wedding?"

I stared at the bathroom door, willing it to stay closed. *Just a couple more minutes*. "It's been fun. The food was pretty good. They had a buffet line with steak and halibut. The venue is a gorgeous barn. And I've met some...interesting people."

"Any pretty girls?" my mom teased. She desperately wanted grandchildren, and after her cancer diagnosis, she reminded me of that fact quite frequently. As her only child, I had the dubious privilege of fulfilling (or crushing) her hopes and dreams.

"Ah, yes. Lots," I said, though I'd really only noticed one.

I turned around when I heard the bathroom door open behind me. Anna wore her shoes and my jacket and had

68

cleaned herself up as well as she could. Her hair was a bit lopsided and there were wet marks on her dress—possibly from the counter, possibly from one of us. But she was stiff as a statue, no longer a playful sex kitten. She stonily shook her head at me and made to slip away back into the party.

"*Ma?* Sorry, I have to go, I'll call you tomorrow, I promise. Wan an." *Goodnight.* I hung up and hurried after her, buckling my belt as I went.

"Hey, hold up, can we talk?" I asked.

She stopped and looked at me, her face grim. "That was a mistake." She tried to turn away, but I grabbed her arm.

"Anna, wait, I—"

She jerked her arm out of mine and walked away. I didn't follow, just stared after her. From the hard look in her eyes and the set of her jaw, I doubted that she would stop and listen to me, no matter what I did.

A moment later, Cassie and her maid of honor (Jessa?) exited the reception area. "Ian!" Cassie walked up and sloppily threw her arms around me. She was clearly drunk, but still blissful and glowing as only a new bride could be. "Was Anna out here with you?" She gave me a sly look and punched my arm. "She looked kinda…" she leaned in and whispered loudly, "sexed up." Cassie winked at me and Jessa cracked up like it was the funniest thing she'd ever heard.

I shrugged. A gentleman never kissed and told.

Cassie put her arm around my shoulders and slurred, "You know, she could use a guy like you. She's always going after wild good-for-nothings. You should totally go after her."

I sighed. "I don't think she'd like that." A thought occurred to me, and I turned to look drunk Cassie in the eye. Surely her filters were long gone by now. "By the way, why doesn't

69

she date Asian guys?"

Cassie disappointed me and shook her head. "Why don't you ask her?" She pulled me and Jessa with her towards the bathroom.

I gently tried to extract my arm from Cassie's grasp, but she was a climber too, and her grip strength was formidable. "I tried, but she wouldn't tell me."

Cassie stopped, then let go of my arm and very solemnly put her hands on my shoulders. "D-daddy issues." She hiccuped.

Ah, Cassie. So reliable. Jessa, who was slightly less drunk, must have realized that that was probably too much information. She squinted at me and said, "You've got a little...something." She gestured at her own chin while pulling Cassie upright and leading her the rest of the way to the bathroom. I wiped my chin off with my palm and turned to walk back to the reception area.

A moment later, Cassie exclaimed, "There's a condom in here!"

I walked faster. I glanced around the dining hall and dance floor, but didn't see Anna anywhere. There was no sign of her, even after checking the cake and coffee area, as well as the terrace. So I headed back to my table and sat down to think.

Daddy issues? Was her dad a misogynistic asshole, and she didn't want to date anyone even remotely similar to him? Or perhaps he was racist, and she was trying (or not trying) to please him? Something else? I imagined the best and worst case scenarios, but I knew that it wouldn't do me any good to guess at what that meant. Only Anna could tell me.

I checked my phone to see if she'd messaged me at all. I'd given her my business card, so she had my number, but I didn't have hers. There were no messages. I sighed and contemplated going back to the hotel to look for her.

Thankfully, after one last song, the DJ announced that the wedding was over, but that an afterparty would be happening at the hotel. Everyone queued up to get onto the shuttles, and I eagerly craned my neck to look around, but still didn't see Anna anywhere. She must've caught an earlier shuttle back.

I got onto the shuttle and ignored everyone. They all took one look at my face and left me alone.

When we arrived back, I sprinted up the stairs to our floor to avoid all of the elevator traffic. As I'd expected, my jacket was on the doorknob to my room. I walked a few feet down and knocked on Anna's door, softly calling her name. No answer.

I went into my room and found a slip of paper and a pen to write a note.

> *Anna,*
>
> *I had a great time with you tonight. I'm sorry if things got awkward. If you give me a chance, I can explain what happened. You're smart, funny, and gorgeous, and I'd love to get to know you better.*
>
> *Hope to see you at climbing tomorrow morning (assuming you're not hungover). 10am at the Granitarium. It'll be "rocking" good fun.*
>
> *Ian*

I folded it twice and slipped it under her door.

She never showed up.

* * *

71

"What's her deal, Cassie?" I asked. I belayed Cassie as she led a 5.10c route at the Granitarium. I didn't give her any details about what happened the night before, just mentioned that I'd been "hanging out" with Anna when she'd gotten mad at me for talking to my mom.

"Don't take it personally. Anna's...picky." She lunged for a jug. Cassie wasn't very tall (maybe only 5'), so she had an extremely dynamic climbing style that was exciting to watch, especially as her belayer.

"You told me before that you thought we'd be great together. Except for the whole Asian guy thing." I gave her extra slack as she clipped in.

She locked off on her right and felt around with her left hand on a large mantle shelf above her, searching for the best hand position. "I...did...still...think so," she said, straining. "Take!" she yelled, a moment before falling. She hadn't gone far from the clip, so she only fell a couple of feet. I caught her, soft and easy.

"So how do I win her over?" I leaned back into the harness to make it easier to look up at her.

Cassie glanced at me from above, shook out her arms, and sighed. "You don't. Not if she doesn't want to be won over."

"You won't give me her number and let me try?" I asked, voice pitched slightly higher with hope.

She stuck her tongue out at me, then got back onto the route. "Chicks before dicks, Ian."

Sigh. Well, it was fun while it lasted.

* * *

With my mom ill and my dad taking care of her, it was a tough time for them both. It always cheered them up to hear from me, so I alternated my calls between them.

On Wednesday morning, on my way to the office, I called my dad.

"Hello? *Ba*. How are you?" We spoke in Mandarin, as usual.

"Ian. I'm fine, I'm fine." His exaggerated sigh suggested otherwise.

"*Ba*, what's wrong? Are you okay?" After retiring last year, he seemed more withdrawn and tired, and he was even less inclined to go to the doctor than my mother.

"Nothing, I'm fine. Just need a break. You know how your *Ma* can be." He heaved another sigh, and I sighed along with him. We both loved her deeply, but my mother was a handful sometimes. "Can we still come see you this weekend? You'll be back from California on Friday, right?"

"Yes, of course you can still come. You know I love seeing you both."

"You sure we're not bothering you?" He often asked me this question.

"No way, I look forward to it. We can go check out this new Italian restaurant that just opened around the corner from my apartment. I've heard it's really good."

He was silent for a moment. "Ian. Are we making it hard for you to date?"

I snorted. "No *Ba*, I'm making it hard for myself. Why do you ask?"

Another brief silence. "Your *Ma* wants to see you get married," he murmured.

"She will. You both will. You're both going to live till you're 100." I hoped I sounded convinced. "She only has a few more treatments left, right?"

"She's so tired sometimes," he said, his tone melancholy. "I'm tired, too."

I clenched my fists on the steering wheel. "*Ba*, you guys are only in your 60s. You have plenty of time to watch me get married and play with your grandkids. Just make sure you exercise and eat well. Don't eat too many of those desserts that you love. And don't make me worry about you."

He sighed. "We try."

I attempted to lighten his mood. "Do your friends have any daughters in mind for me?"

My dad chuckled quietly. "You know your *Ma* would try to find you a wife, if you asked her to. Don't joke about it if you don't mean it."

I smiled, reflecting on my poor dating record. Reflecting on Anna. "Maybe it wouldn't be such a bad thing."

Chapter 7

-Anna-

One month later

I stepped off the subway and was greeted by the familiar, sharp tang of urine. I usually loved New York, but there were days when the reality of it was just too much. Like today, when it was overcast, cold, and windy outside. And the station was crowded and loud and stank worse than usual.

Oh, and I had gotten fired.

I had my suspicions about why. I *may* have been overly vocal in my opinion of our latest client, who'd been accused by multiple women of sexual assault. I *may* have used the words *fucking asshat* and *douche canoe* while I was talking to the secretary about him, right as he walked into the office. I'd *definitely* fucked up, big time. And now it was time for me to find a new job, at least until my music writing career picked up.

Given my ghost town of an email inbox, that didn't seem to be happening anytime soon. I regularly submitted pieces to the biggest music news sites, but I'd only heard back a few times, all rejections. I hadn't gotten paid for a piece since my first, seven months ago. So I still needed a real job, one that left me with enough mental energy at the end of the day to work on my dream job.

Recently, it felt more like a *pipe* dream job. Nothing really inspired me anymore, and my playlists and blog posts were increasingly lackluster. New York was generally a good place for music, but I'd lived there for eight years and it was honestly getting a bit old. Or maybe *I* was uninspiring and getting a bit old. Either way, the venues blurred together, the shows all sounded the same, and with the boring side jobs that I had to work in order to make ends meet, I just never seemed to have enough time or resources to push out new, unique content at the rate that I needed to.

My trip to San Francisco the month before had been a nice change of scenery, and it seemed to have helped a bit. I'd finished the playlist that I'd been working on (one of my better ones), visited some cool record stores, discovered a local band that played psychedelic covers of pop songs, and gotten some ideas for additional playlists. I stretched the experience out into a five-part blog post. It'd been a really productive trip.

The only bad part of the trip had been *him*.

The night of the wedding, I'd taken the next shuttle back to the hotel. It had mortified me to no end that I'd been practically *begging* him to fuck me, and that he'd chosen to leave me there, dripping wet and aching, to talk to his *mother*. What did that say about him? What did that say about me?

Good thing that he hadn't finished the job, and that I hadn't come. Orgasm usually meant attachment for me, and with Ian, I did not want that. He was everything that I'd rejected from my previous life, and there was definitely no future for us. So despite his skilled tongue and his sweet note, I'd completely ghosted him.

But Cassie and Jessa seemed to know that something had happened between us. When we met for drinks on the Sunday night after the wedding, they told me that they specifically had not invited him, even though they had all been climbing together earlier in the day. I was annoyed and vaguely jealous that they'd all gone without me. Not that I hadn't been invited.

"So...what exactly happened between you two?" Cassie asked. It was just me and the girls, Cassie, Jessa, and Lisa.

"Well," I began, taking a sip of my cocktail, "we kinda hooked up. *Kinda.* I was tipsy and thirsty, and he was...convenient."

Lisa giggled. "And *hot*," she added, unhelpfully.

I frowned at her, then continued, "But luckily, his mom called and he started talking to her instead of having sex with me." I sat back and smirked, eagerly anticipating their outrage.

They stared. "He...picked up the phone instead of putting his dick in you?" Jessa asked, incredulous.

"His *mom*?" added Lisa, mouth gaping.

"I *know*, right? Who does that?" I took another sip of my cocktail, triumphantly vindicated.

Cassie studied my face, a small wrinkle on her brow. "You know, we've worked together for the past couple of years, and he doesn't really take time off." She paused. "But he did recently, because his mom has cancer."

I nearly spat out my drink. Instead, I gulped it down, the alcohol burning my throat. "Oh." Giant snakes of guilt writhed in my stomach.

Jessa and Lisa exchanged glances. "It's still kinda weird that he did that," Jessa offered, trying to make me feel better. "He could've just called her back later. He missed his chance with you."

Lisa put her arm around me. "Besides, you have a rule right? No Asian guys."

I plastered on a smile, though the frenzied squirming in my stomach continued. "Yep. No Asian guys!" I raised my glass. They clinked their glasses with mine and we all took a drink. We didn't talk about Ian or guys anymore after that.

* * *

I briskly walked the familiar route back to my apartment in Queens, only half-heartedly glancing at the rock climbers in the gym that I always passed. But a flash of bare, golden skin caught my eye, and I briefly stopped to look.

Fuck. There, on one of the walls nearest to the front, was Ian.

And he was *ripped*.

I'd felt the hard planes of his muscles crushed against me at Cassie's wedding, but I had no idea that he possessed the abs and pecs of an underwear model, all sculpted curves and lines of definition. His shirtless back flexed with pure muscle, bare skin glistening with sweat. The grace and power with which he climbed, the calm precision of his movements on the wall...it was captivating.

He leapt (actually leapt!) from one big green hold to another, catching it easily and pulling himself up and over in one fluid motion. He balanced on the hold on one foot, carefully sliding his hands up along his side and over his head to touch a tiny green speck at the top of the wall. Then he jumped, easily ten feet, down to the mat below. A pretty, olive-skinned brunette wearing only tights and a sports bra gave him a high five. I scowled at her fit, athletic body, the honeyed glow of her skin.

The stunning smile she flashed at him.

I hid in the shadows by the entrance, staring like a creeper. He sat down next to the brunette and they watched as another guy tried to repeat the same moves. The guy leapt, just as Ian had, but his hands slipped off the hold and he ended up belly-flopping onto the mat. He ruefully got up and said something to Ian, who began pointing at the wall and miming climbing movements.

Ian had made it look so easy. I mean, no wonder, with a body like *that*. If only I'd waited for him in the bathroom, maybe I would've—

I shivered. The chill was creeping in, and it was time to move on. I had more important things to think about than who had missed out on whom.

* * *

I wept into my mug. "Cassie...I don't know what to do." I'd just told her about getting laid off. I knew that I'd be okay for a couple of months, given that I had *some* savings, but I was nervous anyway. I needed a new job that paid relatively well, and landing one could definitely take longer than two months.

The thought of going back to being fully trapped...it filled me with dread. Why was it so hard to get on my own two feet, like I so badly wanted?

Cassie typed and clicked on her computer, big blue eyes narrowed in concentration as she stared at the screen. Her bright blonde hair was loose, wavy and wild, perfectly framing her soft, feminine face. She'd insisted that we should keep in touch after my visit to San Francisco, and I'd decided to try, really try, this time. We'd started doing weekly Sunday night Google Hangout calls ever since her wedding, and I was grateful to have such a good friend back in my life.

She stopped clicking. "You probably aren't going to like this...but there's an opening for an office admin role at Stumpstash, in the New York office. I just checked our jobs page." The chat window chimed. She'd sent me a link.

I wept even harder. "*Cassie*, I can't—I can't work with *him*."

"Shhhh, why not? Hey, he's just a guy you hooked up with, it's not a big deal."

"It would be s-so embarrassing." I wiped my tears away and clicked on the link to the job description.

When the page finished loading, my jaw dropped and I immediately stopped crying.

"*$40 per hour?* Is that a typo?" I skimmed the rest of the job description.

"Nope. Welcome to tech, Nana." On screen, Cassie sat back and smiled. "Let's be coworkers!"

"Health benefits? *Three weeks vacation?* What the fuck? This is what tech is like? Why did I waste so much time working for a law firm?" I thought about Ian and his bespoke suit and fancy jeans. Or the absurdly large diamond flashing on Cassie's finger.

"Yup. You should definitely apply! I know the idea of working with Ian bothers you, Nana, but I think it'd be a great role for you. And it'll only be awkward for a minute. Ian's a really nice guy—he's not going to hold it against you. He'll probably even help you. He actually helped me get my job, too."

I was still shocked, but the practical part of my brain started to win over the butt-hurt emotional part. I slowly nodded.

"Ok. I'll think about it. Thanks, Cass."

"Of course! But hey, I have to go. Michael and I are going to catch a movie. Let me know if you want a referral! And if you get a chance, you should ask Ian about what the New York office is like, it might not be run the same way as the San Francisco one."

"Alright, I'll try. Bye, Cass. Thanks for everything." She blew me a kiss through the screen and signed off.

I sighed and closed my laptop, then sipped my tea and considered my options.

A position like this wouldn't be open for long. If I wanted the job, I had to act right away.

I could look around for other jobs, but I doubted that I'd find one as good, or have a friend who could refer me and help me through the process.

And $40 per hour was a lot. *Plus benefits.* My last job had paid less than half as much.

I could eat twice as much pizza, or go to twice as many music shows. I could afford to get a gym membership, or maybe travel more.

But...*Ian.*

The thought of him filled me with a myriad of feelings. Annoyance. Lust. Guilt. Regret. In retrospect, he'd really done nothing wrong. If I'd just waited for him...if we'd just finished what we'd started...maybe it would've been fine. More than fine, the way things had been going. A jolt of need shot through me at the memory of his warm hands and irresistible tongue on my skin, and despite the warm tea in my hands, I shivered.

We likely could have hooked up and ended things on ok terms. Instead, I'd gotten mad at him for talking to his sick mom, and then I'd completely cut him off.

It sucked to be in the wrong, especially now that I needed his help. And though I wasn't superstitious, I couldn't deny the fact that seeing him earlier this evening *seemed* like a sign.

Maybe this was my chance to get a better job *and* to apologize.

So what if he'd almost known me in the biblical sense?

So what if I'd ghosted him, somewhat unfairly?

I could deal with it all for $40 an hour and three weeks of vacation.

I opened my desk drawer and rummaged about until I found Ian's business card. For some inexplicable reason, despite what had happened, I'd decided to keep it. Past-Anna was somehow always looking out for present-Anna.

His smiling face, printed on the card, seemed to mock me.

I imagined his lips curled further up into a sneer. I'd scoffed at him for being a tech bro, and yet here I was, asking to join the party.

Then I imagined his lips doing other things too. *Filthy* things. I shook my head, willing the thoughts to go away.

I lifted my mug and swallowed the last of my tea...and my pride.

Chapter 8

-Ian-

After my conversation with my dad, I'd planned on trying harder to find a girlfriend. Instead, I tried harder in the gym.

Firstly, work picked up and I had a brand new team to manage. I didn't need the additional work of going out to bars or meetups, or carefully reading profiles and crafting messages to people through dating apps. I preferred the more organic approach anyway, as it was easier to tell if we had chemistry right off the bat.

Secondly, I figured that I could just meet someone at my climbing gym. There were a ton of fit, awesome women there. They were usually just there to climb, and not to talk, but occasionally, there were some looking to mingle. My current climbing partner, Lina, was one of them. Even though we didn't talk about anything other than climbing (she was oddly evasive when I asked her about herself), it was a start. Girls knew other girls, right?

Thirdly, I was still a little bummed about Anna. I couldn't shake the feeling that we could've been good together.

She'd been so full of opinions, emotions, feelings...life.

She was like a spicy curry, and everyone else was boiled potatoes.

If only she'd waited for me...I would have devoured her and licked her clean, then come back for seconds and thirds.

But she hadn't, the closed-minded shrew.

Her loss.

So instead of actively hunting for a girlfriend, I climbed hard. There was no trouble, no frustration, that I couldn't climb away. The raw physicality of climbing, the need to push myself and give 110% to my project...it consumed me so that there was nothing left to fuel the other emotions that fought for my attention, like fear about my parents or stress about work. Or loneliness.

Climbing was a form of meditation for me, and tonight's session had been an especially good one. I'd found my flow and finally sent the green bouldering project that I'd been working on for the past two weeks. After so many attempts, so many failures...I was riding high on the feeling of success.

I'd just finished showering when I heard the familiar *ding!* of my phone, letting me know that I'd received a text message. I threw my towel onto the bed and glanced at the screen.

Hey Ian. This is Anna Tang, Cassie's friend from college. From the wedding. I was wondering if you'd be free to meet up for coffee sometime this week? I'd like to talk to you.

I stared at the screen, unsure of how to respond. It had been almost a month since we'd last seen each other, and I was still kinda sore that she'd completely ghosted me. I considered ignoring her, or making her wait for a response...but really, what was the point of playing games? She wanted an answer, I wanted to know what was going on—always better to be direct.

I'm free tomorrow at 8am, I typed, hoping it wasn't too early. *Where should I meet you?*

A moment later, she responded, *The Doughnut Cathedral on 21st?*

See you there, I typed back. I tossed my phone on top of the towel and sat down on the bed, reminiscing about how turned on she'd been that night, about the incredibly sexy sounds she'd made as I ate her out. I'd thought about that night countless times since then. *Maybe she missed me.* I smirked at the thought, however unlikely it was.

* * *

I arrived a few minutes early and ordered a black coffee and two Boston cream donuts, one for there and one to go, the latter of which they playfully termed a *to-gonut*. I didn't usually eat sweets, but Boston creams were nostalgic for me, my dad's favorite. So I sat down in a corner table and waited, leisurely munching on a cream-filled donut.

Two minutes later, the door opened and Anna walked in. She was bundled up in a peacoat with a red scarf and matching red beanie. A short forest green skirt peeked out from beneath her coat, along with black stockings and knee-high black suede boots. She carried a plaid black and white purse, a large black bow on one side. Still as cute as ever.

"Hey! Thanks for coming—for meeting me here." She approached and opened her arms for a hug. I hid my surprise and hugged her back, keeping it brief and casual.

"No problem. Hope it wasn't too early. Morning is the only time that I can get any focused work done at the office, so I usually like to get in by 8:30."

"Nah, it's fine. I'm a morning person," she replied, yawning.

My lips twitched. "Do you want something? Coffee?" I waved expansively at the counter.

"Oh, no thanks," she sighed, staring wistfully at the menu.

"Ah...let me at least get you a coffee." I took a step towards the counter, but she grabbed my arm.

"No no, I really don't want anything." She bit her lip and briefly scanned the display case of donuts before meeting my eyes. Did she want something or *not?*

"*Okay.* Well at least have this donut. I already bought it for you," I lied, sitting back down and pushing the to-gonut across the table to her.

Her eyes sparkled. "Really? Well if you already bought it for me..." She picked up the donut and brought it to her lips, and I sat back to enjoy the no-doubt sexy spectacle of her eating a cream-filled donut, especially after that show at the Ethiopian restaurant in SF.

Anna did not disappoint. I watched in slow motion as she chomped into the donut, taking out a full third of it in one awe-inspiring shark bite. Her eyes closed in ecstasy as globs of cream exploded across her lips, her cheeks ballooning to accommodate the large volume of pastry. She chewed twice, once on the left and once on the right, before her tongue flicked out and around her mouth, smearing the messy cream all over her lips and pushing some up towards her nostrils. She opened her eyes and chewed a few times more (surely not enough for that much donut), then performed a tremendous gulp. Finally, she swiped the side of her thumb across her lips, then licked it like a cat licking its paw...and smiled. "This is delicious."

I coughed and choked down my hysterical laughter. "Ahem.

Hmm. So what can I do for you?"

She looked at me for a moment, then down at the rest of her donut. "First...I want to apologize."

I quickly sobered. "For?" I assumed what for, but I wanted to hear her say it.

"For...running away, at the wedding. For....not talking to you?" Her voice pitched up at the end, as if asking a question.

"For...completely ghosting me?" I added, mocking her questioning tone. I guess I was bitterer about what had happened than I'd thought. I sipped my coffee to avoid saying anything else.

She frowned, then sighed. "Yeah. That. I'm really sorry. I should have just waited for you to finish." Her eyes widened as she heard her own words.

I leaned back and laughed. "I would have loved to have finished."

She shook her head and averted her eyes. "You know what I mean. I'm sorry."

"Not...really. Why did you leave?" I hesitated, then added, "You know I would've come back and eagerly finished the job."

She sat up a little straighter and swallowed. "I mean...what would you do if someone just left you there after you'd been practically begging them..." She trailed off and bit her lip.

"Ok. I get it. But I wouldn't have left you like that if I didn't have a good reason." I sighed, glad for her apology, but not yet ready to forgive. "It's fine, though. There's no need to apologize, really. You had every right to do as you pleased."

"Still...Cassie told me about your mom. I had no idea. Is she doing okay?" she asked, voice sincere.

I nodded. "Yeah, she's getting better. She's almost done with chemo."

Her face broke into a smile, bright and earnest. "That's great to hear."

I popped the last of my donut into my mouth while Anna took another bite of her own. We chewed in silence for several seconds before I asked, "So was there anything else you wanted to talk about?" She seemed nervous, not horny. Not looking for an encore.

"Ah, *yeah*." She hesitated, then sighed. "I actually need your help. I'd like to apply for a job at Stumpstash."

I blinked. "You want to apply for a job there? Doing what? We don't do music stuff."

She took another monstrous bite of her donut, chewing a bit more thoroughly this time. I wanted to brush the sugary flakes of chocolate glaze off her pink lips, but her sweet little tongue beat me to it. "Cassie told me that there was an office admin role in the New York office. She thought it'd be a good fit for me because it's the type of work I do—was doing at my previous job. Unfortunately, she's not that familiar with the New York office so she suggested that I ask you about how it's run. Could you...fill me in?" She casually picked up my coffee and took a sip, then held onto it, clearly not remembering whose it was.

I smiled into my fist as I cleared my throat. "Yeah, sure, I can tell you about it. Is this like a side job, while you work on building up your music following?"

She looked up, relieved. "Yes. I'm really organized and good with people. And I learn really quickly. I specifically want a job like this so that I can work 9 to 5 and then go home and work on my music writing."

She pulled a piece of paper out of her bag and passed it to me across the table. I scanned the contents. *English Major at*

NYU. Office Administrator at Lynd & Cannoli Law Firm. A slew of other odd jobs. While I skimmed the rest, I asked, "Why don't you do something related to the music industry?"

She kept her gaze lowered. "I wanted to work on music right out of school, but paid gigs are rare and it's hard to make ends meet in New York...especially with student loans from NYU." She delicately nibbled her donut, then continued. "I lived with my ex for a few years and that helped a bit, but I didn't want to depend on him. I had to get a job and do my own thing."

"I see." I noted that she hadn't mentioned her parents or family or getting help from any of them. What was that about? But we'd just reached a tentative truce—probably not a good time to ask.

"Okay, I'll help you." Her face brightened, her dazzling smile only slightly diminished by the chocolate on her teeth. "I'll send over some reading materials for you so that you can learn a little bit more about what Stumpstash does. They'll want to see that you're passionate about our mission. I'll also talk to our facilities manager to learn a little bit more about the role. I'll let you know what she says." I glanced at my watch, then stood up—it was time to go.

She put her hand on my arm. "Wait. There's one more thing." She licked her lips and looked up at me. *Damn*, she was cute.

"What is it?" My heart beat faster. *Did* she want an encore?

"Would you...want to go climbing with me sometime?"

I grinned and forgave her completely.

* * *

"*Ba.* What did you do today?"

"You won't believe it. Your *Ma* found a feral hog in our garden."

"*What?* Was it big? Did you call the police?"

"No no, it was just a small one. She got the rake and I got the shovel and we chased it out."

I laughed, imagining my sixty-something-year-old parents chasing a hog around their garden. "How'd it get past the fence?"

"There was a hole in the ground! It was big."

"I see. Sounds like you had fun."

"We did. I haven't seen your *Ma* so lively since...well, you know." He sighed.

"I know, *Ba.* I'm glad the hog paid you a visit."

He quietly chuckled. "What did you do today?"

"I...had coffee with a pretty girl."

"Ah, good. Is she Chinese?" Every time my parents asked me that question, I facepalmed. This time was no exception.

"I think so. I haven't asked, but she looks like it and her last name is Tang."

"Good, good. What does she do?"

"She writes about music."

A pause. "That's not a good job. Is her family rich?"

I nearly facepalmed again, but instead, just rubbed my forehead. "*Ba*, we're not dating or anything. I'll let you know if that changes." *When*, I thought.

Chapter 9

-Anna-

True to his word, Ian emailed me some reading materials about Stumpstash that evening. He also called me after dinner to tell me what the facilities manager had said. Based on that conversation, the office admin role seemed perfect for me. It would be a lot of the mindless, menial tasks that I knew I could easily do while scouting out new tracks, but also some strategizing about resources and event planning that might change things up a bit and allow me to use my brain and creativity sometimes.

After reading the materials that he sent, I also found that I didn't have to pretend to be on board with the mission. Stumpstash supported local communities and helped small businesses get the funds that they needed to get started. I was glad that I wasn't about to sell my soul to an evil corporation.

Ian let Cassie refer me for the position ("She can have the referral bonus to help her pay for the honeymoon," he'd reasoned), but he also put in a good word for me with the recruiter to help speed up the process. By the end of the week, I'd passed the phone interview and was scheduled for an onsite interview the following week.

See what good things can happen when you swallow your pride?

And I was excited to try climbing! Maybe if I got the job at Stumpstash, I could get a membership and finally be one of those fit, hip, happy climber people.

Ian and I had agreed to meet at the climbing gym on Saturday morning, so I showed up in my cutest workout tights and a long-sleeved crop-top sweater, with just a light dusting of makeup. I didn't have the abs of that pretty brunette he climbed with, but I knew I looked *good*.

When I walked into the gym and peered around, I didn't see Ian anywhere, so I approached the attendant at the front desk. He had me watch the requisite safety video, then sign a waiver. The video *guaranteed* that I would fall, and while I wasn't deathly afraid of heights, I definitely didn't like the idea of falling.

"Morning, Anna." A warm, rough hand landed softly on my bare lower back, below where the crop top ended. It was only for a moment, a greeting touch, but awareness of him lingered on my skin.

"Morning, Ian," I replied, more breathily than I'd intended.

Ian talked to the guy behind the counter and used his guest pass to get me in for free. If he hadn't, it would have been nearly $40 for a day pass. *Only an hour of work at Stumpstash.* I shook my head.

The guy behind the counter handed me some shoes and a harness to try on. The shoes were a tiny bit snug, but he said that that was how it was supposed to feel. Then Ian helped me put on the harness. He positioned it on the floor and I placed my feet into the leg loops. He lifted the harness, the outsides of his thumbs caressing my thighs, tracing twin lines of electricity up my legs as he brought the main strap up over my hips and to my waist. He then instructed me on how to tighten the straps.

"How'd the phone interview go?" He already had his own harness on, though he was barefoot. As he led me over to one of the taller walls, I idly noted that he had nice feet. Maybe I *did* have a foot fetish.

Or maybe, as before, it was just Ian.

My voice was slightly too high-pitched. "Pretty good. I have my onsite next week."

"Hey, that's great!" He gave me a high five. "I'm sure you'll crush it." He smiled sweetly, making my heart do a little dance.

I glanced around as he led me through to the back of the gym. The air was dry and cold, and slightly hazy with chalk dust, and I happily noted the minor chords and deep crooning of the neo-soul music that played throughout the gym. I'd seen the area by the entrance before, with walls that were maybe 10 - 15 feet in height, all covered in a multitude of holds (and people!) of different shapes, sizes, and colors. But the rest of the gym was new.

The middle of the gym was filled with benches, weights, cages and other workout equipment, and in the corner, a young, miserable-looking man trudged up a stairmaster with what looked like a *very* heavy pack on his back. As we approached the rear of the building, I had to tilt my head back to look at the walls, which had grown to maybe 50 feet or so tall. I'd only ever seen the shorter walls in the front, never these taller walls, and I gulped at the thought of climbing that high.

"So we're going to do top roping today," he explained,

stopping in front of one of the taller walls. "I think it's more beginner-friendly than bouldering." He explained the difference between top roping and bouldering. I realized that bouldering—climbing shorter, harder routes, without any protective equipment—was what he'd been doing the other day. Top roping involved climbing much longer routes, but with the protection of a harness and rope. It also usually required a partner, someone to belay (or manage rope tension for) the climber as they climbed.

He scanned the wall and selected what I hoped was an easy route. "We'll tie in here." He grabbed one end of a dangling rope that had been anchored by its midpoint at the top of the wall. The other end held a belay device and a carabiner, which he clipped onto his own harness. He stood directly in front of me, tying the necessary knots to keep me secure. I could feel each tug and twist throughout the harness...below my ass...between my legs...and I could still smell his familiar scent. I watched his nimble fingers work, but was too distracted to remember anything useful.

When he was done with me, he said, "Alright, any questions? If not, just get on the wall and try to use only the red holds."

I ran my gaze up the length of the route. It looked even taller up close. I glanced nervously at Ian, then quickly swallowed my fear. I wasn't going to be scared in front of him.

I guess I hadn't swallowed well enough, because he gave me a reassuring smile and a pat on the arm. "I won't let you fall. You should go partway up the wall and let go, just to see how safe it is. And I'll give you a lot of tension so that you can feel the harness keeping you safe."

"I'm not scared," I said. I took a deep breath, grasped the start holds, and began climbing. As I ascended the wall, I noticed that the rope in front of me never felt loose. With each step I took, Ian, as my belayer, took out the slack from the rope below. Relieved, I focused on what was above me and not below, and the first ten feet were surprisingly easy. *I got this*.

"Stop," said Ian. "Try falling from there."

I stopped climbing and looked below me and *oh shit I don't got this*. It wasn't very far, but I didn't want to let go. Letting go was against every instinct in my body, so my arms tensed, elbows bent to hold me close to the wall. My hands felt slippery and tired.

"Hey," Ian called to me. I met his eyes. "Climb down a little if you want, but just let go and sit into the harness. You're not going to fall."

I climbed down a little and the harness *did* feel more secure. I grimaced and let go...and hardly fell at all. Ian was there, holding the rope below, keeping me safe.

"See?" He smiled. "Alright, go to the top! Try to keep your arms straight, you'll tire out less."

Shaky but reassured, and not wanting to embarrass myself further, I focused on keeping my arms straight and making my way up the wall. A third of the way up, my hands couldn't hold on and my legs were trembling. I sat back into the harness. "It's so tiring!" I made the mistake of looking down—it looked *very* high up now. I felt sweaty and achy and scared, and *oh shit I* really *don't got this*.

"You're not coming down until you ring the bell." *What?* I glanced up and noticed a small red bell at the top. It was maybe only five feet away, but with my limbs as tired as they were, it seemed impossibly far.

"I can't. Let me down!"

95

Ian didn't answer. He simply stood there, watching me. Then he shrugged and called up, "Shake your arms out. It'll help."

"Let me down!" I kicked my legs at him.

"Ring the bell!" He smirked.

I let out a frustrated snarl. I was at his mercy, suspended in midair, and he wouldn't respect what I wanted. I *hated* that. I shook my arms out and found that after a minute, I could grip the holds again. I took a deep breath, focused on going *up*, and resentfully climbed the rest of the way up the wall. Despite one kind of reach-y move (I was only 5'4"!) and my foot slipping off once, I angrily rang the bell.

"Nice!" Ian yelled up. "Okay, let go of the wall, I'm lowering you. Hold the rope."

I clutched the rope as Ian lowered me, and I glowered the whole way down. He laughed at my expression as my feet touched the ground, and then my legs collapsed and I was sitting on the floor, glaring up at him. He crouched down next to me. "Hey, you did a great job! You only had to rest a couple of times. I knew you'd be a natural." He smiled and reached down to help me up.

I took his hand and grumbled, "You should've just let me down."

"But then you wouldn't have known you could do it." He gave me a sweet smile. And while I was still annoyed and shaky and full of adrenaline, I grudgingly forgave him.

The rest of the morning went similarly. He put me on some routes that I was sure I would not be able to finish, but after struggling, thinking, trying different methods, asking for advice, and taking breaks, I'd surprise myself by making it all the way up to the top. I doubted myself less and less with each route.

And it was a full-body workout, so I eventually had to take my sweater off because it was getting too hot. I felt a little bit self-conscious that I was only in my sports bra (there were definitely bits of flabby skin that I was not proud of), but Ian didn't say anything. He just kept encouraging me and giving me pointers on how to improve my technique.

There were a couple of routes towards the end where I could tell that I was actually getting tired and it wasn't just my nerves. It had probably been a bit over an hour by that point. I checked the clock and was surprised to see that it had actually been over two!

"Ugh. Ian, let me down. I'm too tired. *Really*, this time."

He lowered me from the last route that I'd planned to do that day and gave me another high-five. He'd high-fived me after every route. "You're a natural, Anna. If you keep climbing, you'll definitely be a crusher. You've got so much flexibility and a great build." I was pleased, and slightly embarrassed when I thought about how he knew I was flexible.

"Hey, Ian, you ready to switch over?"

I looked up from untying the knot to see that the pretty brunette had arrived. She was dressed like me, workout tights and a sports bra, but she made it look so much better. Muscles and firm skin versus wobbly arms and flab. Model versus amateur. And she wasn't a butterface, either—far from it. She had gorgeous cheekbones, a cute little nose, full lips, and straight teeth. I couldn't quite place her nationality, but she seemed mixed.

Ian introduced us. "Yeah. Lina, this is Anna. Anna, Lina. Lina's my climbing partner." We shook hands. Rather, she squeezed mine with her giant climber claws and my tired hands barely resisted.

"Nice to meet you. How'd your session go?" Lina seemed to direct the question at me, but she was watching Ian.

"It was fun," I answered. "I think I'll be back." I met her assessing gaze.

"Hey, that's great! I'm glad you enjoyed it that much," Ian said, patting me on the back. I must've felt like a slug with how sweaty I was, but I relished the contact anyway and directed a tight-lipped smile at Lina. Then Ian turned to Lina and said, "I'll be over in a few. I think Anna and I just wrapped up, so I'm going to walk her out." He turned to look at me and gave me a questioning look. "You're done, right? You said you were too tired to go on?"

"Psh, I just need a break," I said. "Besides, I did all the climbing this morning—it's my turn to watch *you* struggle. Maybe I'll learn what *not* to do."

Ian grinned. "You're going to be thoroughly disappointed."

I smirked at both him and Lina before going to the counter and buying a protein bar and an energy drink. I knew I was going to be there for a while. *To learn*, of course. I ignored the flicker of displeasure that came from seeing Lina and Ian talking together.

Chapter 10

-Ian-

Anna surprised me by asking a lot of questions during the rest of the session. We'd switched to bouldering so that I could teach without wasting Lina's time, and so that Anna could try it if she wanted to.

As I'd thought, she was a natural. She intuitively understood the principles behind the techniques that I showed her, and while she'd started out pretty scared, she quickly gained confidence. She did try a few bouldering routes, but was too tired to really do much.

Lina didn't really help things. She got on some routes that were definitely not for beginners, then encouraged Anna to try them. "This one's easy! You can do it!" she'd say, clearly missing that it was Anna's first time, and that she was beat from two hours of top roping. Anna tried and failed a few times, then declined to try anymore after that. Something seemed kind of off between them, and they didn't really talk much after that.

By 1pm, Anna had stopped climbing. She was also yawning every other minute, lying down on the mat and watching us with dead fish eyes.

I plopped down beside her. "You okay? You don't have to stay here if you want to go."

She looked up at me from the mat. Then her stomach rumbled and her eyes widened.

"Oh...ah, would you be willing to get lunch with me? My treat, because you taught me so much today. And I'd like to ask you more questions about Stumpstash."

"Uh, sure." I wasn't sure what else she could ask about Stumpstash because she'd already grilled me about it the other night, but I wasn't going to turn down lunch with her.

"Hey Lina, I'm going to go grab lunch with Anna. I'll see you tomorrow?"

"Can I come?" asked Lina.

Before I could answer, Anna said, "Oh, it's probably going to be really boring. I'm going to ask him a bunch of questions about his workplace, so you probably wouldn't want to come."

Lina arched an eyebrow at her, but said, "I see. Alright, I'll see you tomorrow, Ian." We high-fived.

I packed up my gear and put on a little extra deodorant in the men's locker room. Better to be safe than sorry. I met Anna by the entrance and asked, "So whereto for lunch?"

"You can pick," she said.

"Uhhh, there's a really good Chinese restaurant around the corner. You cool with that?"

She hesitated. "I...guess that's okay. If that's what you want."

"We can do something else, if you'd prefer. There are a lot of places around."

"No no, Chinese is fine." Her smile didn't quite reach her eyes. "Let's go."

I decided not to dig. Besides, the Chinese place was

objectively the best lunch spot in the area, and one of the cheapest.

"So," she asked, "how long have you been climbing with Lina?"

"A few months now. We met at a partner meetup night and we climb at roughly the same level. She's been a good climbing buddy."

"She's...really good at climbing," Anna said. I glanced at her, but she just looked straight ahead.

I playfully put my arm around her shoulders as we walked. "Are you *jealous?*"

"No!" She glared up at me and I smirked at her, our faces inches away. She lowered her eyes and glanced at my lips, then turned and looked ahead, but didn't shrug my arm off. *Interesting.* Maybe she did miss me after all. I considered kissing her then and there, but decided not to rush things. Let her make the first move this time. I let her go as we approached the Chinese restaurant and opened the door for her.

The restaurant was old and dingy and smelled of grease, as all great authentic Chinese restaurants do. A giant hand-written "Cash Only" sign was posted in the window, next to a yellowing menu that was almost exclusively in Chinese. Old Chinese pop music played in the background, and an older woman in the back of the restaurant greeted us in Mandarin and told us to sit anywhere. I led Anna to a booth by the front.

We spent a few minutes perusing the food-stained menus that were taped onto the table. A minute later, the waitress came over with some hot tea.

"What do you want?" she asked in Mandarin.

I responded in the same language and ordered an authentic

spicy braised pork dish.

"I'll have the General Tso's Tofu," said Anna, in English. I had the courtesy to wait until after the waitress left to chuckle.

"What?" she asked, annoyed.

"You can clearly read the Chinese menu. If you can read, you can probably speak it. And then you ordered the whitest thing on the menu, in English."

"So? I like General Tso's. And my Mandarin is rusty." She poured herself a cup of tea, hands shaking. Had she pushed herself that hard today?

"Here, let me help you." I put my hands over hers and helped her steady the teapot as we poured each of us a cup. She looked away and quickly slipped her hands out of mine when we were finished.

"Do you like authentic Chinese food?" I asked.

"I...used to. I grew up eating it, though, so I'm pretty sick of it." She stared into her teacup.

"All of Chinese cuisine?" I teased.

Without looking up, she answered, "My dad was a chef in a Chinese restaurant, so we ate it all the time." She didn't elaborate further, and I didn't want to start on the daddy issues. I simply nodded and sipped my tea.

Minutes passed, and still she didn't say anything...just yawned and absently looked around the room. At the old cash register. The lucky bamboo on the counter. The giant fake tree in the corner. Only occasionally did her eyes slip my way, then past me. Was she *nervous*?

I cleared my throat. "So...what questions do you have for me about Stumpstash?"

"Oh." She sat up straighter and met my eyes. "Um...how do you like it there?"

I raised an eyebrow. "That's what you wanted to ask me?"

She scowled. "I want to make sure it's a good culture fit for me."

Fair. I knew from personal experience the importance of finding a non-toxic work environment. "I really like it there. The company takes its mission seriously, and the CEO sets a clear, ambitious vision. And my coworkers are mostly great. I mean, I get to work with people like Cassie, and both of us have been with the company for over three years."

"Mostly? Are there people there you don't like?"

I snickered. "There's always gotta be someone." I threw back my tea and reached for the pot to pour myself another cup. "Let's just say that I've stepped on a lot of toes as a tech lead."

She was silent for a moment. "Cassie mentioned that you helped her get her job."

"Yeah. I'm in a professional society that promotes women and minorities in tech. Cassie was part of the network and she reached out to me through another member. She was a shoe-in for the role, so I'm really glad she did. Plus, it's been really fun working with her."

Anna nodded...then slouched again and stared wanly at the table. Silence descended, thick and palpable, broken only by the clinking of her fingernails tapping on her ceramic tea cup. Did she actually have more questions for me about Stumpstash? Was she just that tired? The easy chemistry between us this morning was gone, replaced by a stifling awkwardness.

"So what did you think about climbing?" I asked, genuinely curious. She'd stayed for hours, but it was unclear if she'd actually had any fun towards the end.

Her eyes flared to life and she snapped out of her stupor. "I really enjoyed it. It was nice to have tangible, bite-sized goals to focus on. And my body is totally wrecked. I'm looking forward to being sore tomorrow. I love being sore." She stretched her arms over her head, arching her back, her cropped sweater rising to bare her smooth, pale stomach.

I smiled at her admission. "Me too. So you'll be back?"

Her bright smile said it all. There was definitely a climber in there. "I hope so! I really want to get that blue V3." One of the ones that Lina had encouraged her to try.

I chortled. "Not bad for your first time, going from *'I can't do this!'* to projecting V3. At this rate, you'll be crushing V8s next week."

"Is that what level you...crush...on?" she asked, hesitating on the usage of *crush*. "V8?"

"What *grade*. I *project* V8s. I *crush* V7s. I *have* a crush *on you.*" I winked.

She laughed softly and looked down. "Is that how you use those words? There's so much jargon to learn."

"Yeah. You crush problems, you crush *on* people. Though I guess you could crush people, too."

"Ha, I see," she said, yawning infectiously.

I leaned back in the booth and stretched my legs under the table, accidentally brushing against hers.

We locked eyes. She licked her lips and sucked in a breath, skimming her leg along mine as she sat up straighter. Awareness sizzled between us, and the amusement in her eyes was gone, replaced by something...hungrier.

Good thing that, right at that moment, our food arrived.

The dishes smelled wonderful, sweet and savory and perfect after a long morning workout. The braised pork was delicious, with a thick, spicy brown sauce that made my eyes burn and my nose run. I made Anna try a bite, and she seemed to like it, but had to wash it down with two cups of tea. She also scarfed down all of her General Tso's Tofu without offering me any. Stingy.

Afterward, I was stuffed and ready for a post-climb nap. Lethargy set in, and the energy between us fizzled, the moment past. Anna got up to use the restaurant's ATM, then paid the bill.

"Was that all you wanted to ask me about Stumpstash? Nothing else?"

"I don't remember the rest, unfortunately." She yawned. "I'm too tired. I know there were at least one or two more things. I'll text you if I think of them." She picked up her purse, the same black and white plaid one from the other day in the donut shop, and got up to leave.

"Alright. Thanks for lunch." I went in for a casual hug. I might've held on for slightly longer than was necessary, but she didn't object. If anything, I could have sworn that she was sniffing me. Good thing I'd put on more deodorant.

"Thanks for climbing with me! It was so fun!" We walked to the door.

"When will I see you again?" I asked.

"My onsite is next week! Maybe I'll see you then?"

"Okay." I held the door open for her as we exited the restaurant. "I'm this way," I said, gesturing to the left.

"I'm this way," she said, pointing right. "See you!" She gave a little wave and walked away.

I put my hands in my pockets and turned to walk towards the subway station. I nearly collided with a short guy in a beanie and a leather jacket who had been standing close behind me. I muttered an apology and kept walking.

Chapter 11

Well, that was awkward.

I wasn't sure what had induced me to invite him to lunch. I knew that he climbed with Lina all the time, but the thought of leaving them alone together, while I went home by myself...I didn't want to be alone.

And I should've let Lina come. Maybe she was a nicer person than I'd thought, and I definitely could've used another friend. I should've given her a chance.

But if I had, then Ian wouldn't have held me close on the walk over. We wouldn't have played footsie under the table, and shared that sweltry moment. I was exhausted from the day, but I still felt a flutter at the memory, at the keen look in his eyes.

Unfortunately, we'd gone to a Chinese restaurant, of all places.

Chinese food was delicious, and the place he'd taken us to was really quite good. But whenever I smelled the familiar mixture of oil, garlic, ginger, five spice...my memories always dredged up.

My parents couldn't afford daycare (hadn't even considered it, really), so they often took me to the restaurant that they worked at. The other employees and the customers all doted on me (let's be real, I was *adorable*)...but my parents were strict. Mean. And they fought viciously, both with me and with each other, whenever my dad made a mistake on an order, or whenever my mom flirted with a customer for tips. Whenever business was bad. They put on a good face for everyone else, but I didn't count. With me, they were brutally honest. They each confided in me, cursing the other, telling me their deepest, darkest desires.

I wish we'd never met.

I wish your father were a real man.

I wish I were dead.

I wish he were dead.

The memories made me nauseous.

I pushed the thoughts away and trudged home, taking stock of my body. It'd been a long time since I'd last exercised, and climbing was *tiring*. Every muscle, from my core out to my limbs, fingers, and toes, was already beginning to feel sore. My apartment was only a couple of blocks away, but it felt like miles to my aching legs. I had to walk slowly, limping ever-so-slightly with each agonizing step.

Footsteps behind me. I turned to look—

My purse was wrenched from my shoulder and I was shoved from behind. I lurched forward and fell to the pavement, grateful for the thick fabric of my peacoat. My hands grabbed for the purse, but they were weak from climbing and could not resist the hands of my mugger, who tore the purse away from me. I whipped my head around and watched as a figure ran off in the direction I'd just come from. *Shit!* I got up to chase after him, cursing my tired legs as he turned the corner.

When I arrived at the corner, I fully expected to find no sign of the thief. Instead, he was in a game of tug of war with Ian—and Ian was winning!

As the thief swung an arm back, I shouted, "Ian, look out!" Ian ducked, his face narrowly missing the thief's fist, then countered with a knee to the man's gut. The thief let go and fell backwards, clutching his stomach and wheezing. Ian leaned over and panted, then muttered something to the man, stood up, and walked towards me with my purse. Thankfully, he didn't seem to be harmed. But a moment later, the man rolled to his knees and started to get up, his face twisted in a snarl.

"Ian, come on!" I waved at him to hurry.

He glanced behind him, then sprinted towards me as the man began to rise. I grabbed Ian's hand and ran with him for two blocks until I finally pulled him up the steps of my apartment building. The man didn't seem to be following us, but I didn't dare stop for breath. With shaky hands, I reached into my purse and pulled out the keys. As soon as the door opened, I pulled Ian in and shut the door, then secured the deadbolt. Only then did I lean against the wall and allow myself to breathe.

"Are you—are you okay?" I asked Ian, who was leaning against the other wall.

"Yeah, I think so," he panted. "You?"

I nodded.

We stayed like that for a few minutes, calming our breaths, not saying anything. Finally, I asked, "Do you want to come upstairs for a bit? Maybe just until we're sure that guy has disappeared?"

"Yeah. I think we should report what just happened."

He followed me up the stairs to the third floor apartment. I was a little bit embarrassed by how old and decrepit my apartment was, but it was all I could afford, and *my landlord* didn't care to fix anything. The stairs leading up to it were covered in dirty orange shag carpet. The walls, once white, had water stains and peeling paint. One of the stairs had fallen in and I had to skip over it each time I went up or down.

I unlocked the apartment door, glad that it was marginally nicer inside the actual apartment than in the hallway. I glanced around, taking in what he must be seeing. The dirty dishes in the sink. The dim lighting provided by the only working lightbulb in the corner. The worn-out furniture and old, yellowed kitchen appliances. At least I had taken out the trash yesterday, so it didn't smell too bad.

I was also glad that my roommate / landlord was away this weekend. I *definitely* didn't want them to meet.

Ian didn't say anything. He just took his phone out, walked to a corner of the apartment, and after a few moments, began providing details about the incident to the police. I sat on the couch and waited, somewhat in a daze. After several minutes, he hung up and walked over.

"They said they'd send someone to come and check the area out. I gave a description of the guy. Hopefully they catch him." He went to the sink to wash his hands, then came over to the couch and sat down next to me, taking my hands in both of his.

"Are you okay?" he asked.

I looked up into his face. His eyes were dark with concern, his thick brows furrowed as he waited for me to answer him. His full lips were slightly parted, as if ready to say something...or do something.

Ian.

He was so earnest, so sweet...so handsome. So close. Rationally, I knew that no good could ever come of hooking up with him—not with our sizzling past, and certainly not with our possible future as coworkers. But the adrenaline was still coursing through my veins, my pulse beating wildly, and I couldn't resist any longer.

I slipped my fingers into his hair and pulled him to me, closing my eyes as his lips met mine. He cupped my head and kissed me back, sighing, his lips tender and soft. I leaned in and got up onto my knees to straddle his lap, deepening the kiss with my tongue as I pushed him back against the couch cushions. His hands went to my thighs, and his fingers gently rubbed up my tights until he cupped my ass, pulling me onto the growing evidence of his arousal. We simultaneously moaned. Then we both laughed.

"Seriously," Ian said. Kiss. "Are you." Kiss. "Okay?" His fingers fumbled as he slowly unbuttoned my pea coat. I impatiently pushed his hands aside and undid the buttons myself, then threw the peacoat onto the floor. He busied himself by pulling his sweater and t-shirt off over his head, revealing his delectable chest. It was as smooth, tan, and muscled as I remembered seeing that one cold evening, not too long ago...and now it was on full display, all mine to explore. I placed my hands on either side of his face, trailing my fingers down his thick neck to rest on his round, muscular deltoids. I knew it was just meat, but there was so much of it, and it was so *hard* and so *hot*. Sexy as fuck. I shivered.

But, later. First order of business was his mouth.

"I'm fine." Kiss. "Shut up." I crushed my lips to his, teasing them apart until I could suck on his tongue. It was thick and wet and deliciously warm, and I cradled his head in my arms, urging him to fill my mouth. He complied, running his tongue along mine, molding his lips to my own. I drank him in, wanting to drown in the taste of him.

Below, I felt his hard-on through my thin tights, an answering dampness seeping into my underwear. I shifted my hips up, up, left, until—there! *That* was the spot.

His hands cupped my ass, pressing me harder against him, as if sensing that perfect position. I groaned, rubbing myself against him, the tension in my belly growing, the pleasure nearly unbearable. He left my hips to their own devices and trailed his hands up my sides, slipping his fingers underneath the band of my bra, but stopping there, teasing, as if unwilling to cross the boundary.

Screw boundaries—we were well beyond that by now. We were technically only on first base, but with the flimsiness of our gym clothes and how hard I was rubbing on him, we were basically toeing home plate. So I broke our kiss and pulled my sweater and sports bra up and over my head, together in one motion. We paused then, and Ian eyed my bare chest appreciatively...hungrily. I was usually self-conscious about my small breasts, but my nipples pebbled to little hard points under his heated gaze.

Any remaining reservations evaporated.

His rough hands came up and cupped my breasts, gently kneading them. I held his face in my hands and kissed him again as he ran the pads of his thumbs over my nipples, his mouth capturing my pleading sounds. He stopped kissing my lips and planted a string of tender kisses from my neck down to my breasts, where he took my nipple into his mouth and laved it with his tongue. *Oh fuck.* He gently sucked on one while rubbing the other with his hand, then switched, tracing another line of kisses between them.

My panties were positively soaked.

I reached down and slipped my hand between the elastic band of Ian's workout shorts and his rock hard abs, seeking my prize. His cock was breathtakingly thick and rigid, the skin velvety smooth. He bucked in my hands as I stroked him with my fingers, his mouth once again claiming mine.

I couldn't wait any longer. I broke away, stood up, and shimmied out of my tights and my underwear. Ian watched me intently, licking his lips and slowly stroking his dick with his right hand.

I stood before him completely naked, completely unashamed, consumed with the need to have him inside of me. I reached down to tug his shorts all the way off, but he put his hand on mine, grinding things to a halt. "I don't have any condoms on me."

That's all? "It's fine, just pull out." I kept tugging, but he once more resisted.

"Are you serious?"

"Yeah. Just pull out. I'll take Plan B if I need to." I tugged again, but he still seemed reluctant to let me take his shorts off. "I was tested a few months ago. I don't have any STDs, if that's what you're worried about." I met his eyes. There was no way a goody-goody like *him* would have any STDs. At least, I hoped not. Slowly, he nodded and let go of his shorts. I pulled them off, and his erection sprang fully free.

Fuck. His cock was so thick and juicy, and slightly canted towards the left. I shuddered with anticipation, the emptiness between my legs aching to be filled.

But first...I wanted to taste it.

113

I got down on my knees between his legs and took his cock all the way inside my mouth. Clearly not expecting *that*, he bucked, driving himself deep into the back of my throat. I could feel his engorged veins on my tongue, almost as if he was about to come. But he didn't.

I slowly lifted my head, keeping my lips and tongue molded firmly along his shaft as I did so. He pushed my hair out of the way, his eyes intent on the show. Then I circled the head of his penis with my tongue and slowly licked the shaft from top to bottom and back up again. It was hot and slightly salty, utterly delicious. I loved how he filled my mouth, and I *dripped* at the thought of him filling me elsewhere.

Finally, I planted a very chaste kiss on the top, right where a bead of moisture had started to form. He gave a deep, throaty laugh.

I needed him inside me, *stat*.

I straddled his lap again and slowly lowered myself onto him, and felt myself stretched and filled all the way to my core. I moaned his name and closed my eyes in ecstasy, taking a moment to savor the feeling. *Fuck*.

Then I began to ride.

He placed his hands on my hips and supported me as I gyrated my hips, guiding me up and down. I hadn't had sex without a condom since college, and the bare sensation was almost too much, too intimate. I bit my lip and placed my hands on his shoulders as we rode closer and closer to the edge, eyes narrowed and locked, the pleasure in our faces reflected at one another.

His erection was like hot steel inside of me, the pained look on his face exposing how hard he was trying not to come. At one point, I stopped going up and down and he did all of the

114

work below, planting his feet on the floor and thrusting his hips up into me while holding me in place, deeper and with more force than I'd been able to muster. I closed my eyes and sighed his name over and over, coming utterly undone.

Just as I was about to orgasm, he groaned and pulled himself out of me, spilling himself onto my chest. I cried out in surprise, but also in frustration at the sudden loss of him. Not yet content, I continued grinding myself against his muscled leg until I finally found my own release.

Even though I had asked him to, I couldn't help but regret the fact that he'd pulled out at the last second. My orgasm had been a whimper instead of the massive bang that I'd been anticipating. So as the small waves of pleasure receded, I kneeled on the couch and pouted.

Ian's eyes met mine. He was breathing heavily, but he chuckled at my expression. He pulled me down to sit on his lap and held me close, smearing the wet mess he'd made all over both of our chests. I giggled.

"Anna," he whispered into my hair, his breath a sweet caress. I stayed there like that for a moment, just letting him hold me. Then I turned my head and kissed his warm neck, and I wrapped my arms around him, too.

Chapter 12

-Ian-

I was almost a second too late pulling out. I'd never had sex without a condom, let alone pulled out of someone before, and with Anna riding me like she was, as gorgeous as she was...no man could have blamed me for coming inside of her.

Luckily, I'd been just in time. I think.

I held her close and breathed in her rose shampoo, the feminine scent mingled with the tang of our lovemaking. She wrapped her arms around me and I sighed into her hair, cementing the memory into my brain. She'd been so passionate, so sexy, so sure in her desire. And as I held her in my arms, so sweet. Paired with the fact that she liked climbing and was funny and adventurous...I could easily imagine falling fast and hard for her, if I wasn't careful. She was definitely special.

"Ian?"

"Yeah?"

"I'm starting to get cold." As if to prove it, she shivered in my arms.

"Oh. Yeah, let's get dressed." She eased away from me, cold

air rushing in to fill the space between our bodies. We both looked down and giggled at the twin sticky messes on our chests.

With a cute little smile, she skipped her way to the bathroom to wash up, while I wiped myself off as well as I could with paper towels from the kitchen. I began to put on my clothes again when I heard her turn on the shower. *Lucky her.* I desperately needed a shower after today's exertions.

She stuck her head out of the bathroom, the rest of her tantalizingly out of view. "Hey. Want to join me?" She waggled her eyebrows at me and I laughed. I knew then that I was a hopeless cause.

I stripped off the clothes that I had put back on and joined her in the bathroom. I opened the glass door to the shower to find her standing under the shower head, rivulets of water streaming down her beautiful, naked body. She made room for me and I stepped inside, closing the door behind me. The glass immediately began fogging up, and warm tendrils of steam curled around our bare bodies.

I came up behind Anna and stroked the sides of her breasts while she lathered shampoo into her hair. The familiar scent of roses permeated the moist air, beyond intoxicating in the small enclosed space. She backed up until her ass was right up against me, prompting me to chuckle and grow hard again. I kissed her temple and wrapped my arms around her waist, my fingers gently pressing into her belly, considering whether or not to go lower.

She turned around in my arms, arching her back and neck to let the water wash out the shampoo. I stared at her pert little breasts, her nipples dark pink and stark against her pale skin. I lowered my head and sucked on one of them, her eyes

117

opening a tiny bit to watch me while she rinsed. Before I could move to the next one, she finished rinsing her hair and straightened, leaning into me and gazing longingly into my eyes.

Her hands trailed up my arms, pausing to squeeze my triceps, then up around my shoulders and down to flatten against my pecs. She splayed her fingers across them and gently groped me. *Squeeze, squeeze.* I laughed softly as she smiled and slid her hands lower over the crest of each of my abs.

Instead of going lower, she slipped her arms around my neck and stood on her tiptoes, pressing herself against me. My hands closed around her ass as she leaned in and exhaled softly into my ear. "Just come inside me."

"Uhhh, what?"

She pulled out of my arms, turned around, and planted her hands against the wall, looking at me over her shoulder. "Just do it. Fuck me again, but come inside me this time."

I laughed, but my body responded eagerly at the thought. "Why would I do that?"

She lowered her eyelids, giving me her best seductive look. "Because you want to." She licked her lips and continued, "Because *I* want you to." She stuck her ass out farther until she could rub it up and down on my increasingly hard dick.

I don't think so. But I still grabbed my penis and stroked it a bit, getting it ready to penetrate her again. "You know, it's going to take a lot longer for me to come this time."

She gave me another sultry look over her shoulder. "I'm counting on it."

I chuckled, slipping my fingers into her hair and gently but firmly pulling her head back as I slid into her. Her moan filled

118

my ears, the sound heavily amplified in the small space. I leaned into her so that her breasts and face were pressed up against the wall, though not painfully so.

Damn. Even though we'd just had sex, she still felt so tight. Maybe I wouldn't last that much longer, after all.

I started slowly, teasing her by going almost completely out and then back in. I reached in front and fondled her breast, my hand pressing up against the wall as I pinned her in place.

"Faster, *please*," she begged. I continued my slow pace. In...out...in...out...in...out. I wanted to draw out this pleasure between us, grow—

"Ian, please, *please* fuck me harder."

Well. If she was going to ask so nicely.

I rammed into her, hard and deep, and her groan of approval filled me with satisfaction. I plunged into her, faster and faster, smiling at the hot moisture that was dripping down my leg. It was definitely from *her* and not from the water. She was so deliciously wet.

"Fuck. Fuck. Fuck." With every two thrusts, Anna let out a "Fuck." Like a sex metronome. I smirked and thrust harder.

I could feel the pleasure mounting, and I quickly had to decide—did I want to come inside of her or not? As if reading my mind, she growled, "You'd better fucking come inside me this time. I'll take *all* the Plan B. Just. Don't. Pull. Out."

I leaned into her and murmured, "Wasn't planning on it." Even though I kind of had been.

She rubbed her clit with her fingers, frantic, her legs shaking uncontrollably. With one last hard thrust, my fist clenched in her hair, I cried out and unloaded myself inside of her. She groaned deep within, deep enough for me to feel, and her muscles quivered and clenched around me as she came. It was so deliciously intimate, so satisfying to feel the confirmation of what I'd done to her. Infinitely better than pulling out.

I kissed her hair and leaned into her, pressing my forehead against the back of her head. We were both breathing hard, quietly collecting ourselves after that explosion of pleasure. But after a moment, I realized that she was still shaking. It sounded like she was whimpering. I immediately pulled out of her and turned her around.

"Hey, are you okay?" She was crying. She sank down and sat on the floor of the shower. I turned off the water and retrieved the towel from behind the door, then wrapped it around her. "What's wrong? Anna, tell me what's wrong."

Her sobs came harder, so I pulled her into my arms. She came willingly, crying for a few minutes longer until all I heard was the occasional sniffle.

"Anna. What's going on?"

She looked me in the eyes and sniffed, wiping her nose on the towel. "That was...amazing."

I was very confused. "Are you crying because the sex was...so good?"

She whimpered. "Partly. I think I'm just...tired. Emotional. And it's been a long time since I last, you know..." She trailed off.

She hiccuped once, then was quiet. "It's just been a long day," she whispered. She glanced up at me, then looked down at her hands. "Thank you."

I stroked her wet hair. "Of course," I replied, though I honestly wasn't sure what precisely she was thanking me for. She started to shiver, so I scooped her up, opened the bathroom door, and carried her into her bedroom. The furnishings were sparse, but the few things in the room were

120

cleaner and more tasteful than the furniture in the common area had been. I laid her down in the bed and pulled the covers up, but when I went to go close the door, she grabbed my hand and wouldn't let me leave.

"Please stay." She looked at me with wide, pleading eyes. "Don't go."

"I'm not going anywhere," I promised, gently pulling my arm away. I went into the living room and picked up our clothes, brought them into her room, and closed the door. I slipped into her bed and held her close as we both fell asleep, exhausted from the day.

Chapter 13

-Anna-

I woke up languid and pleasantly sore, but also way too hot. No wonder—Ian was plastered against my back, his arm tucked protectively around me, hand cupping my breast. I sleepily stretched, pausing when I felt his erection pulsing against my ass.

"Oh god." I sat up and rubbed my face with my hands. My hair was wet and my eyes were puffy…and my inner thighs were still slick.

I'd asked him not to pull out. *What the fuck was I thinking?*

Ian stirred but didn't wake up. He must've been just as exhausted and wrung out from the day as I was.

I slipped out of bed and pulled the towel around me, then creeped to the bathroom to relieve and cleanse myself. I did *not* want to get pregnant. Not with Ian's child, not *ever*.

No matter that he had completely and utterly blown my mind with his lovemaking…*twice*. In a row. Way more than anyone else had ever done.

I didn't want a family.

I tiptoed back into my room and stood next to the bed,

watching Ian sleep. His breathing was even and blessedly quiet, unlike Asher, who was a prolific snorer. I could never sleep when he was around.

With his eyes closed, Ian looked so young and innocent, and not like a total sex demon. Without me in the bed, he'd curled up around a pillow, one well-muscled leg thrown out over the covers. I sat down on the bed next to him and stroked his hair until he opened his eyes.

"Hey," I said, smiling slightly at him.

"Hey," he replied, smiling back. He sat up and glanced around the room, then dry-cleared his throat. "Is there water somewhere?"

I grabbed my water bottle from my purse, glad that I had filled it up at the gym. He took a long drink, then handed the bottle back to me. I drank deeply too, surprised at my own thirst, then capped the bottle and put it away.

Ian held his hand out to me and I took it, allowing him to pull me back into bed. He wrapped his arms around me and I placed my head on his chest, quietly listening to his heartbeat.

"Do you...want to talk about it at all?" he quietly asked.

I was silent for a few moments. Then I giggled. "Sorry if I scared you. I think I just had a lot of...pent-up something." I wasn't sure if my tears were from relief, frustration, sadness, or satisfaction. Possibly a bit of all of the above. But I didn't want to try to psychoanalyze myself, to him *or* to me. Ian and I hardly knew each other, and I didn't want to scare him away. I wasn't exactly sure if I wanted him to *stay*, either, but I wanted to have the option, at least.

He interlaced his fingers with mine, rubbing his thumb along the outside of my hand. "Is there anything you need? Anything I can do for you?" He kissed my hair and I snuggled closer, wrapping my leg around his hips. What I felt against my thigh confirmed what I had already suspected as soon as I'd woken up: he was ready for round 3. I was too, but I needed something else, first.

"Get me some Plan B? And some condoms?" No earth-shattering orgasm was worth getting pregnant for.

"Of course." Ian got out of bed and quickly got dressed. He kissed my forehead on the way out the door and said he'd be back in a few.

I shut the door behind him, then went back to my bed and curled up under the blanket, still warm from his body heat.

Through the window, I watched the dark sky brighten from the occasional flash of lightning, followed soon after by a low rumble of thunder. The tree branches rattled against the glass as the wind howled through a tiny crack in the frame. I curled further into the blankets, covered my head and burrowed deep...and sighed.

What was I doing?

Ian was undeniably sweet. Charming. Fun to hang out with. An amazing lover. I hadn't felt so happy and at ease with someone in a long time.

But there was no way that it could work out between us long-term.

Firstly, I definitely didn't want to deal with his undoubtedly fobby (i.e., judgmental, traditional, fake, etc.) family. It sounded trite, but there was too much trauma from my own dysfunctional family to allow me to deal with someone else's. It was still too much to even think about right then.

Secondly, we'd soon (fingers crossed) be coworkers. I wasn't sure what the workplace policy was around dating, but I knew at least that if we broke up, it would be unbearably awkward, even more awkward than it already was...and I really needed this job.

Thirdly...he was too dependable, someone who seemed like he would always be there for me. That was dangerous. I didn't want to be dependent on yet another guy. I was working on getting a new job, and after that, I was going to make it *on my own*. I'd been trying to make it on my own for months, and a guy like him would make it easy to fall back into old habits. He was a crutch, an escape hatch, and I just wanted to be independent and free. My own person.

But, overall...he was wonderful. And I really liked him.

What to do?

* * *

"Pizza?"

Thirty minutes later, Ian had come back with what I'd requested, as well as a large Sicilian pizza and a bottle of wine.

I wasn't sure how I'd keep my walls fortified against him.

I took the pizza and wine to the kitchen while he took off his shoes. While I rummaged around for the bottle opener, he came up behind me and slipped his arms around my waist.

"Anna."

I turned around in his arms and he leaned into me, gently pinning me against the counter.

"Ian. We should—"

He surprised me with a meltingly tender kiss, thoroughly dispelling all thoughts from my mind. My hands gripped his sweater, pulling him close and holding onto him for dear life, molding my body against his. It almost hurt, how well we fit together.

He broke the kiss. "We should what?"

I met his questioning gaze, then looked away. "We...ah..." I sighed. "I shouldn't date anyone right now."

He slipped a hand into my hair, cupping my head and gently turning it back to face him. He searched my face. "Why?"

I leaned into his touch. "I'm just...working through some stuff. Trying to focus on my career. I don't want to be distracted. And I mean, we'll be coworkers soon. Hopefully. I think it's for the best if we don't...start anything." I hoped he understood what I was trying to say. My thoughts were a jumbled mess.

"But...we like each other." He cocked his head a little, unable to compute.

"Yes. But I shouldn't—I can't be with you. With anyone, right now."

He let go of me and took a step back, disappointed. "I see. Then...do you want me to leave?"

I mourned his warmth, the weight of him against me. I knew that I should say yes, that I should start distancing myself from him as soon as possible. There was no point in prolonging the inevitable—it would only make things worse. But with the way he looked at me (a little bit sad, a little bit hopeful), his soothing scent, and the cold creeping into my skin...

"Not yet." I wrapped my arms around him and pulled him to me, kissing him like it was the last time. It very well might've been.

But after that, we went through rounds three and four. Then I knocked him out in round five. By then, I think I'd finally gotten the "pent-up something" out of my system.

I tried to enjoy myself that weekend. I would worry about

the long-term issues later.

* * *

Ian kissed my hair and removed his arm from around my shoulders. We were lying in bed on Sunday evening, listening to an old playlist that I had made on my laptop. He hadn't left my apartment, other than to grab more food. "I should go."

"Okay." I paused the music and sat up, then watched as he got dressed, enjoying the shadows that played across the ridges on his sculpted body.

A familiar tone began to play from my laptop. I checked the time. *Oh!* It was Cassie calling for our weekly chat.

Ian looked up, one sock halfway on. "It's Cassie," I explained. I connected the call, glad that I had already been wearing a t-shirt.

"Heyyy!" Cassie's voice came through, followed by video footage of her smiling face a moment later.

"Hey, Cass." I met Ian's eyes. He made to continue leaving, clearly willing to keep our hookup a secret, but I shook my head and waved him over. I'd been planning on telling Cassie anyway—there was no reason to hide it.

Cassie said, "What are you look—"

He came up before the laptop and leaned over so that his head appeared upside down on the screen. "Yo, Cassie."

Her eyes widened. "Whoa! Ian! What are you doing over there on a Sunday night?"

Ian looked at me to respond.

"He was helping me prepare for the interview." He raised an eyebrow at me, eyes full of laughter, but he didn't contradict me.

127

"Is that so?" asked Cassie, utterly unconvinced. "What kind of prep—"

"Hey Cassie," Ian interrupted, "I'm going to go. Unless you want me to push tomorrow's deadline on the design spec?"

"No, I need that spec! Go away and do it."

He chuckled. "Alright, alright. Talk to you tomorrow." He met my eyes, grinned, then let himself out.

"Girl, you need to tell me what's going on." Cassie demanded.

I rubbed my chin and feigned thoughtful innocence. "Ah, well...we went climbing today. No wait, that was yesterday—"

"You had sex, didn't you?"

"Yes, but—"

"You look like you've been having sex all weekend."

"Wow, what does *that* mean? How can you even tell?"

"Nana, your face has *severe* post-sex glow. I can always tell when you've gotten laid. I can even tell how good it was. You are positively *radiant* and you can't stop smiling!"

It was true. I couldn't stop, and my cheeks hurt a little. "Okay, fine, we had a lot of sex this weekend."

"Thought so. How was it? I assume if you did it all weekend, it must've been—"

"Yeah, it was amazing. He's just so...attentive. And patient." I shivered at the memory of his hands. That mouth. *Mmph.*

"Wow, good job, Ian. So what now? Are you guys together?"

I sighed. "No."

"What! Why? Didn't you just say the sex—"

"Sex isn't everything! And we're going to be coworkers soon! And like...this weekend was nice, but I hardly know him, and what little I do know of him...I'm skeptical."

"Nana. There are plenty of Stumpstashers who are dating,

so don't worry about that. But tell me more about why you're skeptical." Cassie crossed her arms and sat back, eyes hard. Her arguing pose.

I didn't want to tell her the full truth of how I felt. I knew that some of my reasons would not hold up to scrutiny well, even if I felt strongly about them. So I listed some modified reasons off on my fingers. "Well, one, he's a tech bro. All tech bros I have ever met have been basic nice guys who just like to watch movies and go hiking. *Snore.* Two, he's Chinese, and his parents speak Mandarin with him, meaning that his family is probably pretty fobby, and therefore, not one I want to deal with. *You know why.* Three, I've been trying to focus on myself and my career. I'm not ready to date again, not until I get my shit together."

Cassie sat up and started listing counterarguments on *her* fingers. "One, he also likes climbing, which automatically elevates a guy, in my book." She winked. "And not all tech bros are the same. Michael is a software engineer and he's really into art and photography, and he's super fun to be with. Two, the way Ian talks about his family, they seem totally chill. He told me that when his mom first came to the US and learned about high-fives, she started giving them to everyone. How cute is that? And he's pretty progressive, not old-school. Whatever his family is like, it can't be anywhere close to as bad as what your family was like. Third, you've been single for seven months. You told me that you felt like you were in a slump with your music writing. Maybe he can help you get out of it. Music is about feelings, right? Maybe he'll help you feel something? Inspire you?"

That was what I was afraid of. I didn't want him to make me feel anything. Feelings made things complicated, and I needed life to be simple right now. To Cassie, I grumbled, "Sure, *maybe*, but all you've told me about him is the good. What about the bad? What are his flaws?"

"Uhhh. He...works too much? I'm honestly impressed that you got him to stay with you all weekend because he works his *ass off*. And he can be very blunt, sometimes. He's usually a really nice guy, but if he thinks you're wrong or being unreasonable, he can get kinda scary. Not someone you want to argue with. He's definitely made some enemies at Stumpstash with this bluntness." Cassie tapped her chin with her finger. "I think that might be it."

I shook my head. "Just means you don't know him well enough." That list was too reasonable—there had to be *something* else wrong with him.

"Just give him a chance," said Cassie. "What's the worst that could happen?"

I sighed. I could think of lots of things.

He could turn out to be an asshole, and then we'd break up and I'd be miserable at work.

He could make me lose my mind with lust and I could accidentally get pregnant. I vowed to be more careful from now on.

Or he could make me fall madly in love...and utterly break me. Given our explosive chemistry and my fucked-up past, this seemed the strongest possibility of the three.

On screen, Cassie was rocking side to side, waggling her eyebrows and and holding two thumbs up. "Dooo it! Nana! Dooo it! Nana!"

I laughed. "*Fine*! I'll give it a shot. But Cassie...if you're wrong, I'm never taking dating advice from you again."

She grinned. "I'll take that risk."

Later that evening, I texted Ian. *My onsite is on Wednesday. Dinner after?*

He responded immediately. *Absolutely.*

Chapter 14

-Ian-

I thought that after such a restful, lazy weekend, I'd be more productive at work.

Instead, I found myself constantly distracted by anything that reminded me of Anna. And that was a lot.

A teal-colored backpack. Bananas. Pizza. Indie music. Cassie.

"Soooo. *Anna*." Cassie and I had a conference call scheduled to review the design spec, but I could see that it was going to be derailed from the start. Her eyebrows danced up and down, and I was sure that if I were in the SF office that day, she would've been nudging me in the ribs with her elbows.

"Yep. *Anna*. I assume that you know that I wasn't really helping her with her interview prep?"

Cassie's coy smile said it all. "Of course. She had her post-sex face on."

I laughed and shook my head. "Ah...Cassie. Tell me the truth. Do you think I have a chance with her?"

She took a deep breath. "So, I'm not going to say yes or no, but I will say that she's been through some shit. Just treat her with respect and maybe it'll work out. I think you guys would be great together."

I raised my eyebrows. "You think I wouldn't respect her?"

"*Nooo.* I just mean that she wants to be independent, and she needs someone who can be her partner, not like...controlling her. She's had bad experiences with guys in the past. And her family."

I sighed. "I know. You told me when you were drunk that she had 'daddy issues'."

Her eyes widened. "Oh shit. I said that?" She paused and bit her lip. "I didn't...say anything more than that, did I?"

"No," I replied slowly, "but should you have? Is there more that I should know?"

She vehemently shook her head. "It's Anna's story to tell, not mine." She pointed an accusatory finger at me through the screen. "And don't go asking me questions about her when I'm drunk."

"Not even about benign things, like what she likes and doesn't like?"

"Psh, c'mon, Ian." She rolled her eyes. "You can ask her those things yourself."

I laughed. "Fine. Now are you ready to talk about this design?"

She heaved a big sigh. "*Fine.*"

* * *

"How many people work in this office?"

I glanced up from my computer at the sound of Anna's voice. She was talking to the facilities manager, who was leading her around the office on a tour. We locked eyes for a second but she quickly looked away, pretending not to know me. As she walked past, I continued to watch her from the corner of my eye, taking in her ponytail, tan cashmere sweater, tight black pants and black heeled boots. The pants and heel combo was very...stimulating. I looked forward to dinner, and to what I hoped came after.

From across the room, I heard Tom exclaim, "Oh HEY, it's you!" Anna responded in an appropriate indoor voice, so I didn't quite catch what she said. Tom's booming voice continued, asking her about what she was doing here, though his voice grew fainter as they moved away. It sounded like he'd joined the tour. I shook my head. Poor Tom. *She's mine.*

Her last interview finished up at 4:30pm, when I saw the recruiter walk her out. We'd picked a restaurant not too far from the office, and we'd agreed to meet there at 5. So at 4:45, I packed up my stuff, much to the surprise of my colleagues, who knew that I almost never left before 7. They shot me curious looks as I walked out, but I just smiled and ignored them.

Dinner was at a new French restaurant that had opened up just a few weeks ago on the third floor of a neighboring building. The floor-to-ceiling windows offered a gorgeous view of the late afternoon sun. The interior was sleek, with endless glass and matte metallic surfaces surrounding a huge, fully-stocked bar in the center. Although there were dozens of tables in the large space, nearly all of them were occupied when I arrived. Luckily, I'd made a reservation.

I found her sitting at a corner table. She'd taken out her ponytail, and her hair fell in long, loose waves about her shoulders. She saw me approach and gave me a brilliant, heart-stopping smile.

134

"I take it that it went well?" I said, putting down my stuff and slipping into the seat across from her.

"I think so. Everyone was so friendly, and the office is *so nice*. I can't believe that you guys get free Flaming Hot Cheetos."

"We also get free ice cream on Fridays." I laughed when her eyes sparkled wistfully at the thought. I'd learned over the weekend that she loved ice cream, as well as most other kinds of dairy. Girls like cheese, indeed.

I asked her about the interview, who had interviewed her, what they'd asked, what she'd answered. She gave me the play-by-play. She was especially excited by the fact that the facilities manager enjoyed a lot of the same music that she did. She'd promised to check out Anna's music blog, and said she'd be in touch soon.

"Sounds like you knocked it out of the park." We touched wine glasses.

"I hope so. It would be so nice to have a job that actually pays well."

"Yeah, Stumpstash definitely pays well." I took a sip of wine. "Honestly, I hope you make enough to get out of that area that you live in. It's not the safest." Saturday being a case in point.

She sighed. "Yeah, I know. I'm still a little shaken by what happened this weekend. I knew the neighborhood was kind of sketchy, but I've never had anything happen to me before. I guess it doesn't seem like anything really happens until it does."

Our food arrived, and her attention turned from me to the sous-vide chicken breast and rosemary potatoes on her plate. She took a bite of the chicken, then fluttered her eyelids closed. I smiled and dipped a heel of crusty french bread into my steaming bowl of bouillabaisse.

After a few more bites, Anna put down her utensils and said, "So I want to talk to you about...*us*."

I looked up, hopeful at her use of the word *us*. "You mean like, define our relationship?" She nodded.

I put my own utensils down and wiped my mouth with my napkin before reaching across the table to take her hand. "I'd love to date you, if you'll give me the chance."

She wriggled her fingers in my palm, then slipped her hand out of mine and picked up her knife to cut into her chicken. "I need to tell you something. About my living situation."

"What's that?" I asked, using my fork to wrestle the meat from a mussel.

She hesitated, took another bite of chicken, then said, "You remember how I told you that I used to live with my ex?"

I paused in my eating and glanced up. "Yeah?"

Her eyes met mine, then slid to the window. "I'm still living with him."

Good thing my fork had been made of metal, or else I would have snapped it in half. "So...he's your roommate?"

She glanced at my hand, then my face, and nodded. "And my landlord. He gives me a discount on the rent."

After a slow breath, I released my death-grip on the fork and began to chew again. "I see."

She stared at me, tense. "You don't care?"

I poked a shrimp with my fork and shrugged, feigning nonchalance. Obviously, I didn't like the idea of them living together, but she'd made it pretty clear to me that she hadn't had sex in a really long time. And she'd called him her ex, not her boyfriend. If they were still dating, she didn't have anything to gain by telling me. "What's there to say? I'd still love to date you and I already said that I hope you find a better place to live."

A pause. Then, "What if I just want us to be fuck-buddies?"

I put my utensils down again and sat back, coolly meeting her gaze. "No."

She frowned. "Seriously? Wouldn't most guys *prefer* that?"

As a gorgeous woman, she was probably used to holding all of the cards in a relationship. Too bad for her—I knew that I was a catch, too.

I shook my head. "You should know by now that I'm not the kind of guy who messes around like that."

Her leg skimmed against mine under the table as she silkily whispered, "Are you sure you don't want to just go to your place after this?"

I sat up in my chair and reluctantly moved my leg away from hers. "I mean, we *can* go back to my place. But is that your answer? You just want us to be fuck-buddies?"

She looked down and fiddled with her napkin. "I think that would be for the best."

I arched an eyebrow at her and tried a different tactic. "So I assume we'd have a lot of sex. But would you be willing to get dinner with me sometimes?"

"Yes?" She frowned.

"Would you maybe want to go climbing with me?"

"Uhhh, sure."

"So you're down to hang out, outside of the bedroom."

She slowly nodded.

I leaned in and gave her a meaningful look. "That doesn't sound like fuck-buddies to me."

She rolled her eyes and threw her napkin onto the table. "*Fine*. Just forget about it."

Maybe it would be better to say yes and just pretend. The

way she'd looked at me the previous weekend, after our sex marathon, I was sure that I could seduce her into an actual relationship. We'd be dating in all but name.

But I really didn't like playing games. I wanted us to be fully on the same page, 100% honest with each other. I shook my head and reached for her hand again. "Anna. I really enjoy spending time with you, and I think you enjoy spending time with me, too. I'd love to get to know you better. Whatever reservations you have about being coworkers or about wanting space so that you can work on stuff...we can figure it out together."

From the purse of her lips and the way her brows drew together, it was clear that she was reluctant to say yes. I kneaded her hand in mine, trying to massage her doubts away, then lifted her hand to my lips and opened her fingers, planting a kiss on her palm. Her eyes slowly softened, and after a moment, she finally nodded. "Okay."

"So you're my girlfriend?" I asked, hope glowing in my chest.

She nodded again. "But I really want to take it slow. Really. I don't want us to see each other everyday. I want space, and I want time to work on my music writing."

"Of course." I beamed and lifted my wine glass. "Cheers to us."

She smiled and raised her own glass. "Cheers." We each took a sip, and I savored the taste of merlot. And of victory.

"So *can* we go to your place after this?" she asked. "I'd like to keep celebrating with you." Her face flushed slightly...from the alcohol, or from her thoughts?

Part of me wanted to go to *her* place and meet her ex-boyfriend. To make her moan loudly enough for him to know that she'd found a new man. But, one step at a time. "Of course."

"Do *you* have any roommates?"

"No. I live by myself."

"Where?"

"In Williamsburg."

"That's a cute area."

"It is. You'll fit right in." She smiled charmingly in response, nibbling delicately at a piece of chicken.

We ate in relative silence after that, with only the occasional question or comment on our meals. Afterward, we glanced at the dessert menu, but found only French vanilla ice cream, which Anna declined—she only liked interesting, adventurous flavors. So I offered to take her out for ice cream after and she happily accepted.

When the check arrived, I reached for my wallet, but Anna grabbed the server book first.

"I want to pay." She opened the server book and glanced at the amount, expressionless, then put her credit card inside.

"This restaurant is expensive, and I'm the one who picked it. You don't have to pay for this." I left out the obvious—that she didn't have a job.

She pursed her lips. "I know that I don't have to pay, but I want to." Her tone was final.

"Alright then. Thanks." No need to patronize her.

She placed the server book on the table and the waiter promptly came and took it away.

"But I'm paying for ice cream," I said.

She smiled. "Deal."

* * *

We took the subway to my neck of the woods, where there was an amazing ice cream parlor not too far from my condo. To my surprise and delight, she ordered three scoops stacked one on top of the other, each a different flavor, in a huge waffle cone. I didn't order anything—there was no way she'd be able to finish the whole thing by herself.

"You're not afraid you're going to fart a bunch tonight?" I joked.

Three scoops was a lot. I watched as she stuck her little pink tongue out and slowly licked from the bottom to the top, then put her lips on the small peak that she'd formed, pulling it into her mouth. Then she offered it to me and said with a straight face, "I'm a lady. Ladies don't fart."

I laughed and followed the trail that her tongue had taken. "I guess we'll see."

And we did. Her lovemaking that night had been decidedly *un*ladylike. And much to my glee, she *did* fart.

Chapter 15

-Anna-

On Wednesdays, Asher and I liked to work on music together—me on my playlists, him on his song writing. He was the lead singer and keyboardist for Spice Dust, and he composed most of their songs, too. So while I sat on the couch with my headphones and laptop, hunting for new music, he sat on the floor with his headphones and keyboard, composing new music.

My phone buzzed beside me. *Check your email.* That's all Cassie's text message said. Curious, I opened my browser and navigated to my email inbox, as directed.

There were two new emails waiting for me, one from Cassie entitled, "Wedding Photos <3" and one from the recruiter at Stumpstash with the subject, "Regarding Your Candidacy."

I wasn't sure if she'd wanted me to check her wedding photos email or the Stumpstash email. Possibly both. She'd referred me, so she'd likely gotten a notification about my job candidacy, about whether or not we were now coworkers.

With a small sigh, I opened her email first.

Hey Nana,

I shared my wedding photos online—you probably saw them already! But I'm sending you a few special photos that I'm sure you wouldn't have wanted anyone else to see ;)

You guys are so cute together!

Love,

C

When I clicked on the link she'd sent, I noticed right away that by *a few*, she'd really meant *way too many*. I adjusted the screen so that I could more discreetly view the dozens of photos of me and Ian.

The photographer must have been keeping a close eye on us that night, because he or she had captured nearly all of our moments together.

Walking together to the ceremony, my arm looped through his, our smiling faces affectionately turned to one another. The sun to my flower.

The moment he'd pressed his lips to my hand, my soft gaze meeting his quiet smolder.

Standing together during the ceremony, when I'd become teary-eyed. He'd been studying my face (and not the ceremony) with a small smile playing about his lips.

The little girl knocking me over (which would have been hilarious, if I weren't the subject of the photo) and the infamous lap dance that followed. The photographer had captured the slight arch of my back as I struggled to stand, my mouth forming a little 'o' as I encountered Ian's bulge. He was smirking and not helping me one whit, the jerk.

Our dance together, bodies crushed against one another,

mouths teasingly close as we whispered into each other's ears.

There was even one of us kissing on the moonlit terrace, passionately embracing, my bare toes curling on the bench.

I quietly groaned. Cassie had seen all of these, maybe Michael, too. What kind of ninja paparazzo had she hired? How many photos had this person taken that night, and were any of them of anyone else? I was surprised there weren't also images of Ian going down on me in the bathroom. Geez.

Even so, I couldn't help clicking through the photos again to study the details, especially of Ian's face. In every single one of them, his eyes, the tender, playful way he looked at me...*sigh*. I wanted to melt and just soak into the couch.

My boyfriend.

My cheeks hurt, and I had to force myself to stop smiling.

Okay, maybe nice wedding photos weren't *so* bad. Not when they were this cute.

I sighed again, suddenly missing Ian, wondering what he was doing. Given the time, he was probably at work.

Oh yeah. Work. Stumpstash.

I clicked back to my inbox to check the other email.

With a long, deep breath, I clicked, then stared.

It took me a few seconds to read and reread the first line. Then I put my laptop down and did my happy dance, pumping my fists from side to side while bobbing my head in the opposite direction.

When Asher looked up and saw me dancing on the couch, he slipped his headphones off and asked, "What's up?"

I flipped my laptop around and showed him what it said, though from that distance, he probably couldn't read it. "I got the job!"

"Hey, that's great, congrats!" He hit a button on his keyboard and put his headphones down. "When do you start?"

"I have a call with the recruiter to discuss, but probably next week!" I scanned the contents of the offer letter and squealed with excitement.

"Nice. So I can start jacking up the rent?" he asked, giving me a wry look. I laughed, but I knew that he was only half kidding. He was charging me well below market rate for the room.

"Nice try, but I've got student loans to pay, buddy. When you start seeing me walking around with Gucci bags and Louboutins, maybe *then* you can consider raising the rent. And only after you fix this shithole, too." Asher's family owned the building, but he was too lazy to deal with the repairs that were so desperately needed. It was one of the things that I regularly nagged him about.

I turned my attention back to the laptop and started drafting my acceptance email. Asher's eyes stayed on me, though. He didn't go back to his music.

He slowly stood up and came to sit next to me on the couch. "Anna."

"Hmm?" I kept typing. I didn't want to hear what was surely coming next. We'd already had the same conversation multiple times before, and I wasn't sure how many more times we could...especially now that I was with Ian.

Asher was a good guy. He was smart and charming, and he loved having a good time. We'd partied a lot while we were together, going out night after night, weekend after weekend. He was there for me when I needed him, didn't bat an eye at helping me out with cash or letting me skip out on rent when I needed a little extra time to get him the money. And we knew how to deal with each other. Whenever I got mad about something, he'd argue half-heartedly, then shrug and let me have my way...or if it was bad enough, he'd leave until our tempers cooled, then come back and apologize and move on. He was generally laid back and didn't really push me for anything.

Until earlier this year, when he'd asked me to marry him. Of course, I'd said no. I'd repeatedly mentioned that I never wanted to get married, but he'd taken my sticking around for three years as a change of heart. It wasn't, and his pressuring me had backfired. He'd left me high and dry in an expensive-ass restaurant, to fend for myself, to remind me of how dependent I was on him. I needed him, but I didn't want to, especially if he couldn't respect what I wanted, couldn't respect *me*. It made me realize that I didn't want to be with him anymore. We were good friends, but we weren't good for each other.

But I couldn't just end things. Asher was my best friend in New York, and his friends were the closest thing I had to my own friends. I didn't have anywhere to go, no one else to turn to. So I'd asked him for space, and for time to get my shit together. Coward that I was, I'd asked him for *a break*, not to break up, even though I already thought of him as my ex.

He was tired of waiting.

My hands shook slightly as I continued to type. He sat silently for a moment, just watching me, then put his hand on my back and said, "It seems like things are going well for you."

I kept my eyes on the screen. "Asher, can we not talk about this right now? I'm still figuring shit out."

"Anna. I don't...I can't keep waiting around." He put his other hand on mine.

I turned and looked at him, removing my hand from under

his and placing it on his shoulder. "Hey. Seriously. I can't talk about this right now."

He huffed in annoyance. "Sorry it's so inconvenient for you, Anna. I've just been waiting over here, celibate as fuck, giving you discounted rent. When *are* you going to be able to talk about it?"

He was usually laid back, but when he felt like it, he really knew how to piss me off. "Just fucking go out and get some then." The words slipped out before I could think. I turned back to my computer and continued typing, but I tensed, bracing myself for his reaction.

He shot me an incredulous look. "Are you fucking serious? You know how I feel about you." Then he narrowed his eyes. "Don't tell me that *you've* been going out and getting laid."

"No, Asher, of course—"

"You've always been bad at lying." His voice was dangerously low.

"Asher." I really, really didn't want to start some shit right now, but he was starting to piss me off. And to scare me. "I haven't, really," I whispered.

"Then why would you tell me to go out and fuck other people?" He stood up, his expression dark. "What the *fuck*. I gave you *space* because you asked for it. I let you stay here for almost *nothing*. Then you take advantage of me and just start fucking someone else?"

I raised my chin, furious, defiant. Part of me knew that I was in the wrong, that I shouldn't have gotten us into this situation...but my emotional defenses kicked in, winning out over my guilt. "So what if I have? It just happened, just this weekend. I *just* met him."

"I fucking KNEW IT. While I was gone? Like, you brought

him home and fucked him while I wasn't here?"

Yes. "No. God, why are you flipping out? We've been broken up for more than half a year, I thought we were good. I thought we were *friends.*" My guilt grew worse, a dense miasma spreading through my chest, crowding out the oxygen in my lungs.

He shook his head and slapped one hand into the other for emphasis, making me flinch and curl into myself. "*Fuck. Friendship.* We had something, you and me. I was just giving you *space*, 'cause you felt too guilty about letting me take care of you. You *know* I wanted to get back together."

I cried out and covered my face with my arms when he turned and punched the wall, leaving behind a hole. "FUCK."

Horror warred with relief. He hadn't hit me, but he'd been violent and shown a side of him that I'd never seen before. The Asher I knew was calm, collected, chill. Even when he was angry, he kept his cool. And he'd never laid a hand on me before...but there was a first time for everything, as my mother had found out the hard way. My eyes blurred with tears as I yelled, "ASHER! Calm down! You're fucking scaring me."

His jaw flexed and he opened and closed his fists, breathing hard. My legs tensed, ready to get away if he did anything else. But all he did was turn away and quietly say, "Get out."

"What?" My heart sank, his words paralyzing me.

"Get the FUCK out of this apartment. You have till tonight to get your fucking shit out of here."

He stormed out of the apartment, slamming the door behind him.

I stared after him, stunned, heart racing. With each beat, his words slowly sank in, deeper and deeper, searing every nerve. Then, with shaking hands, I picked up my phone and called the only other person I could in New York.

* * *

Ian opened the door to his condo and walked inside, carrying in most of my meager possessions. He placed my stuff on the floor by the door and went downstairs to grab the rest from his car.

"Make yourself at home," he softly called up.

I put down my own armload of stuff and walked inside. I'd been there just two days ago, but we'd been too busy *getting* busy for me to notice much. I looked around carefully then, taking in what would be my home for the foreseeable future.

The condo was spacious and well-lit, featuring floor to ceiling windows along two of the walls, shaded with gauzy white curtains. One wall featured exposed brick, from which he'd hung shelves with brilliant green plants that charmingly curled every which way. The remaining wall was painted white, with a series of framed photographs hanging across it. His kitchen was spotless and seemingly well-stocked, with plenty of counter space, including a beautiful marble island. The stainless steel appliances looked brand new.

It was night and day from my old place. I didn't want to develop the same dependency on Ian that I had on Asher, so I didn't think of this as my permanent home. But even so, it felt like I'd upgraded.

Ian re-entered the apartment carrying the last of my things. Most of the furniture in my old room had been Asher's, so all I'd really brought with me was my clothing, keepsakes, and decorations. I didn't have the money for much else.

I stopped looking around when I noticed that Ian was carrying my things towards the master bedroom on the right, instead of to the guest bedroom on the left.

"Hey wait, can I just stay in the guest bedroom? Then you can have your own room to yourself?" I liked Ian, but if we were going to live together, I wanted as much personal space of my own as possible. And luckily, he had a spare bedroom. I marveled at the extravagance of having a spare bedroom in New York City—how did he pay for all of this?

"You'll stay with me in the master bedroom," he said. "The guest room is for my parents."

"Oh." Bummer. "I mean, how often do your parents visit?" I noticed a framed photograph of the people in question. They were a handsome older Chinese couple: a woman with short black hair, permed in the typical old Chinese lady fashion, but with a warm smile and beautiful eyes...and a man who looked just like Ian, but with a bigger nose, thinner lips, and slightly longer, grayer hair. They were holding hands and standing in front of the Golden Gate Bridge with pleasant, windswept expressions.

"Like once a month," he called out from his room.

"That's...pretty often." Maybe too often.

"Yeah. They'll actually be here in a couple of weeks."

I coughed at the sudden bile in my throat. Was he that close with them, that they visited that much? I didn't want to deal with his parents, not this soon. I hadn't met Asher's parents until after a year of dating, and we hardly ever saw them after.

"From where? Where do they live?" I sat down on his couch and focused on breathing.

"They live in New Jersey, in Princeton. They moved there when I was there for undergrad."

Of course he was a Princeton grad.

Another wave of nausea hit at the thought of his parents moving from California to Princeton to be near him. *Who did that?*

Having finished placing all of my stuff in the master bedroom, he came to sit next to me on the couch and took my hands in his. "Hey. You can stay here as long as you like. I know that you want space. I'm not going to expect us to spend every waking moment together. Just let me know when you want to hang out, and otherwise, I'll work, climb, do stuff as usual, ok? You can tell me if—if it's too much."

I took in his earnest expression, the solemn promise there...and after a moment, squeezed his hands, grateful for his understanding. "Thanks, Ian."

I didn't want to get into the parents discussion right then. It was too big, and we could deal with them later. In the meantime, I resolved to find a new place as soon as possible. No need to meet his parents if we didn't live together, right?

He stood up. "I'll cook us some dinner in like an hour. I still have some work to do, so I'm going to go upstairs to the loft and do it." I had completely missed that there was a loft. *There was a loft, in addition to a spare bedroom?*

He kissed my forehead and disappeared behind the brick wall, leaving me to my thoughts.

I sat for a while, taking in my surroundings, letting the situation sink in.

Asher, my ex-boyfriend, best friend in New York, and fellow audiophile, just kicked me out of his apartment, where he'd let me stay for years with reduced rent.

Ian, my boyfriend of less than a week, of whom I knew very little, had just taken me in and offered to let me stay for as long as I liked. We hadn't discussed any rent.

Friend to relative stranger; shithole to Williamsburg condo; and still...dependent.

Fuck.

Chapter 16

-Ian-

I was nervous about having Anna live with me. Things were moving way too fast, when she'd explicitly asked us to go slowly. We'd just started dating, hardly knew each other, and would soon be colleagues, too. It seemed like a recipe for disaster.

But she didn't have anywhere to go, and I didn't want to turn her away. So I gave her space, as much as I possibly could.

She had a few days before starting work at Stumpstash, and I made sure to stay at work for my usual hours to give her time to settle into her own routine.

Her second night living with me, I went to the climbing gym and didn't get home until she was already lying in bed, so I just showered and cuddled up next to her and held her as she slept. Her body was warm and sweet in my arms, and she snuggled close, sighing and fitting against me as if she'd always belonged there. I hadn't known that I'd been sleeping poorly for so many years until I woke up next to her, without an alarm, refreshed and ready for the day.

The next night, I worked late and didn't get home until 9pm.

We fell asleep watching old comedy sketches together and woke up to brilliant sunshine, twin smiles on our faces.

On Saturday, we went climbing together. She was getting better, stronger, and braver, and the V1s in the gym were no match for her. Lina noticed it too, and began high-fiving Anna as often as I did. At one point, I even caught them whispering together and pointing at me, then giggling. Disturbing.

That night, we cooked and ate dinner together. With Anna as my sous chef, we made a green vegetable curry from scratch, with fresh kaffir lime leaves and galangal. Her pride and delight, that mouthgasm look that she wore throughout dinner, made every extra step worth it. It filled me with pride to know that I'd been the one to put that look on her face, and I was glad that she shared my love and appreciation of good food. And based on what happened after, the enthusiasm with which she thanked me for the meal...food was a good way to her heart.

I schemed and plotted out several more meals that we could cook together in the near future.

On Sunday, her last day of freedom before work started, she asked to be left alone. She spent the day in the loft, on her computer, oddly quiet. Maybe working on a playlist? I wasn't sure.

So that night, during dinner, I asked her about it. "Is there a new playlist coming out tomorrow?"

"Oh. No, not this week." She stared vacantly at her plate of roasted asparagus and salmon.

"What were you working on today?"

Her brow furrowed, and she pushed a piece of salmon skin back and forth on her plate. "I was looking at apartments."

"Oh." I knew she didn't want to live with me forever, but

153

the thought put me out a little. It must've put her out too. She sighed.

"You okay?" I asked.

She seemed to snap out of it. "Yeah, I'm fine. Excited to start tomorrow." Her lips tilted into a half-baked smile.

I decided not to press. "We're going to be seeing each other a lot, working at the same place and living together. Hope you don't hate me by the end of the week," I joked.

She looked down at her food. "I won't live here for too long. I've found a couple of possible spots. I'll move after I get a few weeks' pay, once I can afford a security deposit."

"Ok. But if you need to, you can stay here as long as you like, it's no problem at all. It's been really nice having you here."

She pursed her lips. "I shouldn't stay. I don't want to be dependent on you. I don't want to be dependent on *anyone*."

I cut my asparagus stalks in half. "You're not dependent on me. I'm just helping you out for a bit." I glanced up and was surprised to see tears in her eyes. "Anna?"

She got up from the table and walked to the bedroom. I stood up and followed.

"Anna, what's wrong?"

She'd sunk down to her knees on the floor by the bed, tears silently streaming down her face. I slowly sat down next to her and put my hand on her back, not saying anything, just letting her cry it out.

I thought about her words. *I don't want to be dependent on* anyone. No one could be fully independent all the time. What about her family? Did she have parents or siblings? Was she on bad terms with them? Was she an orphan or something? I wanted to know, but with the possibility of *daddy issues* hanging over us, and our relationship as new and tenuous as it was, it didn't seem like a good time to ask.

After several minutes, she finally said, "I'm so tired of depending on people." She sniffled.

"Hey, it's not like that. This is just temporary. You'll get on your own two feet at some point. And I don't mind at all." My hand rubbed soothing circles on her back.

"I've been a fucking leech for *years*. Asher took care of me, and now you're taking care of me. And before that..." She angrily wiped her face with the sleeves of her sweater. "Nothing's different. I just went from one guy to another."

I hesitated, then said, "Maybe."

"*What?*" Her eyes flashed, face taut with anger.

I met her gaze head-on. "So? You did it before, doesn't mean you have to do it again. You're not helpless, you're an adult. It's not like you're incapable of taking control of your life. Don't just sit there and cry, do something about it."

She gave me a withering look, like she wanted to argue, or hit me. The way her fists opened and closed, I think she almost did. But after a moment, her face slackened. "You're right," she whispered.

I kissed her temple. "Everyone needs a little help sometimes." When she didn't respond, I stood up, then held my hand out to her. "C'mon. Let's go finish dinner. You've got a big day tomorrow."

She took my hand and nodded slightly. I helped her up and led her back to the dining table, where we finished our meal in relative silence.

* * *

"Hey, *Ba*. How are you? How's *Ma?*" Anna was in the other

bedroom talking to Cassie.

"I'm okay, just tired. We were pretty lazy today."

"What'd you do?"

"We walked to the grocery store to buy some fruit. And we finished another drama." My parents loved watching Asian dramas. I thought it was cute that they watched them together. Sometimes my dad cried more at the end of them than my mom did.

"What happened in this one?" I asked.

"Well, a hardworking country girl gets raped, and she goes blind and becomes pregnant as a result. Everyone looks down on her, except for a handsome doctor who is traveling through the countryside. He stops and helps take care of her, and eventually she gets her eyesight back and falls in love with him. But then his ex-girlfriend gets jealous and tries to poison her so that she'll go blind again, except that he gets poisoned instead and so *he* goes blind. So the country girl poisons herself and decides to be blind with him, but then she loses the baby." He sniffed. "It was so touching."

"I...see." *Nope.* I cleared my throat. "So *Ba*, speaking of dramas, I have some news."

"Oh? Did you get someone pregnant?" he joked.

I winced at the memory of how reckless we'd been. "*No.* But I do have a girlfriend now."

"Ah, I knew my handsome son couldn't stay single forever. Is she the girl you had coffee with?" Unlike my mom, my dad still had a sharp memory.

"Yes. Also, she's...living with me now."

He paused. "That fast? Is she homeless?"

"No!" *Kind of.* "It's temporary. She just needs to stay with me for a bit while she finds her next place."

"Okay." He paused. "Can we still come over for Thanksgiving?"

"Of course! I'm sure that she'd love to meet you guys." My parents were adorable, and I was sure they'd get along great with Anna.

"Ok. But if it's inconvenient, we don't have to come. Just let us know."

"*Ba*, you and *Ma* are always welcome here, anytime. I'm sure she'll be fine with it."

My dad chuckled. "Uh huh. Why don't you ask her before you say that?"

"I will." I made a mental note to do so.

Then I promptly forgot.

* * *

The next morning, I showed Anna the commute: 10 minute walk to the station, M train for 15 minutes, then another 10 minute walk on the other side. I let go of her hand at the door to the building, as we'd agreed to keep it fully professional during the day.

It was clear that *someone* had let the cat out of the bag, though. I saw Emily and Tom chatting at the snack bar, and when I came up to get my morning coffee, they stopped talking and looked at me. "Hey *Ian*," Emily called in a sing-songy voice, "I heard that you're *dating someone*." Tom didn't say anything, just stared me down, hard.

I shrugged, threw a handful of nuts into my mouth, then grabbed my mug and walked away without answering. Let them gossip.

Surprisingly, I found it easier to concentrate now that Anna was in the office and not off somewhere in my imagination. I got through my backlog of code reviews and created new tickets for my team. Every so often, I looked up and saw Anna meeting someone new, or staring intently at her work laptop, no doubt going through the sexual harassment training materials. I noticed other guys (*too many*—it was a fintech company, after all) checking her out, too. By 6pm, I felt like I had accomplished enough and was ready to take Anna home and away from all those lonely men.

"How was your first day?" I asked, as we walked towards the subway.

"Good. Everyone seems really nice. I didn't do much today besides meet people, take stock of what's in the kitchen, and review some materials. I also started the sexual harassment training." She took my hand. "Speaking of, I think Tom finally got the hint. He just waved today and didn't say anything weird to me. Do you think Cassie told him?"

I snorted. "And probably everyone else from Stumpstash who was at her wedding. So, most of the company."

"Oh." She was silent, lost in thought.

"Why do you ask?"

"Do you...think they'll all assume that I got the job because of you?"

"I assume they'll think it was because of Cassie. They know you were her old college roommate."

"But you don't think that they'd think I was just..." She trailed off.

"What? Sleeping with me to get the job?" She didn't say anything, so I continued, "One, I'm not your direct supervisor, nor was I the hiring manager. Two, everyone gets a job in tech through referrals. I got my job because of Emily, Cassie got her job because of me, and you got your job because of Cassie." I squeezed her hand. "Why do you care so much about what people think?"

She let go of my hand and scowled at me. "Wow, that was such a judgmental question."

"Well why *should* you care about what people think? Nobody cares how you *got* the job, as long as you can *do* your job."

She stopped walking, so I stopped beside her. "I thought you said you were an advocate for women in tech. Do you even *know* how hard it is to earn and keep people's respect in a workplace environment? As a woman? People are always all too happy to put you down. I want people to know that I got the job because of my skills, not because I was fucking you—"

"You *did*. You got the job the same way everyone else did. And because I'm not your boss, so it doesn't matter that we're sleeping together, okay? It's not a big deal. Chill out." We stood in the middle of the corridor just after the entrance to the subway station. Commuters streamed past us, ignoring us in typical New York fashion, with only the occasional sideways glance.

Her eyes flashed and she poked an accusing finger into my chest. "*Chill out?* You're so fucking patronizing sometimes, you know that? You think you know everything, don't you? I bet you get off on lecturing me and taking care of me like I'm your pet or some—"

"No, I get off on you being a strong-willed, passionate woman." I grabbed her shoulders, pulled her to me, and kissed her.

At first she froze, her lips clamped firmly shut against me. But after a moment, her body melted into mine, and she met my tongue with hers. Her arms wrapped around my waist and my hands shifted up to cup the back of her head, fingers slipping into her silky hair.

"Get a room!" said an old lady as she walked by. Someone else jostled me as they passed.

We broke our kiss and looked into each other's eyes. Her gaze went from wanton to withering in a heartbeat, and she quickly looked away, clearly still dissatisfied. "Let's take her advice," I said. I took her hand again and we continued on in silence until we reached the subway platform.

I turned to face her and sighed. "I don't mean to be patronizing, Anna. I do think it can be hard for women in the workplace. But I know that you're going to do a great job and I'm also sure that no one will care that we're dating. I can think of at least two Stumpstash couples, and nobody mentions anything about their relationship at work."

She shook her head and continued staring at the tracks, not saying anything.

"Anna, talk to me."

"There's nothing to talk about," she bit out, crossing her arms.

"Anna, don't be like—"

"Are you patronizing me again?" she snapped, turning back to look at me.

I threw my hands up in exasperation. "If you're going to act so fucking immature, then yes! You won't tell me what's bothering you. Let's talk about it like adults!"

A flexed jaw muscle was her only response. She was grinding her teeth.

The train screeched as it pulled to a slow stop before us. When the doors opened, she angrily stepped inside. I followed her in, slowly breathing in and out.

We found a spot near the door that led to the next car, then turned to face each other.

"You know what your problem is? You think things are so simple," she angrily whispered. "Everything is black and white and crystal clear to you. But things are *not* that simple."

"Where is this coming from?" I muttered back. "I didn't say anything was simple. I didn't—"

"You're so happy and optimistic, like everything's always going to work out for you. Things don't always—"

"What do you want me to say? *Geez, you're fucked?* Too bad for you? You have to—"

"God, can you just shut up and stop telling me what to do? Just *fucking let me talk for once?*" She'd shouted that last bit. I glanced around and noticed several people staring at us.

I clamped my mouth shut as a woman's voice called out, "You tell him, sister!"

Anna glanced at me, then looked away and shook her head. A moment later, she quietly hissed, "I'll tell you when we get home."

I grimly nodded and reached for her hand. She let me take it, but her hand stayed limp in mine.

* * *

When we got home, we both went into the kitchen to prepare dinner as we'd planned. As sous chef, she helped me slice vegetables for that night's veggie lasagna.

"Which playlist of yours should I put on tonight?" I asked. It had become a ritual of ours to listen to her playlists while we cooked.

"*Murder at Midnight*," she said, vigorously chopping a zucchini.

"I hope that's not foreshadowing for something," I joked, selecting the playlist that she'd requested on her computer.

She didn't smile, just kept cutting. "I'm having my period."

Ah. At least she wasn't pregnant. "Is there anything I can do for you?" I asked earnestly.

She stopped cutting but didn't look up. "If I want something from you, I'll ask." She wiped a stray lock of hair out of her face, then continued cutting. I frowned, but stayed silent.

A few minutes later, after finishing chopping the vegetables, she washed her hands and sat down with a glass of wine, silently watching me work. I kept my mouth shut, hoping that she'd eventually get around to telling me what was going on.

Finally, she sighed and said, "Look, there's some shit you need to know about me."

"Ok." I started wiping my hands so that I could go sit with her. She held up a hand to stop me.

"Wait. Keep cooking. Just...don't stop, don't interrupt me. If you say *anything*, I'm going to stop talking." Her eyes bored into mine, and I remembered what she'd said on the train. I wanted to let her have her say, didn't want to be a flippant asshole. I slowly nodded, relit the burner, and resumed sautéing onions.

"I didn't...have the happiest past. So I'm going to tell you about it, because I think it will help you understand a little bit more about me, and about my...my doubts. Where I'm coming from."

She took a sip of wine and began.

"My dad was...mostly ok. He loved me and my mom in his

162

own twisted way, and did his best to take care of us. But he was flawed. He drank a lot, and I mean *a lot*." She took another sip.

"When he drank, they fought, and when they fought, he beat her and he beat me too." Her lip quivered.

I burned my hand on hot lasagna noodles and bit back a swear. Her dad had beaten her? Light spankings had been normal in my household growing up, but beatings? *Fuck.* I stared at her as if I could see the scars, but of course they were gone, only left on the inside.

"They mostly fought about money. He was a chef at the Chinese restaurant where my mom was a waitress. They didn't make much, and I think he felt guilty about not being able to earn more. He used to apologize to me, sometimes, and to my mom, when he couldn't afford to buy us things. But mostly, he just got frustrated and beat us for wanting shit that we couldn't have, and called us ungrateful." She twirled her wine glass by the stem and stared into the ruby-red liquid.

"My mom was a beautiful woman, and when he was in a good mood, he'd joke and tell her, 'Beautiful women like you shouldn't have to work.' He kinda meant it, too. He had a weird sense of manly honor or something, and he felt like he should be the sole breadwinner of our family. But I think he mostly said it because my mom believed it too, and that's what she wanted to hear. She was so pretty that her family had always thought she would marry well. Instead, my dad knocked her up, and her family always looked down on him, said that he'd ruined her. They resented him for that, and he hated them right back." She took another sip of wine, a bigger one this time.

"That's why, when I was growing up, my mom's side of the

family encouraged me to marry a rich Chinese guy. *Specifically* a Chinese guy, because my family was pretty fucking racist. They told me that she'd fucked up by marrying a low-life, but that I needed to marry a rich Chinese guy who would help take care of me, and all of *them*." I met her eyes. That explained some things. I thought about how my own family hoped that I would marry a Chinese woman...of how my parents and their generation could be simultaneously so well-meaning yet so closed-minded. I nodded in understanding.

"*'Don't be like your mother,'* they'd say to me. Even my dad said the same. He wanted me to be pampered, and not to have to slave away on my feet all day like my mom did." She reached over to the laptop and paused her playlist. I'd been listening to her so intently that I'd completely forgotten that it was still playing.

"I think my dad was ashamed that he couldn't take care of us well. He felt guilty. But he made himself feel better by telling us that he'd just work harder and save up until he could open his own restaurant."

She looked down into her wine glass, her hands finally still. "He died of liver cancer when I was in high school. He never opened his own restaurant." She tipped the glass to her lips and drained the wine, then poured herself another glass.

My hands froze and I looked up. My legs twitched to go to her, to comfort her, but I could tell that there was more to her story, and I didn't want to disrupt. I took a deep breath and focused on seasoning the sauce.

"My mom took her family's advice the second time. My grandma had a friend whose son was single, an older Chinese lawyer. He lived in a nice house, drove a fancy car. On paper, he seemed like a perfect guy, and she was so pretty and charming that he proposed right away. Without my dad around, and after paying for his medical bills, we desperately needed cash. So my mom ended up marrying him."

She clenched her fist around the stem of the wine glass.

"And they had this big, grand wedding, a huge to-do, with over 200 people there. And my mom...she was so beautiful. She looked so happy, so much happier that day than she'd ever been with my dad. And I think she really believed that it was going to be happily ever after for her."

She forced her hand to open and gently placed the glass on the table.

"But he fucking *sucked*. He was so much worse than my dad. He thought that just because he was rich and educated, he could look down on *everyone*. He expected my mom to be perfect and loyal to him in every way, and he expected the same of me. He called my mom a slut if she so much as talked to another man. All he ever cared about was *appearances*."

"My mom's family changed their opinion of him when they saw his true colors, but they still outwardly bragged about him to others. About him being a lawyer, or driving a Mercedes, or being so rich that my mom didn't have to work. They never mentioned how he loved verbally cutting everyone down and making people cry. Bending people to his will. My mom resented him, too, but she felt like she couldn't leave. She didn't want to deal with the shame of a divorce, and she'd gotten used to the lifestyle. She would rather put up with his bullshit than be a divorcee or work in a restaurant again."

I shook my head and forced my hands to relax. My parents had fought prodigiously when I was younger, and they'd half-heartedly mentioned divorce once or twice, but they'd never hit or verbally abused each other the way that Anna's parents had. I shot Anna a sympathetic look before mixing together the egg and ricotta.

Anna continued. "Everything was about appearances and reputation to my family. Everything had to *look* good. That was their guiding principle—do whatever looked best to the outside. Whatever happened in private didn't matter, as long as no one found out." Another sip of wine.

"I avoided him as much as possible during high school. He yelled at me over nothing and everything. Any time I so much as raised my voice or gave him a dirty look, he slapped me." Her voice quieted. "And sometimes when he slapped me, I'd see...something else in his eyes. Like he wanted to do other things to me."

I channeled the overwhelming desire to nut-punch her step-dad into angry sauce stirring. I ended up having to wipe some off of the counter and off of my shirt, and I scalded my hand on the side of the pot.

Fuck that fucking guy. I began layering the lasagna.

"The last straw for me was when I'd just started college. I finally had the freedom to ignore them, so I did. But he was paying for my tuition, at least at first, and he was a fucking control freak...so when I didn't pick up their calls, he and my mom just showed up to visit me one day without telling me. I'd just started seeing this guy who was half-black, and when they showed up at my dorm, they found us in my room alone together, and my step-dad *lost his shit*. My boyfriend didn't know what to do, so he just left, even though I'd asked him to stay. Then my step-dad chewed me out and started hitting me, saying all of this terrible racist shit about how bad it would look for our family. And my mom...she agreed with the things he'd said. She scolded me just as badly."

166

Anna looked straight into my eyes, her own eyes brimming with unshed tears. I finished layering the lasagna as quickly as I could. I knew that it was hard for her to tell me all of that, but why *the fuck* was I making lasagna? There was so much that I wanted to say to her...but still, I kept my mouth shut like she'd asked and just worked faster.

Voice high-pitched and trembling, she continued. "She eventually realized that he was going overboard. She tried to get him to leave, but he refused, just told her to go wait in the car. I think she could tell that he'd lost it, that something was wrong with him, because she refused to leave us alone together."

Anna held a hand to her cheek. "So he slapped her. I remember her holding her hand up to her face, shocked and hurt. He used to hit me all the time, but he'd never hit her before that. She'd thought she was safe from him, that he was different from my dad...but she knew then that he wasn't. She was stuck with him as much as she'd been stuck before. She was helpless, and she knew it." Anna stopped to blow her nose into a napkin.

"But at least," she whispered, voice thick, "at least she still refused to leave me alone with him. She stood her ground that day, just that one time, for me." She sniffed. "And that's...that's when he started beating her in earnest."

I hurried to put the lasagna in the oven and wiped my hands on the dish towel, then went to sit with her. *Finally.* I took her hand and gave her my full, undivided attention. A lone tear slipped down her cheek.

"He hit her and said that it was her fault that I was such a slut. I tried to get him off of her, but he was stronger than both of us, and he hit me too. Luckily, Cassie came into the room and she grabbed her tennis racket and started threatening him. Jessa and Lisa were living in the room across, and they heard the noise and came in too and got him out of the room. He finally gave up and ran away before the campus police could get there." The lone tear had turned into a stream, steadily dripping down her face.

"I never pressed charges," she sobbed. "My mom asked me not to. She never *fucking divorced him*. She even defended him and told me that he was *right—*" I pulled Anna to me and held her close as she shook and cried into my shoulder, scrunching my shirt in her fists.

"I never want to be like her. I don't want anything to do with them. That's why I cut my family off. I don't fucking talk to them anymore and I never will."

I kept silent and just held her, stroking her hair and occasionally wiping her tears away. Inside, I boiled with anger, trying to envision what her step-dad looked like so that I could imagine beating *him*. Why the fuck were people like him allowed to exist? Allowed to terrorize and abuse innocent people like Anna? My hands itched to strangle him. Instead, I reached over to the nearby tissue box and handed her a kleenex. She noisily blew her nose and sobbed.

After a couple of minutes, she quieted and stopped shaking. She lifted her head and looked at me, inspecting my face, then wrapped her arms around my neck, her voice heartbreakingly raw as she said, "I'm so glad you're not an asshole."

I held her close and stroked her back. *Me too*.

Chapter 17

-Anna-

I wasn't sure how Ian would react to my past. He'd finished prepping the lasagna, then sat there quietly, not judging, not trying to fix anything, just listening to my story. He held me at the end and just let me cry onto his shoulder.

I'd found myself a wonderful human being.

"Thanks for telling me," he finally said, kissing my hair. I nestled my head deeper into the crook of his neck.

"Thanks for listening. And for not saying anything." I really appreciated that he'd just let me talk, like I'd asked him to. It would have been difficult for me to tell the whole story, had he interrupted me. For that reason, I hadn't even tried with my exes. All Asher knew was that I didn't talk to my family anymore. He hadn't cared about the rest, and likely wouldn't have fully understood.

With Ian...I saw the sympathetic looks he gave, his nods of understanding when I explained what my family was like. The fear of shame, the paramount importance of appearances. He *knew*.

I loved that I could share my burden with him.

"For what it's worth," he said, "you're nothing like your mom. You're passionate and independent and I—"

"Shhh." I put a finger on his lips. "You don't have to tell me that stuff. I know that I'm not as strong and independent as I want to be. I'm trying, but it's hard, and it really triggers me when people point out that I'm doing a shit job of it. I just...wanted you to understand. Like why I find it hard to depend on people. And why I don't like feeling trapped."

He kissed my hand. "And why you don't date Asian guys."

I kissed his neck. "Why I *didn't* date Asian guys."

We turned our heads and kissed each other. Then kept kissing, and kissing, until the oven beeped and the lasagna was ready.

I'd never tasted one better.

* * *

That night, while we lay cuddling in bed, I asked him, "So how *did* Cassie end up telling you about me?"

Ian massaged my scalp with his magical fingers. I closed my eyes and leaned into his touch. "I had just broken up with my girlfriend at the time and she was going through her roster of female friends to set me up with. And I wasn't lying—she really did say that you'd be perfect for me, except for the No Asian guys thing." He kissed my hair. "Guess she was right."

I snuggled closer to him and drew circles with my fingers on his smooth pecs. Totally hairless. I filled my lungs with him, practically snorting from his skin, then sighed contentedly. His scent, once so aggravating, was now so soothing, so utterly addicting.

"She's a really good friend," Ian commented, oblivious to

my huffing.

"Yeah, she is. I'm really lucky to have her." I rubbed my nose along his bristly jaw. It was the perfect scratching post.

"No, *I'm* really lucky that she brought us together."

"Yes, *you're* really lucky." I laughed and kissed his cheek, shifting my leg up onto his hips. As usual, his penis was rigid and ready beneath my thigh. I giggled. It was still so gratifying to witness my effect on him.

Maybe he'd get even luckier tonight.

I traced my fingers along the ridges and valleys of his abs, sighing. "Mmm, your abs are so hot. Like a sexy ice cube tray."

He snickered. "Thanks?"

"Or like...a sexy lobster tail." He laughed as I lowered my head and planted kisses in the valley between his pecs, all the way down to his belly button.

I stopped and lifted my head, inspired. "No! I know. It's like sexy day-old challah bread." I licked his abs as if tasting the golden egg wash crust. "I want to turn you into bread pudding and eat you up."

He jerked his knees and rolled onto his side, guffawing. "Is that how you like your dirty talk? Are you still hungry or—"

I pushed him back down and shut him up with a long, tender kiss. "There's just something about you that makes me want you in my mouth."

His eyes danced with amusement. "Same here." He lifted his hands to my chest and kneaded my breasts through my oversized sleeping shirt. "I want to...juice your overripe oranges."

I struggled to keep my face straight, fighting both laughter and the feeling of his wicked hands. "I want to suck on your...giant...rod of ginger."

171

"It's a *knob*, not a *rod*," he corrected, deadpan. He slid his hands down from my breasts to my ass, pulling me against him. "And your ass is like...two big, juicy...cloves of garlic stuck together. Goes great with my ginger."

I laughed and kissed him, once, twice, three times. "We make a really weird meal together."

He smiled up at me, his sweetest, most heartbreaking smile. "It's perfect." Then he kissed me back, his delicious, soft tongue brushing against mine. I traced my hand from his challah bread down along his happy trail, then slipped my hand under the waistband of his boxers. His penis rose to greet me, and I leisurely brushed my fingers up and down his shaft, relishing every answering twitch of his cock.

He broke our kiss, his breathing shallow. "Aren't you on your period?"

Still stroking him with one hand, I rose up onto my elbow and knees and kissed a trail down his neck. "So? Maybe I really do want to suck on your *knob*." I scuttled further down the bed and lowered his boxers over his hips, then slipped them off his legs and tossed them onto the floor.

"Anna," Ian breathed, eyes hooded. He was so gorgeous, naked. All perfect lines and curves, golden skin and tantalizing shadows. I groaned, just taking in the sight of him and his thick, rigid *knob*.

I really *did* want to eat him up.

Keeping our eyes locked, I placed my hands on either side of his hips and slowly bent down. I kissed the tip of his penis, then continued kissing down the shaft, down, down, until I could swirl my tongue on his salty sac…then licked all the way back up to leisurely circle my tongue around the head, taking my time, loving the sound of his labored exhalations, the feeling of his legs tensing below me. His penis was rock-hard and ready to eat. I took the tip into my mouth and gently sucked while curling my tongue around him, barely able to wrap my hand around his thick shaft.

After a moment, I popped his penis out of my mouth, leaving a trail of saliva that dripped down his full length. I met his hungry gaze.

"Fuck." Ian had one hand behind his neck, holding himself up in a crunch position to watch me. *Damn.* Those abs would be the death of me.

I rose and kissed Ian on the mouth, slowly, deeply. I poured all of the emotion, the affection and gratitude that I felt for him into that kiss...and I melted at all of the passion and tenderness, the reverence that he gave back.

Then I broke our kiss, gave him a mischievous look, and returned to sucking his cock in earnest.

He groaned as I took him deep into my mouth and swirled my tongue again, bobbing my head up, then down, up, then down, faster and faster. His free hand brushed my hair aside and held it out of my face, on top of my head. I made eye contact with him as I sucked, wanting him to see and feel how much I savored him.

"Fuck!" Ian was still staring at me, his face contorted as he struggled not to come. "Anna...Anna...just get on."

"Wha?" I said, mouth still full.

He gently tugged on my scalp and lifted my head up. "Just let me fuck you."

I raised an eyebrow at him and smirked, continuing to lazily pump his shaft with my hand. "You don't care about my period?"

"*Fuck no.* Just get on." He eyed me thirstily, like he really

173

could use some fresh squeezed orange juice.

I grinned at him wolfishly. "Can we take this to the shower then? Spare your sheets?"

He smirked. "You really seem to like being fucked in the bathroom."

I giggled and pulled him out of bed and towards the shower.

* * *

The next day, we were back to our giddy, affectionate selves. I openly held Ian's hand as we entered the office, and the many looks from our colleagues did not escape me. I didn't care.

I even changed my laptop background to my favorite photo of us from Cassie's wedding, the one of us walking towards the ceremony, laughing and smiling together. I constantly had spreadsheets and emails up on my laptop, so I hoped that no one would see it but me. But whenever I did glance at it, my heart fluttered and my chest swelled with emotion. It was a perfect photo.

I met more people, got set up with a company credit card, introduced myself to some of our vendors, and started working on some plans for the company holiday event. I actually had fun at work that day, way more than I'd ever had at Lynd & Cannoli.

I left the office and went home late with Ian that night, energized and ready to work on my music writing again. It was a little bit odd that I was busier than before, yet also more motivated. I guessed it was because I had more stimulation, more things going on in my life that I could draw inspiration from. I was no longer isolated and lonely, and it felt good.

And while we worked in the same office, Ian and I hardly

ever interacted. He was a busy guy, often running in and out of meetings or being pulled into discussions about *this problem* or *that tool*. When he wasn't in meetings, he was laser-focused on his computer. He didn't stand around and shoot the breeze by the coffee machine, like many other Stumpstashers did, and he left me to my own devices for lunch (which he hardly even ate, most days). He gave me the space to mingle with our coworkers and make friends, and for that, I was grateful.

I didn't have to try very hard—my fellow Stumpstashers were so friendly and welcoming, and nearly everyone stopped by my desk to introduce themselves. I was invited to lunch, coffee, and drinks by multiple coworkers that first week, although some of those people were definitely asking me out on dates. I erred on the side of caution and only accepted an invitation to the weekly company happy hour. Emily, whom I remembered from Cassie's wedding, had been the one to ask me. So on Thursday at 5pm, a group of roughly 20 of us headed over to the bar next door to the office and took over the back room.

"Are there always this many people?" I asked Emily as we settled into our seats.

"Ha, no. The group is usually much smaller. But more people come out when there's a special occasion, like a product launch or when there's a new Stumpstasher. I think most of these people are here for you!"

Tania, my boss, suggested that we all go around and introduce ourselves. There was Emily, as well as Tom and a few other people whom I remembered from Cassie's wedding, Priya, Rich, and Tony. Besides one female software engineer named Laila, everyone else was a dude, and even though I repeated their names in my mind, I just could not keep their names and faces straight. There were too many hoodies and too much flannel.

A waiter came by with waters for everyone, then went around and took our drink orders. Multiple people offered to buy me a drink, but I only accepted Tania's offer.

As the waiter made his way around the table, Emily looked around and asked, "Where's Ian?"

Rich snickered. "Ian never comes out."

"He came out once, when we launched the new mobile app," offered Priya.

Rich rolled his eyes. "For like five minutes. That guy never hangs out, never even tries to talk to us except about work. He's so unfriendly." The intensity of Rich's dislike surprised me.

"He's not that bad. Just kinda awkward sometimes," said Emily, who was watching my face.

"We're software engineers, we're all awkward," said someone whose name I'd just learned a minute ago, then promptly forgot. Matt? Mike? "But Ian doesn't even try."

Rich continued, "I'd be surprised if he had any friends."

Priya turned to me and asked, loudly enough for everyone to hear, "Anna, aren't you dating Ian?"

I nodded, meeting Rich's widening eyes. "Yeah, I am."

Rich didn't say anything, just looked away and sipped his water.

"Did you guys start dating after Cassie's wedding?" asked Tom, eyes a bit too wide.

"Ah, kinda." I nervously sipped my water.

"If you guys are dating, then he can't be that bad, right?" Priya asked, clearly trying to throw me a bone. "Have you met his friends?"

Did Ian have friends? I decided that Lina didn't really count, as we only ever saw her at the gym. I slowly shook my head. "We've only just started dating, so I...I haven't met his friends yet."

Silence. Rich and Matt / Mike exchanged a meaningful look.

Emily came to the rescue. "So you were Cassie's roommate in college, right?"

* * *

A couple hours later, Ian and I were making a pizza together for dinner. I chopped the vegetables while he worked on the dough, skillfully flinging it into the air, stretching and flattening it out with each upward toss.

"The happy hour today was interesting," I said, slowly slicing a bell pepper.

"Oh yeah? What happened?" Ian asked. He set the prepared crust on the floured countertop and stirred the sauce.

"I kinda got the impression that some of our coworkers don't really like you."

He chuckled. "I can guess who. I've killed some projects because they didn't make sense for us as a company, and it definitely upset some people."

I nodded. Typical office politics. "But they also asked me if I'd met any of your friends. I said that we just started dating, so I hadn't met them yet."

Ian continued stirring the sauce and didn't look up. "I see."

When he didn't say anything more, I innocently asked, "So when will I meet them?"

He finally looked up and met my eyes. Exhaled slowly. "I

don't have that many friends here. Most of my friends from high school and college live elsewhere. You've met Cassie and Lina, at least, and I chat with other folks at the climbing gym sometimes. I'll introduce you to them next time I see them." He went back to tasting and seasoning the sauce.

"I see." I did, and I knew that I had no right to judge. I didn't have that many close friends in New York, either. I had a bad habit of just hanging out with whichever guy I was with at the time and *his* friends.

I hoped that wouldn't remain the case, or else it would just be the two of us. And maybe Lina, I guess.

* * *

On Saturday, Ian brought me along to the climbing gym again. Lina was there, too, as usual.

"Hey, how's it going?" she cheerfully asked, patting my back. "Ready to send that red V1 today?"

Sending a route meant successfully getting to the top of it, and there was a red bouldering problem in the corner of the gym that I hadn't been able to send the last time I'd been there. It was the only V1 left in the gym that I hadn't completed yet, so out of pride, I'd refused any beta (climber lingo for *advice*)—I wanted to get it on my own. Lina and Ian respected my wishes and kept their beta to themselves, but despite trying over and over, and even secretly watching both of them warm up on it, I just couldn't send it.

With his height and long arms, Ian had swung up through the hardest part and easily caught the next hold, which I'd dubbed the devil hold because of its deep red color and horn-like, curved shape, as well as its ability to bedevil me. But when I tried to copy his motion, my fingers barely curled over the lip of the hold, then slipped off, each and every time. Maybe if I jumped and committed harder...but no, no matter how much I threw myself at it, I just couldn't stick it.

Meanwhile, Lina gracefully rocked her body over a foothold and maneuvered into a position where she could easily reach the devil hold, despite being slightly shorter than Ian. She was still taller than me, though, and when I tried copying her method, I still couldn't quite get my fingers fully over the lip before my foot slipped off and I banged my knee on the wall.

Random strangers in the gym tried to help me too, even though I hadn't asked for their advice. "Lean into the wall!" or "Swap your feet on that lower footchip!" they said. I gritted my teeth and grew more and more annoyed until Lina told them to stop "spraying beta" at me.

After several more tries, I slumped down between Lina and Ian and grumpily watched as a tall teenager warmed up on my project. With her smooth and steady movements, she made it look ridiculously easy, and was up to the top and down again in less than ten seconds. I huffed in annoyance and said to no one in particular, "Ugh, I wish I were taller. I'm too short to get this stupid problem."

Lina coolly shrugged. "Being taller isn't necessarily better. There's no single best body type. Everyone has their own unique strengths and weaknesses, and climbing well is about finding your own method, a balance of things that works for you and your specific situation." *Psh*, easy for her to say—she was tall and totally shredded.

Ian chuckled at my dismissive eye roll. "Lina's right, though. Check this person out." He gestured with his chin towards an older woman who was around my height or slightly shorter, and who had just hopped onto my project.

The start was straightforward, and she cruised through it the same way that I did, grasping and stepping easily through a series of large holds, which Ian had told me were called *jugs*. But when she got to the crux, the big move where I kept getting stuck, she put her leg up onto a higher hold, much higher than the one on which Lina's or Ian's legs had been. I hadn't even considered that my foot could reach that high. The woman successfully grabbed the devil hold, then was all the way at the top and back down again in a flash.

Lina's eyebrows and lips quirked up at me, as did Ian's. I grimaced and looked away, but got up and tried the V1 again. Using the higher foothold that time, I finally sent it.

I was grateful when Lina and Ian didn't say anything, just high-fived me when I went to sit back down.

"Okay, fine, teach me everything," I told them.

So throughout the rest of that session and the sessions after, they did. *Flag your foot out here for balance. Engage your core and keep your hips close to the wall. Don't overgrip, drop your knee in, maintain tension...*They were two climbing encyclopedias, and I absorbed as much from them as I could.

And just as I'd suspected I would, I enjoyed climbing. A lot.

I loved the sense of accomplishment after conquering my fear and successfully sending a route. My progress was measurable, concrete, and steady, and it was gratifying to improve in something that was both physically and mentally stimulating.

I loved the muscle soreness after a long session. I felt stronger, more confident in myself, and more at ease with my body, proud of my newfound ability to do a full pull-up.

And I loved watching Ian's rippling back muscles as he made

his way up the wall. The way it looked...*mmm*, I was going to turn into a *back* girl instead of a pecs girl. He was such a beautiful physical specimen, and I wanted to explore every dip and curve of his body.

I couldn't keep my hands off of him when we got home.

In general, life at home with Ian was as blissful and passionate as you could imagine. I was worried that we'd become attached at the hip, but we didn't. He gave me space, more than Asher ever had, yet he was always there when I wanted him. He was careful to invite me to do things with him, to never assume that I would join in just because we lived together. I was glad to have found an easy rhythm with Ian, and things were so good between us that, after the first week, I stopped checking for new apartment listings.

I wish I'd kept looking.

* * *

"Did you want to do something next week? We get Thanksgiving and the next day off!" I'd just received a company-wide email reminding me of that fact. Maybe Ian and I could take a romantic road trip—

"Oh, I forgot to tell you, my parents are coming for Thanksgiving, and they're going to stay with us." It was a statement, not a question. "Sorry, Anna. I thought I'd told you already."

"Oh." Ian had told me that his parents visited once a month, and it made sense that they'd come for Thanksgiving. That's what families did, got together and ate food on Thanksgiving. But things had been so good between us that I'd pushed the thought from my mind. I didn't want to deal with this, not when the past few weeks had been so perfect. "Isn't it a bit early for me to meet them? We've only been dating for..." I counted, "three weeks." *Wow, that was it?*

He glanced up from the Sunday paper, then back down. "It's not like this means I'm going to marry you anytime soon. It's just meeting my parents. They're nice, you'll like them."

I idly stirred my coffee with my spoon, frowning at his mention of marriage. "I'd rather wait."

He looked up again, noticed my expression, then tossed the paper onto the table. "Why? If you're going to stay here, you're going to see them every month anyway. They always look forward to visiting." He eyed me warily.

Why was he so uptight about his parents? "Look, I really like you, but I don't feel comfortable meeting your parents until we've been together longer." I paused, then added, "You know that I completely cut off my own family, right? I don't want to deal with the inevitable questions about my parents. I don't want that judgment right now."

He exhaled slowly and put his hand on mine. "They're not going to judge you. They—"

I pulled my hand out from his. "How can you know that? They're Chinese, right? I've never met a Chinese family that was like, *'Oh, you don't talk to your parents anymore, that's okay, you can still be a good person.'*"

He frowned. "They'll get over it. It's really not a big deal. But really, if you're so sure that you don't want to deal with them, do you have somewhere else to stay for Thanksgiving?"

I shot him an incredulous look, my heart sinking at his tone. "*Seriously?* You know I don't. Why don't you just put them up somewhere?"

"Because this is my apartment, and they're welcome to stay here?" He let out a frustrated sigh. "*Look.* My mom is still

182

going through chemo, and it's hard for her to sleep or be comfortable sometimes. She can be comfortable here."

"Why do they even come here, then, if she's so sick? Why don't you just go to their place?" I hated how petulant I sounded, but I hated the dismissive way that he was treating me even more.

"Why are you asking me to justify having my parents visit?" He ran his fingers through his hair. "My parents like having a change of scenery, okay? They have a few friends in New York that they like to visit, and new restaurants to try. And I'm their only son. I want them to keep having something to look forward to." He stared down at the table, his expression pained. "They're getting old."

He really loved his parents. That much was obvious. But there's loving your parents, and then there's burdening yourself with them, or living your whole life for them, which is exactly what my family had always expected of their kids. Family always came first. What about me and my preferences? Didn't *I* mean something to him? Ian's defensiveness and inflexibility when it came to his family...it put me on edge. *In fact*...I shook my head and laughed mirthlessly. "You are *literally* the Chinese-American dream."

He rolled his eyes and threw up his hands. "Why are we back to that?"

"Because you are!" I snapped, piqued at his tone. "You're a fucking caricature. Ivy League grad, high salary, filial piety. Did you ever, I dunno, have a dream of your own? You literally just became the person that your parents wanted you to be, that all of *our culture* wanted you to be. I have never seen you do anything that even remotely demonstrates that you have a will of your own."

He glared at me, and I glared right back. His parents were obviously a touchy subject. He'd had a scare with his mom's health, so of course he wanted to keep her spirits up. But this was a triggering topic for me too. I'd had enough drama with my own parents—I didn't want to have to deal with his. After what I'd told him about my family, how could he not understand? I was asking for *time*, not to *never* meet them. But *of course* he would get offended at my request. He couldn't fight what he was raised to be.

"Where the hell is this coming from? What, now I'm too perfect for you or some shit? You need a guy who can feed into your daddy issues?"

I scoffed, though his words hit a nerve. "Seriously? You're going to use my past against me? That's fucking *low*."

"You're the one who's telling me that I don't have a fucking mind of my own, just because I have what *most people want*. You think I should quit my job and become a starving artist? Huh? Is that how—"

"You couldn't even be an artist 'cause you don't *have any fucking passion!* Look at what you do every weekend! If I weren't here, you'd probably just be working and climbing all the time, and that's it. When you didn't come to the Stumpstash happy hour on Thursday, everyone told me that you *never* go out with them. You don't have a life and you don't even have any fucking friends!"

"I don't have friends? I don't see *you* introducing me to anyone around here. The only anecdotes I've ever heard from New York are about your ex—"

"Well all your anecdotes are about your fucking family—"

"Just because my family isn't fucked up, and just because *I'm* not fucked up, doesn't mean that I've led any less of a life than

184

you have." His voice was dangerously low, but I was too riled up to care.

I laughed bitterly. "So *I'm* fucked up? Really? At least I'm fucking *alive*. You act like you're a robot, you're so fucking predictable. All you do is work, climb, and fuck. I'm probably just a checkbox on the fucking to-do list that your mom—"

"So your life is somehow more glamorous? You must feel so *fucking self-righteous*, working shit jobs, living with your ex, not giving a damn about anyone but yourself but still needing people to take care of you. Is that what you call *passion*? Or *independence*? Is that—"

I picked up my mug and threw it at him. He dodged it, but the coffee spilled all over his white area rug.

Enraged, he continued, "Is that how to feel alive? Just deny all the things that any sane person wants? You think you're beyond appearances, but you care just as much about your fucking image as—"

I'd had enough. I nearly threw a fucking chair at him. Instead, I stormed into the bedroom, slammed the door behind me and locked it, then began shoving my things into a bag.

A minute later, the front door slammed.

Chapter 18

-Ian-

I went to the climbing gym. It seemed like the best place for me to calm down. My blood was boiling, and I needed to let off a *lot* of steam.

Anna had infuriated me. How could she be so closed-minded, so fixated on her own problems? She was just as much a product of the Chinese-American dream as I was, in her own twisted way. She'd accused me of thinking everything was black and white and crystal clear, but *she* was the one who always assumed the worst about everything. Her negativity was so draining to deal with sometimes, her moods so fickle.

Fuck.

And her line of questioning about my lack of friends, my lifestyle...that had *really* rubbed me the wrong way.

Especially because, to some small extent, I knew that she was right.

I'd lived with my parents during undergrad to save money, so I didn't have as many close college friends. And even after college, I just didn't seem to fit in. It always felt like people were judging me, like everyone else had some mysterious knowledge base that they could draw upon, spoke some secret language that I didn't. It wasn't easy for me to meet new people and make meaningful connections with them. I didn't like the things that other people did, and I wasn't going to change my preferences or lifestyle just to have a few drinking buddies.

And career-wise...I *had* taken the safe route. I didn't know exactly what I'd wanted to do with my life (who does?), so I did what I was told—get good grades, make good money. But fulfilling the American part of the Asian-American dream, finding something that I loved, that was meaningful and helped people...that part was tough. The times that I'd tried to discover my own passions, I'd felt like I was being selfish, putting my livelihood at stake and therefore the hopes and dreams of my parents, too, both of whom had busted their asses to give me the privileged life that I now lived. I didn't want to take that risk. It was easier for me to live my life for the people who depended on me than it was to find meaning for myself. After all, meaning was what you made it to be.

But ultimately, while my parents were proud, I knew that it was impossible for them to be everything that I needed. I did want to set bigger goals for myself. I just...wasn't sure how.

Sigh.

I'd said some things that I was absolutely going to regret. Anna, at least, was trying to live the meaningful life that she'd dreamed of for herself. I admired her passion, her strength of will, her desire for independence. I hadn't meant to throw her past in her face. Even now, I wanted to go back and apologize, to make sure that she was okay.

But first, I needed time to calm down.

So I bouldered, hard. Bouldering required me to clear my mind and be in the moment, to focus on what was in front of me. It required more than strength—balance, precision, and the conquering of one's fear. As always, it centered me and helped me calm down.

Lina eventually showed up. "Hey, I got your text." She studied my face, and her brow furrowed in concern. "You okay? Trouble in paradise?"

I got onto a seriously crimpy blue V7, balancing precariously on the very tips of the fingers on my left hand, then reached straight up with my right to a one-finger pocket. I placed my right foot onto the next highest footchip, nearly level with my hip, then—

My foot slipped and I fell to the mat.

I sighed and stared up at Lina. "Yeah."

She sat down on the mat and I rolled up to sit next to her.

"Do you want to talk about it?" she asked. I liked that Lina was never really one to pry. We were climbing partners, and we climbed together a lot, so she could always tell when I was upset about something and vice versa. But we mostly tried not to burden the other person with our problems, just pushed each other to climb harder. Climbing was what we needed from each other, not idle chat.

But I couldn't help it today. "She's just so...frustrating. I love that she's passionate and strong-willed, but she's also just...kinda messed up." I sighed and lay back down on the mat. "This has been the craziest three weeks of my life."

Lina laughed and leaned back onto her elbows. "It's only been three weeks, and you're already climbing out your problems with her? That's not a good sign."

"I've just never felt so..so..."

"Alive?" she offered, chuckling.

It wasn't quite the word that I was looking for, but maybe it fit. Anna had a knack for bringing out the worst in me, as well as the best. She had upended my peaceful world, like a force of nature, and I both reviled and revered her for it. It'd only been three weeks, but maybe...if we could just get past our differences and learn to communicate better...maybe I could love her more than I'd ever loved anyone. I heaved another sigh.

"Hey." Lina poked my arm. "What are you doing here?"

"What do you mean?" I sat up. "I'm climbing." I went to attempt the blue V7 again (same sequence, same result) then came back to sit down.

Lina stared at her fingers, then casually said, "You know, I was married briefly."

I gaped at her. "Before...we started climbing together?"

"Yeah. He used to be my climbing partner. I met him on a climbing trip, and it was the most passionate relationship I've ever been in. Towards the end, we both quit our jobs and spent the year climbing in some of the most beautiful parts of the country." She smiled fondly. "It was the best year of my life."

She picked at some dead skin on her palms. "We had such a rocky start, though." We both chuckled. "No pun intended."

After a brief pause, she continued. "It was so rocky in part because he was already doing van life as a dirtbag, whereas I was in grad school. So he'd be away for weeks at a time, chasing crags, only coming back to check in with me and his sick dad every so often. Each time he came, I savored our moments together. He was such a beautiful human being, so full of light and life. But whenever he was about to leave, we fought, about anything and everything. We almost broke up a couple of times because he accused me of not 'being at his level,' of holding him back. And after his dad passed away, he gave me an ultimatum—get married and do van life full-time for a year, or end things between us. I thought, you know, maybe I *should* try to live a little. Life is so short. So I took a break from grad school, we got married, and we toured the country together." She chuckled. "The marriage was for insurance purposes."

She leaned back on the mat and looked up at the ceiling, legs crossed and hands behind her head.

"But living in a van together, climbing together full-time...you can imagine how hard that would be for any couple. At the beginning, the fighting was even worse. We'd go to bed so *mad* at each other. We'd wake up and keep fighting and our days would just be ruined. So one day, we agreed to never go to bed mad. We always worked it out before going to sleep, no matter what, and it made things so much better, because we'd start each day happy and loving each other. We found that there's nothing that can't be resolved with full honesty, with ourselves and with each other." She closed her eyes. "It's what saved our relationship."

"I see." My mom had said something similar to me before—she'd told me to never leave the house angry. Whoops. "So...where's your husband now? Is he still chasing crags?"

"He died." She smiled, but when her eyes opened, they were full of tears. "He was such a good climber, he regularly sent 5.13." She paused, and tears leaked from the corners of her eyes. "But he got careless and just...rappelled off the end of his rope."

"That's terrible. I'm so sorry." I awkwardly patted her leg, unsure of what else to say or do. This was the most about herself that Lina had ever told me.

"So again," she said, sniffling and wiping her tears away to give me a meaningful look. "What are you doing here?"

* * *

I arrived home to find no one there. I called Anna's name. No response.

I walked past the ruined area rug. The mug was still on its side on the floor, as if the fight had just happened instead of over two hours ago. I strode past and into the bedroom. Froze.

Her stuff was gone, just vanished into thin air. She must have packed up fast and called a friend to help her take her things away. I could guess which friend, and the thought made my jaw clench.

I tried to call her, but she didn't pick up. I left her a voicemail, then texted her too, asking her to call me back. After ten minutes of no response, of aimlessly pacing around in my apartment, I tried calling Cassie.

"Hey, what's going on?" she asked, after picking up on the second ring.

"Did you talk to Anna today?"

"Anna? No. We were supposed to do our weekly Sunday call but she didn't pick up. What happened?"

I told her about our fight.

"Shit. I don't...she didn't call me. I'll try to reach her again. I'll let her know that you were looking for her."

"Thanks, Cassie." I hung up, just in case Anna was trying to call me.

I sat down on the couch and stared at my phone.

I shouldn't have lost my temper.

I shouldn't have said those things to her.

I shouldn't have left. Or let her leave.

Never again.

With deep sighs of regret, I put my head into my hands and waited.

After a few agonizing minutes, I stood and prepared to drive over to her old place to look for her.

But before I could, the phone rang. I didn't recognize the number, but I accepted the call and said, "Hello? Anna?"

Five minutes later, I was out the door and headed to my car.

* * *

My dad was a good man. Had been.

My mother had found him face down on the floor and unresponsive. The paramedics declared him dead on the way to the hospital, likely from a heart attack. I'd pushed past the speed limit and driven over as fast as I could to meet her at the hospital an hour and a half later, where I found her so much more broken and fragile than cancer had ever made her. We held each other and cried for him, for ourselves, and for each other. We cried until our eyes were swollen and it physically hurt to cry anymore.

I took her home and tucked her into bed, then sat in the living room downstairs.

Then I thought about nothing and everything...but of course, mostly about my dad.

My dad really *had* been a good man.

He'd lived an unglamorous life as an HVAC technician. It was hard, physical work, and he often came home with gashes and bruises on his hands. Once, he'd even come home with a black eye because a coworker had accidentally dropped a monkey wrench off a ladder and onto his face. He'd been angry at first, but when he told the story to my mom over dinner, he just laughed at his terrible luck. While his temper had always been quick to flare (a trait that I'd inherited), he was so good natured, and he forgave so easily. A good man.

And he'd always been there for me. Despite having to drive around to installations, he'd always made time to come and watch my tennis matches. Looking back behind the baseline and meeting his eyes, finding his steady encouragement, always calmed me before each serve. He'd trained me too, on the weekends, when he could've been at home relaxing. My dad was always good at sports, no matter what sport it was, so even though we'd started playing at the same time, he was way better than me. So he'd trained me, hard, and I'd gotten pretty good.

It was that way with most things. He was always there to help guide me, to help me grow. To support me, no matter what. He did the same with my mom, even though they didn't see eye-to-eye on everything. He loved his family fiercely, and he would've done anything for us.

So on paper, he may not have lived the most amazing life. He didn't have many friends, didn't travel the world or make a name for himself. But he meant the world to me and my mom, and he enriched our lives with every ounce of his own.

And he was gone.

Gone.

Inevitably, eventually, my thoughts drifted back to my fight with Anna.

The things that Anna wanted, that creative, independent life that she asked for...before, I'd thought it was admirable. Now it just seemed ridiculous, the childish dreams of a spoiled girl.

I'd truly grasped tonight that wholeheartedly loving people was what gave life stakes...it's what made things matter. *Family* mattered.

Family loves you, no matter what. They are a part of you, and you, a part of them. Someone who could just cut out her own family didn't understand loyalty, what it really meant to fight for what you love, to cherish people despite their flaws. It was selfish and naive.

Anna just...didn't get it. She'd left my apartment after a simple fight. She'd abandoned her family, had left her mother to fend for herself against her shitty situation.

She wasn't a fighter. She was someone who gave up and ran away.

It could never work out between us.

Some time later, I sent an email to my manager asking for the week off, explaining the situation. Then I turned off my phone and fell asleep on the couch.

Chapter 19

-Anna-

Things had been too good to be true. We'd had three glorious weeks together, week after week after week of sensual pleasure and fairy tale romance. But of course it couldn't last. Fairy tales weren't real. I'd simply...forgotten for a moment.

Outwardly, he'd respected me, treasured me, even made me feel things that I didn't care to name. But deep down, he'd thought that I was broken. *Fucked up.* And not worth staying and fighting for. He'd left and slammed the door on his way out, just as Asher had. I hadn't upgraded. Things would always be the same. Every man I cared for and depended on would just get up, walk away, and slam the door on me. It was inevitable.

Because the truth was, I *was* fucked up. I *was* broken. And I didn't deserve him.

Not that this was completely one-sided. He had his issues, too, and I'd meant what I'd said. By any standard, he was a great guy, a dream boat. But he was a dream boat that was sailing nowhere, and I didn't want to go nowhere. I had aspirations, life goals. Things to do, places to be.

So while part of me knew that it was rash to leave, that we, like billions of couples before us, had simply had a fight...the other part of me couldn't bear to stay. I felt trapped, mired in emotions, and I had to get out.

I called the only other person that I could in New York.

"Please," I sobbed, "You can charge me more rent or whatever. I just...I don't have anywhere else to go right now."

I could hear Asher thinking through the phone. Finally, he sighed and quietly asked, "Anna, where are you?"

I told him the address. Within the hour, he swung by with his band van and helped me haul my crap into the back of it. It took only two trips up and down before we were done. We closed the rear doors of the van and he got into the driver's seat while I ambled back upstairs to return the key.

I numbly swept my gaze around Ian's sleek apartment, one last time. It seemed cold and sterile, with no hint of the warm happiness that Ian and I had shared together. It was merely a place now, no longer a home. No longer *my* home.

I closed the door, locked it, and slipped the key under the door. Then I went downstairs and slid into the passenger side of Asher's van.

He didn't say anything, just pulled out of the parking garage and onto the road. We sat silently for a long time, with only the occasional rattle of my things in the back of the van.

"Thank you," I whispered, hands fisted in my lap.

He kept his eyes on the road, but I knew that he was hyper aware of me, of my every word. "Did he hurt you? Did he do something to you?" His knuckles whitened on the steering wheel.

Not physically. I shook my head. "No. We just...we're too

different. I don't know what I was thinking."

Asher kept silent, mulling over something. Then, "I'm sorry, Anna. If I hadn't kicked you out, you wouldn't have had to deal with this." He put his right hand on top of mine, glanced at me, then looked back at the road. "I'm glad you're coming back."

"Me too," I whispered. My heart squeezed painfully at the lie.

* * *

I considered calling in sick the next day. I wasn't sure that I wanted to see Ian again. I imagined him greeting me coldly, maybe walking by and not meeting my eyes. Or perhaps pulling me into a conference room to talk it out, trying to kiss me and hold me to make up for things. I wasn't sure which of those possibilities I wanted.

But none of them happened. He wasn't at work that day. He never missed work, so where was he? Had he taken my leaving so poorly that he was at home, nursing a broken heart? Was he still angry and just unwilling to face me?

I thought about calling him. I saw that he'd texted me and left me a voicemail, asking me to call him back. Cassie called me too, but I didn't pick up—I didn't want to talk to her about it. But when she called me again in the afternoon, I picked up.

"Anna, where are you? Are you okay?"

I slipped into an empty conference room. "I'm okay," I said quietly, muffling my voice with my hand. "What's up?"

"You know that Ian's been looking for you, right?"

"Yeah. But I can't...I don't think we can be together. We're just totally different people."

"You know, it was just a fight. Couples do that. You might not agree on some things, but you're supposed to talk about it and figure it out. Michael and I used to fight all the time. We still do sometimes."

"Cassie, we can't agree on this, okay? He is literally just living the life that his parents want him to. I cut my family off because I didn't want to have anything to do with stuff like that. He stands for everything I reject." I paused to wipe my tears away. "Besides, I'm pretty sure that he doesn't want to be with someone as broken as I am. He deserves a happy, healthy, *normal* person."

"Anna! How can you say that! He obviously loves you."

I cry-snorted. "We've been together for three weeks, and all we've done is fuck and fight. How can that be love?" I tried to stifle my sobs and turned away from the glass door so that my coworkers couldn't see.

"Anna. Listen to me. You *are* a happy, healthy, normal person. You're not broken. You're strong and beautiful and—"

"Cassie, stop. Just stop. I know you mean well, but you know what I've been through and what I'm like. I don't want to hear it right now."

Her tone hardened. "So what, you just want to wallow in self-pity and let Ian be miserable? He was frantically trying to get in touch with you last night. He's probably sitting at his desk, try—"

"He's not here." I sniffed. "He didn't come in today."

"Oh," Cassie said. "That's...odd. I hope nothing happened."

"What do you mean?

"Ian's never missed work except because of his mom."

Shit. *Fuck.* I was always thinking about *me me me*, never about the bigger picture. Guilt set in, and I panicked. "I...do you...should I—"

"Just *call him*, Anna. I know he'll want to talk to you. Good luck." Cassie hung up.

I tried calling him right after, but the call went straight to voicemail. I hung up and tried calling again. I left a voicemail that time, telling him that I was staying with Asher for the time being and that he should call me back when he could.

He never called me back.

* * *

When I came home from work that day, Asher was there, getting ready for a show that night in Hell's Kitchen.

"Hey." He walked up to me and reached out as if to put his hand on my arm, but then thought better of it and dropped his arm to his side. "Can we talk? I just want to make sure that we get off on the right foot this time."

I nodded and glanced at the fist-shaped hole in the wall. He hadn't patched it yet, just like he hadn't fixed anything else in the apartment. "Yeah, that's a good idea."

He walked over to the couch and I followed. He turned to me and said, "While you were gone, I did a lot of thinking. I shouldn't have assumed that we'd just get back together. I know you were trying to work through some stuff, and I shouldn't have pressured you or held our friendship over your head." He paused. "I should've been more understanding."

I smiled. Asher was a good guy. Quick to anger, quick to forgive. But my smile faltered as I forced myself to say, "It's not your fault. I should've been honest with you. About everything. And I will be, from now on." I meant it.

"Me too." He took my hand in both of his. "Anna, I don't

199

want to pressure you or anything, but I'd like you to know that I would love to get back together with you. I know it might not happen right away, or maybe at all...but you're welcome to stay here and we can figure it out."

I wanted to *want* to kiss him. I really did. But all I could think about was Ian.

"Thanks, Asher." I patted his hand. "I'm really lucky to have you."

He pulled me in for a hug, and we held each other for a long time.

* * *

Ian didn't show up the next day, either, and he still hadn't called me back. I began to assume the worst and started to panic, so I texted Cassie to let her know that he hadn't come in. She tried calling him, too. He didn't pick up her calls, either.

I saw his manager, Isaiah, later that day, so I stopped him in the hallway. "Hi, Isaiah. Has Ian mentioned anything to you? About...why he's out?"

Isaiah gave me a pitying look and patted my arm. "Anna. He didn't tell you? His father passed away."

My ears began to ring, and my vision tunneled into the office carpet. Had I just heard him right?

Ian's *dad* had...died?

Shocked, I thought back to the argument that we'd had, where I'd told him that he didn't have a real life, just lived for the sake of his parents. That he didn't have any passion.

I thought about his pained look when he mentioned that his parents were getting old.

We'd fought because I hadn't wanted to deal with *meeting*

them. Because I'd been so wrapped up in how judgmental they'd be, so offended that Ian couldn't understand my point of view, and cared more about their comfort than my own.

And then...his *dad had died*?

All at once, my hearing returned to Isaiah calling my name, his hand on my shoulder, asking if I was okay. The tension in my chest burst, morphing into full-blown heartache, and I crouched down and hugged myself as hot tears spilled over. Our coworkers came over to see what was the matter, and soon they were all patting my back and offering me their condolences.

I hadn't even met Ian's father, hadn't *wanted* to, and here people were comforting me about his death. But they had it wrong. I *was* crying for Ian's father, a little, but I was mostly crying for Ian. And part of me knew, I was also crying for myself, and for our relationship. There was no way that Ian would forgive me now.

Before this, I'd mentally told myself that it was over between the two of us...but my heart hadn't really given up. Not yet.

But now...now it really *was* over. And I mourned.

The rest of the day passed by in a blur of tears and condolences. By the end of the day, all I could do was stare mindlessly at my laptop background. It was the photo of us from Cassie's wedding. I still hadn't changed it. The way that Ian looked at me in the photo, like I was precious and perfect and *not* broken or fucked up...I'd seen that look on his face countless times during our weeks together. I could almost believe what Cassie had said. Maybe he did love me, once.

I sat up straighter, still staring at his expression. What if he *did* love me? What if he was suffering, alone with his grief, wishing that I were there with him? What if he needed me?

We'd had a fight, but couples fought all the time. It meant that we were being honest with each other, that we wanted to make things work between us. We'd also had a connection, a bond, one that I knew in my heart was strong. It was wrong of me to give up on us so easily, especially in his time of need.

I suddenly had to see him, to make sure that he was okay. I checked the time—it was 4:37pm. Close enough, and my coworkers would understand. I packed up my things and rushed to Ian's place, not remembering a single step of the journey. I smoothed my hair out of my face and knocked on the door, once, twice. There was no answer, and he still wasn't picking up his phone.

I found an old receipt in my purse and wrote him a note on the back of it.

> *Ian,*
> *Please talk to me. I'm so sorry for everything. I'm here if you need anything at all.*

I hesitated, then added,

> *My heart goes out to you and your mom.*
> *Love,*
> *Anna*

I slipped it under his door.

Chapter 20

-Ian-

I was glad that I'd decided to stay for the week. My mom was in terrible shape.

I had to encourage her to get out of bed, to eat, to do anything other than lie there. If I hadn't been around, I don't know what would've happened. I gently tried to remind her that she had to eat and keep strong, so that I wouldn't lose her too. But sometimes she'd just look at me and look away, as if that weren't enough. As if *I* weren't enough to keep her around.

Those moments killed me inside.

It helped me to have someone else to care for. I couldn't wallow in sadness because I had to be strong for the both of us. And while I grieved in private for my father, I could only imagine the pain of losing a partner of 30 years. My brief forays into love were a joke in comparison.

The hardest part of that week was calling our family and loved ones and telling them the news. Most times, my mom broke down and cried before she could get the words out. She couldn't even say his name. Eventually, she just turned off her phone and went to lie down in her room. I ended up calling my mom's sister and my dad's brother and telling them what happened, and I asked them to spread the word for us. We were tired of talking about it, and of needing to make other people feel better as they tried to console *us*.

We decided to bury him in California with the rest of his family. There was nothing special about Princeton or New York. My parents had only moved out there to be close to me during undergrad and after, as I was their only son, and not for lack of trying. Besides, there were more HVAC jobs on the east coast than in California, and the cost of living was lower, so they'd lived in relative comfort. But ultimately, they belonged in California with their loved ones. Both of them.

I arranged the funeral services and body transport for that week and began contemplating my mother's situation. She belonged in California, too. I wouldn't be able to take care of her on my own, and she certainly wouldn't take care of herself. I was the one who kept her going, who cooked meals for her, who made sure that she actually left the house. Sometimes we'd walk around the neighborhood a little bit, but she was too tired to do much, so we mostly just sat around and watched TV. Her dramas didn't pull her in or excite her as much as they used to, though, and sometimes she'd just look away and stop watching, or change the channel. She usually switched to the news, even though it was depressing and her English wasn't that great.

There was good news in terms of her health, though. I took her to the doctor for her last round of chemo, and they told us that she was good to go—her next check-up wasn't for another three months. I was relieved, so relieved that it was over, but she cried, great big sobs racking her tiny body. I couldn't tell if they were tears of relief, of sadness...or of disappointment.

* * *

In the evenings, I sorted through my dad's things. The first night, my mom tried to stop me from touching anything. She said that she wanted it all left alone. I told her that we couldn't leave it there, that it wasn't good for her to keep seeing his stuff. That he wasn't coming back. She weakly pounded my chest with her fists until I crushed her to me and let her cry it out.

The next night, she didn't say anything, just walked out of the room and let me go through his stuff.

I sorted them into three piles: trash, donate, keep.

Most of it went into the donate pile, like his clothes, his shoes, his tool chest, and his old accordion (which, sadly, neither of us could play). I trashed some of the clothes that were too old or worn to donate, as well as some old documents that he'd just kept lying around.

The keep pile was the smallest. It contained a few items of clothing that I'd bought for him that happened to fit me, too. Some old photos in a shoebox. His favorite watch. A mix cd of songs that he'd asked me to download for him when I was in high school. Most surprising, I found a pocket-sized sketchbook that was filled with little doodles. It seemed to be for work, with some ductwork diagrams and drawings of houses and such. But every few pages or so, there were sketches of other things. A woman who looked a bit like my mom. Hands in different positions. Birds and plants. I smiled sadly at a sketch of a donut next to a bowl of ice cream. The words "Everyday is sweet" were written underneath.

* * *

On Friday, we packed up our things and flew to San Francisco. We were greeted at the airport by our entire family, my mom's sisters, my cousins, and my dad's side of the family, too. My mom and I both cried as we were enveloped by relative after relative, every one of whom shared our pain.

Family. Something Anna would never understand.

* * *

I showed up to Stumpstash's SF office on Monday. As soon as Cassie spotted me, she ran over and gave me a hug. My coworkers also came over and said comforting words or put their hands on my shoulders, awkwardly patting me. I gritted my teeth at the polite bullshit. They hardly knew anything about me and certainly knew nothing about my father. But I thanked them for their concern anyway and made to walk to the guest seating area, when Cassie took my hand and pulled me into an empty conference room.

"Ian. I'm so, so sorry for your loss." She bit her lip. "But why didn't you pick up—"

"Cassie," I interrupted, sighing, "I'm sorry for not picking up. I had to talk to so many of my relatives, I didn't want to talk to anyone else."

"I'm sorry." She patted my arm. "I didn't...will you...did you at least talk to Anna?"

I shook my head. "I'll talk to her when I get back. I don't want to deal with her right now."

"Why don't you just—"

"*Cassie.*" I stood up. "I've gotta catch up on work." I squeezed her shoulder. "Thanks for caring."

I quickly walked out of the room and left her behind.

But when I got to the desk, I took out my phone and texted Anna. *Let's chat when I get back next week.*

She responded a few minutes later. *Ok. Are you okay?*

I didn't respond. She knew the answer.

* * *

"We should move back here," I said in Mandarin, spooning fish onto my mom's plate. We were at dinner at her sister's house with my uncle and my younger cousin.

"That's a great idea," said my aunt. She patted my mom's hand. "Come live with us. Lianyang moved out, so you can take his old room."

"Or you can stay with me, *Ma.* I'm going to move here, too." I bit into a slice of roasted duck meat.

She looked at me. "You're going to move here?"

"Of course, if you do. My company has an office here. And it'll be nice to be closer to family."

"Don't you have a life in New York? Friends? *Girlfriends?*" She gave me a meaningful look.

I think my dad had told her about Anna. Not that it mattered now.

I shook my head. "I can have all of that here." I smiled at her and piled more fish onto her plate. "C'mon, let's just move here."

She didn't say anything after that, but I could tell that she liked the idea. My aunt and uncle did, too, and they talked about it as if it were a done deal. So that night, I started looking into selling her house in Princeton, as well as my condo in

New York. It was time to come home.

* * *

After the funeral, I left my mom in the capable hands of my aunt and uncle, then caught an early morning flight back to New York on my own. When I arrived at my apartment, I opened the door and saw a slip of paper on the floor, as well as a key. I read Anna's note and felt a pang of regret that things had ended up the way that they had.

But it was what it was. And I was moving back to California. I breathed deeply, shrugged the feeling off, and looked around for things to do, now that I was back.

I walked past the area rug with the large coffee stain. It was well beyond saving by this point, so I moved the furniture and rolled the rug up, then placed it by the door. I'd put it on the curb the next morning.

Then I went into the bedroom and stood there, looking down at the mussed sheets, the bed not in its usual made state. I sank down onto the bed, then slowly burrowed into and hugged the pillows. The pillowcase still smelled faintly of rose shampoo, and I breathed deep, filling my lungs yet somehow not feeling like it was enough. How long would it be before the scent of her faded? Or before the pain in my chest subsided?

I rolled the sheets and pillowcases up and threw them into the washer.

With not much else to do, and not feeling like working, it was probably a good time to talk to Anna. The clock read *7:21 PM*. I could call her or invite her out to ice cream or something. Maybe she hadn't had dinner yet.

Instead, I sighed, then took out my phone and texted her. *Talk tomorrow, if you're free for lunch?* I wasn't ready, not yet.

Her immediate response: *Yes, please.*

Another sigh escaped my lips. I tapped my phone against my hand, pacing back and forth, restless.

So I texted Lina. *Sunday night primetime climb time?*

Her immediate response: *Let's do it.*

I put on my shoes and headed to the gym.

* * *

"Hey Ian. I'm so sorry about your dad." Lina appeared behind me and patted my arm, then tossed her shoes onto the ground. Her face was sympathetic, but not exaggeratedly so, not one of the over-the-top anguished looks that people had been giving me all week. And I was glad that she hadn't asked me about any details of his passing or about how I was doing. Everyone wanted to know how I was holding up, wanted to offer their condolences or ask me about all of these intimate details that they had no right to know. I was tired of talking about it.

As she pulled on her harness and tightened the straps across her hips, I remembered that her husband had passed away not that long ago. Maybe she understood.

"Thanks. Did you warm up yet?" I asked. We each had our own warmup routines. Well, she *actually* warmed up with cardio and stretching. I just bouldered on lower grades.

"Yeah, I did. Did you?" she asked, clipping on her chalk bag.

"Yeah. Did you want to get onto that route I did a few weeks ago? The 11c? You mentioned wanting to do it last time." *When Anna was here with us.*

"Sure." Harness on, she sat down and began pulling on

209

her shoes, eyeing me curiously. "Don't you usually work on Sunday nights?"

I pulled on my own harness and smiled grimly. "I didn't realize you kept track."

"Oh, I notice these things. You're my climbing partner. I have to." She stood up, grabbed the rope, and tied into the route. "The last time you were here on a Sunday night was after your fight with Anna, and that was two weeks ago, when I last saw you. What's going on with you guys this time?"

I snorted. "You know, for someone who doesn't really talk about her own life, you sure know a lot about mine just from my climbing schedule." I clipped the belay device to my harness and clicked the carabiner twice to check that it was locked. "Climb on."

She did a quick safety check of my harness and carabiner, and I did the same for her knots. For such an experienced climber, she'd always been really anal about the safety checks, and I'd never known why until recently. No wonder.

With a quick nod of approval, she got onto the route and began to climb, rocking over onto a high left foot, getting just enough height for her fingertips to hook onto a tiny crimp. "So did you take my advice? Did you guys work things out?"

I shook my head, even though she was concentrating on the wall and not looking my way. "No. If anything, we're probably going to break up tomorrow." I wasn't sure why I'd said *probably*. More like *definitely*.

"Why?" she asked through gritted teeth, belying the effortless way she moved between the shallow holds. I'd thought this route was *crimpossible* (Lina's word—she liked puns and wordplay) when I'd tried it, but she was making it look easy.

"It's just not going to work out. We want...different things

210

in life." I sighed. That seemed like the easiest explanation.

"Ok. Still, it seemed like you guys were good together. And she would've made a great climber, too. I liked her."

I sighed. "I know. I liked her, too. But I'm also moving to California, so—"

Lina's foot slipped and my hips jerked as I counterbalanced her fall. "Shit. Seriously?" She looked down and shook her arms out at me. "You're moving? Why?"

"To be closer to family. My mom is alone now. Our family is in California."

"Ah...I see." Lina nodded, no judgment or questions in her eyes. "I get it. I'm lucky, my family is in Philadelphia."

I leaned back in the harness to get a better look at Lina. She was smart, beautiful, a great climbing partner...and she loved her family. We enjoyed each other's company, and whenever I had trouble with Anna, I found myself hanging out with Lina. Maybe she liked puns a little too much and made up weird words, but I could get used to it. Why couldn't *we* have gotten together?

But even as I had the thought, I saw the answer on Lina's subdued face. She didn't have Anna's liveliness. That spark, that flame to my moth. She was too similar to me, maybe, too somber. We probably would have bored each other to death.

And perhaps most importantly, she wasn't interested. Lina and I had been climbing together for months, yet she hadn't really spoken to me about anything other than climbing until I started dating Anna. She was clearly rooting for us.

"Long-distance is doable, you know. I did it with my husband half the time while we were dating and he was driving around chasing crags. You should try it before you just give up on her." She stretched her hands and rolled her wrists.

"That won't change the fact that we want different things."

"Why don't you invite her here tonight to talk it out? I'm sure she'd be reasonable," she called down, her voice too pleasant.

I frowned. "Are you just trying to get me to stay with her so you can groom her into your new climbing buddy?"

She snickered. "Ah, Ian, I knew you were smart. Guilty as charged. But also, really. She's great! I'm sure you could work it out, no matter what it is. And for real about the long-distance. We live in this amazing age. I know you're in tech, so maybe you've heard of it...there's this really cool invention called a *phone*..."

I rolled my eyes.

"...and maybe you've only ever used it to text and watch porn, but there's this really sweet feature..."

"Lina."

"...called *calling* and you can literally talk to someone, whenever you want, in like two seconds. And planes—okay, I won't *belabor* the point. Heh, get it? Belay-bore? But yeah, long-distance really isn't that bad."

I snorted. "Lina, you are...weirder than I thought. I'm gonna miss you."

"I know. I'll miss you, too. Let's keep in touch, for real. *It's not hard these days.* And hit me up if you're ever back in the city." She got back onto the route, gracefully flagging out and easily climbing through a section that I'd burled through (with poor form) only a few weeks ago.

"I will." I meant it, too.

Chapter 21

-Anna-

I got into work 30 minutes early that day, and even then, he was already there, hard at work.

I dropped my stuff onto my seat and walked over to his desk. He briefly glanced up from his computer, then went back to typing. "Hey."

"Hey." I expected him to get up and hug me, but he didn't. Just sat there and kept typing.

"Do you need something?" he asked without looking up, face expressionless.

"I…" I glanced around and noticed that a couple of other people were already in the office, including Tom, who was watching us keenly from the water cooler. "No. I'll talk to you later." I turned on my heel and walked back to my desk. I could see how our conversation today was going to go, and my breakfast threatened to resurface.

I sat down and compiled a mental breakup checklist.

1. Change desktop background image
2. Delete photos and text messages from phone

3. Never go climbing again

As lunch drew closer, my queasiness only grew, and my eyes periodically misted for no apparent reason.

He didn't look up from his computer again, except when coworkers came up to him and gave their condolences, or asked him something about his projects. His responses to them were as terse and unfeeling as they had been to me, and I saw more than one frown or confused look thrown his way.

At exactly noon, he got up from his desk and came over to mine. "Ready to chat?" He sounded as if we were colleagues going on a walk to discuss a work dispute—tense, yet blandly cheerful.

"Yeah, can I use the restroom first?"

"Sure, I'll wait."

I walked to the ladies room and checked my makeup. My eyeliner was smudged in the corner, the usually-sharp wings smeared and sagging. I suspected that it was going to look far worse by the end of the day, but I cleaned it up anyway, washed my hands, squared my shoulders, and went out to meet him.

He was waiting for me out in the hallway, reading an article on his phone. He looked up as I approached and fell into step beside me as we walked towards the elevators. I let my hand hang by my side, close to his, hating myself for how hopeful and desperate I felt...but he didn't take it, just kept holding his phone.

Instead of going out, we went to the dining hall on the second floor. I think it was a good call on his part, as we weren't likely to kill or fuck each other with our coworkers looking on. We each grabbed a tray and waited in line for different things. I got the Cobb salad, he got the noodles. We met at a table in the middle, then picked at our food in silence.

Finally, he said, "Anna, I want to apologize for all of the things that I said the last time I saw you. I didn't mean any of it. It was just my temper talking."

He'd dropped the cool coworker act, and his voice was low and filled with regret. I knew that he hadn't meant the things that he'd said, but it still cheered me up to hear him apologize. But the pressure in my chest was only marginally relieved. "It's...okay. I said some terrible things, too. I didn't mean it. Any of it." I poked at my salad. No appetite.

"You were right about some of it, though. I won't deny that...I've lived my life according to a plan, one that my parents were proud of. But that's what I wanted. And honestly, it's pretty clear to me that that's not what you want, so...I think we should call it quits."

I blinked, utterly dumbfounded. We weren't going to talk things through? Not even a little? We were...over that quickly? How could he just end things between us so horribly, with so few words?

My brain latched onto the only rational explanation. "Yeah. I guess so. You can definitely do better than a wreck like me."

He shook his head. "That's not—"

"It's fine. I think you deserve someone more...more..." I struggled to find the word. Gave up. "Like you." I blinked even harder.

He hesitated, then reached across the table and took my hand. "I know you won't believe it, but you're not a wreck. I'm lucky to have had a chance with a wonderful, fierce woman like you. You're gonna make someone really happy, someday."

My heart clenched at the genuine look on his face, and my

eyes watered once more.

He drew his hand back down to his lap. "Besides, I'm moving to San Francisco."

"What?" I gawked at him. The shock of his news stemmed the tide of tears that were threatening.

"I'm transferring to the SF office and moving over there. I want to be closer to my family."

"But...when?" My fingernails dug into my palms—this was really happening.

"As soon as the transfer goes through, and as soon as I can put the condo up for sale."

"You *owned* the condo?" Fuck, how much did tech leads make?

He smiled grimly. "What did you expect? I'm the Chinese-American dream."

"Ian." I wanted to reach out to take his hand again, but it wasn't on the table. "I'm so sorry about everything. Really." I rubbed my eyes, not caring if I looked like a panda.

"There's nothing to be sorry about. We're both adults. People make decisions and move on. And they get old and die." He went back to eating his noodles. "That's life."

"I guess," I whispered, sniffling and wiping away two stray tears. I didn't even try to pretend to eat my food anymore, just shoved it away from me and delicately dabbed a napkin to my eyes.

After a moment, he pushed his plate away too. "Are you done?" he quietly asked.

I nodded, sniffed, and stood up to go. He rose and walked with me towards the elevator.

"Anna, I...I really appreciate the time that I had with you. It was...thrilling." His voice cracked before he cleared his throat and added, "I hope you'll find the right person for you. And that we'll remain friends."

He'd put on his bland colleague voice again. I was no better to him than Tom, Rich, or Emily. The elevator doors opened and he placed his hand on my back and walked me in.

But when the doors closed with just the two of us in the elevator, he turned to me and surprised me with a hug. He pressed my face into his chest and I couldn't help but inhale his familiar scent. I wrapped my arms around his waist and he held me close, blanketing me with his warmth, cradling my head in his hands, his fingers in my hair. He took a deep breath. Then, as the elevator slowed to a halt, he let me go.

I turned to catch his arm. "Ian—"

He firmly pulled away and walked out without a word, not meeting my eyes.

I stared after him as my coworkers got onto the elevator. They stepped in and turned their backs to me, facing the front, their eyes carefully averted. The door closed.

The waterworks were on full blast by the time the doors next opened.

Where was the anger? The hatred? The pride or sense of self-preservation? The only thing in my chest was emptiness, like a core part of me had just suddenly disappeared, collapsed in on itself. Where Ian's steadfast support and tender compassion once existed, there was just a huge, gaping vacuum, a black hole eating me up inside.

It was clear that he'd already checked out of the relationship, had moved on without me. And he was literally moving away, to San Francisco, without me.

I would never hear his boisterous laugh again, the one he saved only for me, for our private moments together. I'd never again feel the perfect fit of his body against mine, the feel of him *inside* me, his weight so comfortably crushing me into the bed.

His smell, his smile, his eyes, his hands...his affection...they were no longer mine. And it fucking *hurt*.

After one full elevator ride down and up, I walked back into the office and asked my boss for the rest of the day off. She took one look at my face and said, "Take tomorrow off, too."

* * *

"Yeah, he told me while he was here." Apparently, Cassie already knew that he was moving to San Francisco.

"I guess that's all. He just wanted to apologize, say it's over, and tell me that he's moving."

"I see. Nana...you going to be okay?" On screen, Cassie's face was scrunched up with sympathy.

"Yeah, I'll be fine." I'd cried it all out at the office earlier. And I knew that we weren't right for each other. It was a painful truth that I just needed time to accept.

Cassie bit her lip. "You know...*you* could move to SF, too."

The thought had crossed my mind earlier, but..."No thanks. My life is here."

"So don't take this the wrong way, but what's so great about New York? You told me that you mostly just hang out with Asher and his music buddies." She bobbed her head around, excited. "If you came here, we could meet at a bar every Sunday instead of on Google Hangouts!"

I slowly shook my head. The idea was tempting, but I didn't want to just follow Ian, and I didn't think that it would actually make me that much happier. I needed to figure things out on

218

my own. For real this time.

Part of me knew that I'd been a hypocrite with Ian. I'd judged him for not living a life for himself, but at least he acknowledged that he'd *wanted* to live for others and went all out for it. He'd been successful, in his own way. I supposedly knew what I wanted...but how much was I really doing to achieve it?

I'd felt helpless for so long, stuck in situation after situation, with no easy way out. My solution had always been to run away or blame others. But deep down, I knew that I had only myself to blame. I wasn't helpless...just scared.

Tears flooded my eyes when I thought about the first time we'd ever gone climbing together. How he'd believed in me and helped me learn to believe more in myself. Or about how, even though we'd lived together, he'd given me space to grow on my own, like I'd asked him to. Or when I'd admitted that I was serially dependent on others, how he'd looked me in the eye and challenged me to do better.

Don't just sit there and cry, do something about it.

He hadn't let me wallow in self-pity, something I regularly did and hated about myself.

Something I was doing even then.

I sighed. There was no reason to dwell. He was a great guy, and I was broken. I really didn't deserve him.

But maybe...maybe I could.

"Cass, I need your help. I need you to hold me accountable."

"For what?"

I gritted my teeth. "I'm going to fucking take control of my life."

Chapter 22

-Ian-

It took a few weeks for the transfer to happen, and for me to arrange for my mom's and my belongings to be shipped to SF. She'd opted to stay with my aunt and uncle, so I decided to just rent a place in Pacific Heights instead of buying. I wanted mobility, the option to move when I figured out what I wanted to do next...because something definitely needed to change. I used to think that I was still young, still had time to figure things out, but now time just felt so short. I was getting old, and *Stumpstash* was starting to get old.

I wasn't sure how much longer I could work there. I wasn't excited about my projects, nor about tech at all, really...yet I was living in the thick of it. Every company that I looked at seemed to think that it was somehow saving the world. It was certainly truer in some cases than in others, but most of the time, it was a gross exaggeration. Software engineering paid well, and it was easy for me, but I wanted to do something that *actually* made the world better, or brought people joy, or that I truly, genuinely cared about. But what?

I didn't know, and I didn't know how to figure it out. And

with my dad's passing so young (he was only 63), I could feel death lurking around the corner, waiting for me. The days started to feel a little bit like I was just killing time while I slowly crawled towards my appointment with the afterlife. Going to the gym, eating, sleeping, taking care of myself...all of that was just delaying the inevitable. Why bother?

I even lost interest in climbing. Every route in the gym felt the same. Getting to the top of a finite wall, following a route that someone else had set...climbing in a sea of indifferent, or deluded, tech people. None of that held any appeal to me. What was the point of getting stronger? Of facing fears or challenges that were artificially constructed? And continuing to do so, over and over and over? It just seemed like an unnecessary hassle, not worth the effort anymore.

Eventually, I stopped going to the gym. Most nights, I just worked late, ate at the office, and went straight home.

The only thing that kept me going was my mom. I'd wanted to be strong for her, to keep *her* going...but instead, I found myself holding onto her like a lifeline. The knowledge that she needed me was what got me out of bed each morning.

I visited my mom, aunt, and uncle for dinner every few days. While she was still quieter than before, her spirits seemed to have picked up with the added company. Each time she smiled or laughed, I was a little bit more relieved.

My mother was a very intuitive woman, and it wasn't long before she noticed that something was wrong with me. One night, she pulled me aside after dinner. "Let's go walk around the park." She put on her walking shoes while I told my aunt where we were headed, then we set out towards Dolores Park.

Even that late, there were people still hanging out on the grass, talking and smoking. My mom dramatically held her nose and waved her hand in front of her face at the smell of marijuana. I jokingly breathed in deep, and she slapped my arm and told me to stop. I laughed.

"Ian. Don't do that. You'll get cancer."

"I'm young and healthy, *Ma*, I'll be fine." But I did stop. Shame filled me at the thought of how insensitive my joke had been, given her health scare.

"Ian. You need to take better care of yourself. You're young, be happy. Don't look so sad all the time."

I was surprised. Whenever I was with my mom, I always tried to act happier than I was. In some perverse way, sometimes I actually believed it. "I am happy, *Ma*." I grinned. "We're here in beautiful California, with our family. And I have the best mom." I put my arm around her shoulders.

She frowned, not buying it. "You need to get married."

Sigh. Not this again. I shook my head. "I will. I'll go home and start messaging women right after this, just for you." I squeezed her shoulder.

She looked up at me, still frowning. "Ian. What do *you* want to do?"

I stopped walking and turned to face her. "What do you mean? I'm happy to get married, I just have to find the right person, first."

She reached up and patted my cheek. "You're a good boy. But what do you *want*?"

I frowned. "I still don't understand. What does that mean?"

She took my hand and pulled me towards the park, continuing our walk. After a few minutes, she asked, "Do you know why we watched so many dramas, your *Ba* and I?"

We crested a hill, and I turned to take in the San Francisco evening skyline. "Because you were bored?"

She shook her head. "Because they represent the lives we could have had, but were too afraid to try for. Oh, we were happy together," she said and waved a hand at me when I tried to interrupt. "I'm not saying we wanted to experience crazy romance stories. Though I wouldn't have minded if your *Ba* were a CEO who beat up bad guys and swept me off my feet. The point is, those characters always have to choose: do they stick with what they know, with what's safe, or do they follow their hearts? In the dramas, they always follow their hearts. But when your *Ba* and I first came to the US, life was hard. We didn't have choices. We *had* to do what was safe so that we could have a good life together. We did what we could to survive, so that we could raise you responsibly."

She kneaded my hand in both of hers. She'd been a masseuse, and it was her subconscious way of comforting people. "But we'd always dreamed of more," she sighed.

The faraway look, the sparkle in my mom's eyes...it reminded me of Anna, her expression when she talked about music.

"You know, when your *Ba* was younger, before we got married, he wanted to be an artist. He used to draw all kinds of things...people, animals, food...himself. When I first met him, he didn't have any photos of himself as an adult, so he drew a self-portrait and gave it to me. He was so handsome. I wish that we had kept his drawings. They were good." She sighed. "But when we came to the US, he had to pick up a trade. He had a friend who did HVAC, who was willing to teach him the skills. It was hard work, and it paid well. But it wasn't art."

I remained silent, shocked at these revelations about my dad. I thought about the sketchbook that I'd found among his belongings. What else had I not known about him? Why hadn't he shared those dreams with me?

My mom sighed again. "And I was almost a professional ping pong player."

I stopped and gaped at her. *"You were almost a professional ping pong player?"*

She nodded and swished her hands around as if she were grasping an invisible paddle, penholder style. "I was number one in my school. But your grandparents convinced me to come to the US with your *Ba* instead."

I shook my head, astounded. "Why didn't you tell me?"

She shrugged. "We didn't have a ping pong table. If we did, I would have taught you. And besides," she said, leveling a look at me, "you never asked."

"Seriously?" How could my parents not have mentioned these things to me before? These secret dreams of theirs inspired me more than their lectures or praise ever did. They added color and beauty to the simple reality of their lives—rough and plain on the outside, but with a dazzling, kaleidoscopic interior that I wished I'd known about earlier. I smiled, eyes misting, and silently vowed to learn more about my mom and her secret life. And maybe, when it didn't hurt so much, she could tell me more about my dad's, too.

My mom continued walking, so I followed, placing my arm around her shoulders again.

"The point is, we came to the US and had to start from scratch. We gave up our dreams so that we could survive, build a life together, and have you. But there's no reason why you have to give up *your* dreams. We're fine now." She smiled. "You don't need to watch Asian dramas like we do."

My tears spilled over, and I pulled her in for a hug. As

their only child, I'd thought that their dreams for me were so simple, and so different from my own—that I had to sacrifice something for them to be happy. But really, our dreams were the same, a beautiful jug shimmering just out of reach, waiting for me to make a big, committed move.

I'd given up without even trying. That was the worst kind of climbing mentality.

She briefly patted my back before releasing me and saying, "Speaking of dramas, we should go back so that I can watch my show. It starts in ten minutes."

I laughed, wiping my tears away. "You don't have to watch them anymore, either, mom. Maybe you should pick up ping pong again."

She waved her hand, dismissing the idea. "No way. I like dramas. This one is especially good. It's about the ghost of a man who possesses his former wife's dog and saves her from constant danger. The last episode ended with her stuck on a cliff. I want to know what happens."

I roared with laughter. "Is the dog going to climb up the cliff and save her?"

She patted my hand and walked faster. "Let's go find out."

We got back in time and I ended up staying to see what happened.

The dog climbed up a cliff to save his lady love. He even did a slow motion doggie dyno.

Arrrrrrrrrrrrrf.

My mom, aunt, and I were all crying, but I was the only one rolling on the floor.

* * *

Cassie could also tell that there was something a little off with me. She checked in on me frequently and invited me over for dinner sometimes. I usually refused, citing too much work to get through, which was often true. But by the fourth or fifth time, I felt rude refusing any longer, so I gave in and promised to come over on a Tuesday night after work.

"How are you doing, Ian? What's going on in your life these days?" She popped the cork out of the bottle of wine that I'd brought and poured me a glass, followed by another glass for herself. We walked over to the dining table, where Michael was already sitting with a neat glass of Bulleit.

"I'm okay. Just trying to figure stuff out." I took a sip of wine and sat down at the table.

"Like what?" she asked. She picked up the salad tongs and began serving each of us some strawberry arugula salad.

I laughed dryly. "Ah, everything. What I want to do with my life. My goals, my dreams…" I paused and gave Cassie a *look*. "Relationship stuff."

She nodded knowingly, then glanced at Michael. "You know, Ian," she said, putting more salad onto my plate, "Michael and I were thinking about doing shrooms this weekend."

I raised my eyebrows. I'd known that things like acid and shrooms were pretty common in Silicon Valley, but I hadn't thought that Cassie was a user. She seemed so innocent sometimes. Except when she was drunk, which she currently was not.

Michael also raised his eyebrows. "We were?"

Cassie glared at him. "Yes, we *were*. Remember?" She placed more salad onto his plate too, though he tried to move his plate away and she had to chase it a little. I smiled at their antics.

"Oh yeah? What's it like?" I asked, genuinely interested. I'd toyed with the idea of trying psychedelics before, but wasn't sure how to get my hands on any.

Cassie sat down and steepled her fingers. "Well. Let. Me. Tell. You. They totally blew my mind." She spread her fingers out from her temples and made a "bwah" sound, demonstrating the blown-ness of her mind.

I laughed. "Uh huh. In what way?"

She went on, her eyes wide with enthusiasm. "It's different for everyone, but for me, I just felt so...content. It's such a mundane yet underrated feeling, contentedness. Like you realize, things in life aren't that bad, and everything's actually kinda nice. There's always an upside to things, you know?"

Michael snorted. "That's what you remember the most? I remember you taking off—"

"Bupbupbup," Cassie warned, frowning at him. She looked at me again and said, "It also made me really appreciate what I have with Michael. It brought us closer together in a way that I never could have imagined. It was like we were in our own little world...and I guess I'd acted like we were, even though we were out in Big Sur with a bunch of our friends." She blushed.

I chuckled. Shroomed-out Cassie must've been even crazier than drunk Cassie. "I see. Sounds pretty fun."

Cassie glanced at Michael again, then looked at me. "I was wondering if you wanted to join us this weekend? For your first time, you might just want to be somewhere safe, so we were thinking about doing it here. We wanted to keep it chill anyway."

I chewed on a strawberry and thought about it. I *had* been wanting to find new inspiration, especially after my talk with my mom, and all the VCs and big shots in tech seemed to swear by psychedelics. Besides, I hadn't yet decided what my "big thing" for the year was going to be. I'd considered quitting my job and taking three months off to climb around Europe, hoping to rekindle my love for climbing out in Spain or in the Italian Dolomites...and maybe I still would. But I could do this, too.

"Y'know, honestly, that'd be awesome. Thanks so much for the invite."

* * *

On Saturday, I went over to Cassie's again and ate a handful of shrooms.

For the first fifteen minutes, nothing happened.

"It takes a little bit to kick in sometimes," Cassie explained. She'd told me to dress comfortably, so I was wearing joggers, a t-shirt, and a hoodie, the same one that Anna had borrowed on the plane. It was comfortable, but also *comforting*. I'd wanted both, just in case my first experience with shrooms went south.

Cassie was wearing a green dinosaur onesie, of all things, and Michael wore a matching pink one.

They were disgustingly cute.

"What do you do when you're tripping?" I asked. Their living room was cozily furnished with a thick, navy blue area rug and light gray sofa set. Michael's dog, Frankie, lay on the floor by my feet, busily tearing apart a chew toy.

Michael put his hands behind his head and leaned back against the couch. "We usually just like to chill, listen to music. Maybe put on some cool visual stuff to look at."

Cassie swiped and tapped on her phone, then music began to play from their surround sound speakers. "I like to put on Anna's playlists. She makes the best playlists to get high to."

I could see that. Her music was so dreamy and sensual, so different from the repetitive tunes that I heard on the radio. My stomach clenched at the thought of her.

Michael nodded slightly when I put my hand on my stomach. "I see it's starting to kick in." In answer to my quizzical look, he added, "It often causes some stomach discomfort."

Ah, that explained it. Not Anna.

My eyes began to swim, and the lines around the furniture became fuzzy. I closed my eyes against the sudden brightness of the room, and my legs prickled with numbness. I'd been sitting upright in the loveseat, but I abruptly needed to lie down. I sank into their rug.

"Whoa," I heard myself say from far away.

Cassie giggled, then nestled into Michael's lap. "I'm starting to feel it, too."

Newly aware and hyper-sensitized, there was so much for me to examine, even with my eyes closed. My fingers dug into the shag rug, the long, thick fibers dry and slightly abrasive against my skin. The ripe, savory tang of Frankie's saliva tickled my nose, along with the spicy scent of my own deodorant, which I hardly ever noticed anymore. But the highlight, the most glorious part of the experience, was the music. It *invigorated* me. I breathed deeply, as if the music were infused into the air, as if it would continue to resonate in my lungs. It filled my core and stimulated every cell in my body.

My cheeks hurt from how much I was smiling.

Before, my practical brain had simplified sound down to

mere vibrations of different frequencies and levels of loudness. I'd never before appreciated the sheer *range* of frequencies, or noticed how moving the interplay of notes of different pitches, tones, and lengths could be. The memories that were attached to them, and that they evoked. The staggering power and emotion of the *human voice*. How had I gone so long without noticing?

I'd liked Anna's playlists when we'd listened to them before. They'd always been in the background while we did other things, like cooking, cleaning, or making love. But there, at that moment, they were a focal point. Each synth, beat, and note perfectly resonated with my emotions, and I *felt* the music as I never had before. I sighed with pleasure at discovering this new power, this new part of myself.

I pulled out my phone and briefly forgot how to unlock it, as my eyes struggled to focus and the screen seemed three-dimensional. Eventually, I unlocked the thing and found Anna's Spotify profile and hit subscribe. I could not believe that I hadn't recognized how good her music taste was until just this moment. Had *she* done shrooms before?

The thought drifted away and my vision blurred once more. I struggled to keep my eyes open.

So I closed them, and remembered.

* * *

As Cassie had described, I felt so at peace. So content. I found myself revisiting fond memories of other moments in my life when everything had felt *just right*.

I remembered my grandpa walking around the house, shirtless and singing Chinese opera off-key and at the top of his lungs. My dad told him to stop singing and put a shirt on because my mom was around. She just laughed and told him to do as he liked.

I remembered my grandmother's cooking. She practically lived in the kitchen, trying to keep enough food on the table to feed our giant family. I loved the simple things she made, like pan-fried Chinese sausage and eggs with pickled turnips. She always gave me a little extra meat because I was the eldest grandchild, and she'd wanted me to physically *be* the biggest.

I remembered my mom staying up late one night, her cool hands on the nape of my neck as she held my head up to help me drink her homemade ginseng tea. I'd hated the taste at the time, so she'd added honey to help it go down. The flavor combination was so soothing to me now.

I remembered my dad...and for the first time in a while, the memory was full of joy and laughter, not grief.

I was eight, and my dad was eating his half of a Boston cream donut. He'd given me the other half, and I'd already shoved the whole thing into my mouth.

"*Ba*, do you know how to make these?" I'd asked him, mouth still full.

Dad chuckled. "No, I don't know how to make donuts. Your *Ayi* on your *Ma*'s side knows how to make something similar, though. "

"*Chinese* donuts?" I looked at him, wide-eyed.

"*Jiandui*." Sesame balls.

I frowned. "Those aren't the same at all." My aunt's fried sesame balls had red bean paste in them, and they weren't as sweet.

He chuckled. "They're still good, though. You should ask your aunt to try to make one for you with cream inside

231

sometime."

The memory shimmered away as I opened my eyes and smiled. Then I fumbled with my phone again and sent a text to my aunt. *I hope I don't sound obviously high*, I thought, closing my eyes again.

I released another contented sigh and slipped back into my memories. Memories of Anna.

The silkiness of her hair between my fingers, the weight of her head on my chest as we lay languid and spent, cuddling in bed after a long bout of love-making.

The sound of her laugh, so loud and full-bodied, honest and pure, whenever I tickled her stomach or told her an especially corny joke.

Her utterly euphoric expression whenever she discovered a new song that she loved, and her boundless excitement when she shared it with me.

Then...the hurt in her eyes when I'd betrayed her trust, and belittled her, the day of our fight. The moment I'd lost her.

That night when she'd told me her story, I tried my best to just shut up and listen, to be sympathetic. But deep down, I couldn't believe that she'd just throw away her family forever, especially her mom.

And after experiencing the shock and pain of a parent's death, I'd thought that she didn't know what it meant to truly cherish someone, to compromise and fight for them. If you really love someone, how could you just give up on them like that?

But looking back...maybe I was the one who'd given up too easily.

I sighed, long and wistfully.

* * *

Later that evening, sober and more clear-headed than I'd ever been, I called my aunt.

"Hi, *Ayi*," I said. *Ayi* meant *aunt*.

"Ian. What did your text mean? 'Crem balls = $$$'. I don't understand."

I laughed. "Sorry, *Ayi*. That was a reminder for me. I wanted to ask you to teach me how to make *jiandui*."

"Oh, *jiandui*. Why do you want to learn how to make *jiandui* all of a sudden?"

"So that I can spend some quality time with my aunt?" I teased, though I did want to get to know her better, too. What were *her* secret dreams? "But really, I have some ideas for fillings and different flavors. I'd like to try making them with you."

"Mmm, I can never say no to my nephew. I can teach you. When?"

"Are you free tomorrow? I can come by anytime."

"Sure. Come here at 10am. Can you pick up the ingredients?" She told me what they were and I jotted them down.

After she hung up, I looked up recipes online, just to get some additional ideas for things to try. I went out and bought some ingredients, then stayed up late trying different variations on the recipes that I'd found.

By the end of the night, I fell into bed exhausted, yet proud and excited. I finally looked forward to what the next day would bring.

* * *

A month later, I told Cassie, "I'm opening a food truck."

I'd just turned in my two-weeks notice to Stumpstash and Cassie had been the first to know, other than Isaiah. She pulled me into a conference room to discuss the details and started flipping out.

"No way. Seriously? Oh my god." Cassie held her hands against her forehead, as if I were completely boggling her mind. "What kind of food?"

"Sesame balls. You know the kind you can get at dim sum, with red bean filling? I'm going to have different fillings and toppings and put my own unique spin on them."

Her eyes widened. "Wow. That sounds SO GOOD. Oh my god. You need to bring some to the office before you quit."

I chuckled. "I will. I'll need you guys to help spread the word."

She squealed in excitement, hopping from foot to foot. "Ah, Ian, I am SO EXCITED FOR YOU!" She paused, then quickly sobered, her voice dropping an octave. "But seriously...I'm going to miss working with you. You always made meetings more entertaining. And I really loved that you got your team to deliver pretty close to on target, most of the time."

"I feel like that was mostly you, breathing down everyone's necks."

We both laughed. Then I got up and hugged her. "Thanks for everything, Cassie."

Chapter 23

-Anna-

There were three excruciatingly awkward weeks between when Ian and I broke up and when he moved to San Francisco.

We nodded at each other in passing and exchanged pleasantries in the elevator, faces carefully neutral. He spoke civilly to me when he needed more office supplies, and I politely requested his attendance in meetings and interviews that he was needed in. And at the end of those three weeks, I casually hugged him, just like everyone else, at his office goodbye party, which as the office admin, I'd helped to organize.

Outwardly, I think I succeeded in seeming fine.

Inwardly, I had to hold the pieces together with musical crazy glue.

I made so many new playlists during those three weeks. Some of them, understandably, were about heartbreak. The volume and fervor of those playlists kind of surprised me though, given that our relationship had been so brief and tumultuous. But maybe it made sense. After all, the sex had been mindblowing, a total dopamine rush, and my body craved him like it craved sugar and fat.

But more than that, I'd been vulnerable with him...and he'd turned it against me. And even though he'd said he hadn't meant it after the fact, it made me feel like no sane, whole person would accept me for who or what I was, no matter what they promised me. I was broken and couldn't be fixed, even by a guy as sweet and caring as Ian had been. Maybe I was lamenting the fact that my heart would *never* be whole.

And now that I was back at Asher's place, it felt like nothing had really changed. Like I'd gone one step forward and two terrible, heartbreaking steps back.

But you know...that was how life was. You fell, you got up, and you kept trying until you got to the top. I wallowed at times, and I cried, maybe a bit too much. But with each new tear, my determination grew. My days of running from my problems were over. I was going to get my shit together and live the life that I wanted.

My life.

* * *

I started by telling Asher the truth.

We were sitting together, him on the floor, me on the couch, splitting a pizza from the place right down the block. We'd spent the evening watching the trashiest of television together and laughing at the ridiculous couples that got together. After one particularly terrible quote from a guy who'd been catfished, we were both howling with laughter. He took my hand and kissed it, smiling so sweetly at me from where he was sitting.

I slowly pulled my hand away.

"Asher...we should talk."

236

He sighed and pinched the bridge of his nose. "It's...hopeless, isn't it?" The commentators on the show guffawed at yet another catfishing victim. Asher reached for the remote and turned off the TV.

I slipped onto the floor to sit next to him, then took a deep breath. It was time. "You know how much I love you, Asher. I really, really do love you, but...only as a friend. I don't want to lead you on or give you the impression that things are going to change. I'm sorry."

He nodded, taking things in stride. "I figured. I just wish you'd told me sooner."

I looked down, ashamed. "I know. I'm sorry. I was just...scared that you wouldn't let me stay. And I didn't know what else to do."

He laughed mirthlessly. "I'm not a kid, you know. We can talk about things like adults." He ran his fingers through his long, curly hair. "And you can stay as long as you want. Just...let me know how I can help."

I placed my hand on his shoulder, relief flooding through every cell. I hadn't lost him. "Thanks, Asher. I mean it. I'm so grateful for everything you've done for me. But I definitely don't want to hold you back. I'm going to find a new place soon, I promise."

"No rush," he said, getting up and pulling a beer out of the fridge. "It's fun having you around." He tentatively smiled, and I smiled back. Friends.

* * *

Because I was back at Asher's, I also walked past the climbing gym everyday. Just another painful reminder of Ian, of what

I was missing. As were mentions of California...anytime I heard the word Europ*ean*...the eggplant emoji...ginger. *Sigh*. I still peeked in when I walked by, but I knew that I wouldn't find what I was looking for.

But one day as I was walking past, I saw Lina on her way in. On instinct, I waved. "Lina!"

"Anna!" To my surprise, she came up and hugged me, long and hard. "Long time, no see! Are you climbing today?"

"Oh, no, I don't...I mean, Ian..."

She held up a hand to stop me. "I know you used to climb with him, but you were making progress on your own. If you keep at it, you'll be a crusher in no time."

My eyes filled with tears. I *wanted* to be a crusher. I wanted to crush at everything.

Lina put her hand on my shoulder, her big brown eyes full of compassion. "It looks like you could use a climbing session. Want to come in? I've got a guest pass."

I looked down at my clothes. Luckily, I did have leggings on, but my sweater was cashmere. A lucky thrift store find, one that I didn't want to muck up with sweat. As if reading my mind, Lina said, "I've got a spare t-shirt if you need to borrow one."

I nodded, grateful. I could really use the endorphins. And maybe a friend.

* * *

Without Ian around, Lina was totally different.

Before, she mostly just talked to us about climbing. We focused on the problems and worked through them together, and that was the extent of our relationship.

She still pushed me to climb hard, same as before. But now, she actually talked to me ("Guys always think I'm flirting if I talk about anything other than climbing," she'd laughingly explained). She asked me about work, about my weekends, about music. I did the same, and was thrilled to discover that we had a ton to talk about.

She was doing her PhD in Chemistry at NYU. I'd gone to NYU for undergrad. We compared notes on the best work nooks around campus.

She'd grown up in Philadelphia, just like I had, and neither one of us really liked Philly cheesesteaks much. And our schools had actually been field hockey rivals, though neither of us had played on our respective teams.

And we were both happily *single*. After that first climbing session together, we agreed to go out dancing that weekend. And, I agreed to get a membership to the gym so that we could keep climbing together. She was so sweetly thrilled about both.

For someone so hot, Lina was surprisingly bookish. She worked in a chemistry lab all day, so she dressed for function, not for fun, and her wardrobe consisted almost exclusively of workout clothes, jeans, and t-shirts. Asher's band was playing at a swanky venue in Bowery and could get us in for free, but she needed to meet the dress code. We agreed to meet at my place on Friday so that she could borrow one of my dresses.

I heard her knock on the door while I was in the bathroom, where I was finishing up with my makeup. "Asher, can you get it? It's my friend Lina."

"Yeah," I heard him call back.

I couldn't hear what they said to each other, but a moment later, Lina was knocking on the door to the bathroom. I pulled it open.

"Hey!" We hugged. "Ready to look sexier than ever before?"

Lina grimaced. "No?"

I laughed and tried not to mess up my eyeliner. "The dress is on my bed. Shoes, too. Go try them on!"

She entered my room and closed the door. I finished applying my makeup, then went and knocked on the door. "Lina, you ready?"

"I guess so," she quietly replied.

I swung open the door and stared.

Wowza. The dress, a halter-top backless bodycon dress, was meant to be form-fitting and kinda short, but she was taller and had broader shoulders and bigger boobs than me. And a bigger ass. Her legs looked miles long with the heels on, which she probably didn't need, given her 5'10" height. She was a natural beauty, and even without much makeup on, she looked like a supermodel, especially with her perfect little beauty mark on the left above her lip. The only flaw was her hair, which was tied back in her typical messy bun.

I walked over to her and pulled her hair tie out, then fluffed the resulting curls out.

"Asher," I called. "Come here, we need your professional opinion."

"What? No!" Lina tried to cover herself with her jacket, but I pulled it away, laughing.

Asher showed up at the door. "What's up—"

He froze. And he stared. A moment later, he whistled. "Damn." Lina bit her lip and tugged the hem of the dress down, so bashful and sexy.

Asher continued, "No offense, Anna, but that dress looks way better on her than it ever did on you."

240

I gave him the finger and said, "Yeah, yeah, it's true. It's Lina's dress now."

"What? I'm just borrow—"

"Hush! You're going to seduce the shit out of people with that dress. It's yours now—use it wisely."

Lina looked at me, so sweet and so cluelessly hot...then looked at Asher.

And kept looking at Asher.

Asher licked his lips.

"Oh my god, get a room guys, stop eye-fucking each other."

Lina laughed nervously and took her jacket from me. "Let's go before I decide to change."

It turned out to be a really fun night. Asher's band was on fire, and the crowd was really feeling it. Lina was putting on quite the show herself, and I was impressed with how well she could dance, despite wobbling on my borrowed heels. I caught Asher staring at her during his set significantly more than once. I smiled at the sight, and wondered if that was how it had looked when Asher and I'd first met.

* * *

"Hey. I found a place. I'm moving out." Cassie had helped me find the place on Saturday evening, so I'd gone over to the open house on Sunday with my checkbook and rental application filled out. I'd gotten approved then and there—my tech job had done wonders for my credit.

Asher looked up from his keyboard. "Oh. Where? When?"

"It's in Jackson Heights. A little bit farther of a commute, and super tiny, but it's totally affordable. I move next week."

"Nice, that's great." He frowned, distracted, and after a

moment, added, "Hey...I hope you aren't mad about what happened on Friday." He met my eyes. "You know, flirting with Lina."

That's all? I shook my head and smiled, relieved. "If you guys got together, I'd be really happy for you both. For real."

He got up and hugged me. "Thanks, Anna." He patted my back and let me go. "Speaking of, could you give her my number, or give me hers?"

I laughed. "I'll see if she's interested, first."

And later that night, at the gym, I found out that Lina *was* interested.

"Did you used to have a thing for *Ian*?" I blurted out, after giving Asher's number to her.

She snorted. "Are you asking me because I was kinda cold to you that first time?"

I nodded.

She shook her head. "Sorry about that. Some climbers are pretty 'polyamorous' with their climbing partners. I'm not. Once I find a partner I like, I don't like it when they start climbing with new people." She met my eyes and smiled. "I thought you were taking my climbing partner away, but he was just introducing me to a new one."

I was relieved to hear it, even if I was no longer with him. "I'm not as good as he is, though."

She smiled wolfishly. "Not yet."

* * *

Under Lina's patient coaching, I got better at climbing. *Way* better, if I do say so myself.

It was still scary sometimes, falling from the last move of a boulder problem, or throwing myself into a dyno, even really short ones. Or committing to a move at the top of a 40ft wall when top roping, even knowing that it was pretty darn safe (assuming you follow all the safety checks and don't horse around). But with each successful send, and more importantly, each successful *fall*, I grew more confident. I'd trusted Lina from the first, and I increasingly trusted myself.

When I got good enough, Lina convinced me to take the Intro to Lead Climbing class at our gym. Lead climbing requires you to attach the rope to your harness and pull it up behind you, then clip it into fixed draws that are placed periodically along the way for your protection. There's no rope pre-attached to an anchor at the top, so if you fall, you fall down past where you last clipped in below, and hope that your belayer is paying attention and gives you a soft catch. During the class, I was *required* to fall about eight feet. It was terrifying (I hadn't wanted to let go!), but also incredibly empowering. I knew it might be a while until I was totally chill about falling (or maybe I never would be), but I was slowly but surely getting better at dealing with it.

That was the most important thing in climbing mentality—not the fall itself, but how you approach it. Do you accept that you might fall, and try hard anyway? And when you do fall, do you give up, or do you try again?

* * *

One day in early spring, Cassie asked me if I wanted to try climbing outdoors. She was going to be in New York for work and was planning to tack on a trip to the Adirondacks to climb. She'd never been to "the Dacks" before, but she'd heard good

243

things, and she wanted to take me on my first outdoor trip. Lina told me that she used to go out to the Dacks all the time, so when I mentioned it to Cassie, she suggested that I invite Lina, too. Lina gladly accepted.

The getting-to-know-each-other began well before the trip. Cassie organized a conference call a month before for the three of us to discuss logistics. Cassie loved planning things, so she took charge in researching the climbs, looking into weather, campsites, etc. But Lina was the local, and she possessed the ultimate guidebook and plenty of experience. Watching those two lady crushers interact was absolutely awe-inspiring.

"So you've climbed in the Dacks before? Which areas?" asked Cassie. She was sitting back in her chair and casually sizing Lina up.

"All of them," said Lina, matter of factly. She wasn't bragging; it was just true. "I spent a lot of time climbing there with my husband."

My jaw dropped. "Wait, what? You're married? And you never told me? Where's your husband?"

Lina blinked and looked away, taking in a deep breath, then exhaling slowly. On screen, Cassie's eyes widened. "Wait. Are you *Lina the Crack Queena?*"

Lina nodded and chuckled softly. "Yeah. It's been a while since someone last called me that, though. I haven't been outdoors or on crack since...you know." She sighed. "But I'm ready to get back out there now."

Wait, what? *Lina had been on crack?*

Cassie nodded, her face sympathetic, not at all concerned about Lina's admitted crack habit. "My husband's not a climber, so I never have to worry about him being reckless. I

244

was so sorry to hear about Craig. I never met him, but I have friends who have climbed with him. They said he was a really smart, funny guy."

Lina shook her head and muttered, "Not smart enough to knot his ropes."

I glanced between the two of them, their sad faces, understanding dawning. "Your husband...*died?* While out climbing?"

They both nodded. When Lina didn't say anything more, Cassie explained, "His nickname was Craig the Cragster. He was really well-known in the community. He died in a rappelling accident...maybe a year ago?"

Lina sighed. "Yeah. But the point is, I've been around the Dacks and I know the best places for us to go to get a good mix of stuff, some easy routes for Anna to get her toes wet, then maybe some harder routes for *us* to play on," she said, pointing between the two of them. They began a detailed discussion of which regions to visit, which routes to try, and what gear to bring. From their smiles and playful exchanges, I could see the mutual respect growing between them with each passing minute, proportional to my bewilderment at all of the terms that they were throwing around. I had no idea what I was getting into, but I knew that I looked forward to their in-person meeting, at least. I busily took notes on my phone, vowing to watch every online video about outdoor climbing later that night. And to read up on rappelling accidents so that I could make sure they never happened to me.

* * *

A month later, they finally met in-person, and I was not

disappointed. Two goddesses (one, short and blonde; one, tall and bronze) had come together and mutually recognized one another. They firmly shook hands and smiled, nodding, and with their meeting, my world shined a little bit brighter. I literally shivered in anticipation for the weekend—it was going to be a kick-ass time with those two.

And it really was. By the end, my ass was *so* kicked.

I'd obviously known that it was going to be different from climbing in the gym...but it was *totally* different.

In the gym, the route-setters make it very clear where your hands and feet are supposed to go. The routes are clearly delineated, and the holds, bolts, and ropes are all routinely cleaned and inspected for safety.

When you're outdoors...anything goes. And shit happens.

Lina and Cassie did all the hard work of leading and setting up the top ropes for me to climb more safely...but even so, it was so much more nerve-wracking than climbing in the gym. Instead of cheery, brightly colored holds, all you've got to work with are these tiny little cracks and crevices, which are often difficult to spot and even harder to trust. And *damn* they were sharp sometimes. Some of the routes were a little wet or mossy, and even home to some nasty bugs. Climbing in the shade was freezing, but climbing in the sun was sweltering. Rocks came loose, holds broke, ropes snagged, etc. After a month of watching online videos about the hundreds of ways that things can go wrong, I was slightly rattled by each of these little occurrences, which admittedly, mostly happened to Lina and Cassie on the harder routes that they got on. But the two of them—even with their totally different bodies, experiences, and climbing styles—were unfazed. They calmly dealt with these things, one after another that weekend, and patiently taught me what to do and what not to do, what to look out for, how to stay safe. The more I learned and the more I watched them, the more confident I grew.

Even so, I'd never been more scared before in my life, even when I was only on top rope with two badass women looking out for me.

It got infinitely worse when Lina and Cassie convinced me to try leading a 5.6 face-climb.

On Sunday, towards the end of the day, Lina looked up from the guidebook and ran her gaze up a portion of the wall. Then she turned to me, a twinkle in her eye.

"You know...this 5.6 here is totally doable."

Cassie shaded her face with her hand and regarded the route closely, then glanced my way, a matching twinkle in her own eyes. "You may be right, Lina. It *does* look doable."

I laughed nervously. "Why are you guys looking at me like that?"

They turned and looked at each other, then smiled and nodded, brain waves synced. "You're leading this one," said Lina, counting out several quickdraws.

I shook my head and waved my hands. "Nooo, no no no. I'm fine with just top roping, thanks." I'd led a few times in the gym, but I was *not* ready to lead outdoors, even on a 5.6.

I backed up as Cassie approached, and I cowered against the wall like her prey. She reached out as if to grope me, but only caught my forearms and squeezed them. "Girl, you are *pure muscle now*. So *burly*. So *ready*. You can do this." She smiled reassuringly and pulled me away from the wall to get a better look at the route. "Just try to read the route ahead of time. Strategize about your moves based on the bolt line, and try to find good rest spots. We can help you out if you need.

You'll do fine."

I glanced at the route that Cassie pointed at. "But what about when I get to the top? I've never rigged an anchor before."

"We've shown you how to lower off a bolted anchor without going off belay, and we can keep practicing it down here until you're ready, if you're nervous," said Lina. She stood up from her bag of gear with a fistful of quickdraws. "Why don't you come here and try?"

"Uh, no." I sat down on a rock and frowned at them. They were like two gentle bully sisters—while they looked totally different, their aggressive support of me was fully harmonized.

Cassie crouched down before me and put a hand on my shoulder. Her face softened. "Hey. We're not going to force you to do anything. We would never do that."

Lina assumed a mirrored pose to Cassie's on my other side. "But we know you can do this. And we think it'll be a great learning experience for you. It's a fun route, easily within your capabilities."

I stared at them, alternating between two sets of confident, supportive eyes. They were total badass women, the perfect mix of brains and brawn. Bold, burly, and beautiful.

And they looked at me like I was one of them. I wanted to belong. I wanted to see myself the way that they did. To believe, and to achieve.

So I nodded.

Lina's answering smile rounded out her big, gorgeous cheeks, and Cassie blinded me with her pearly whites, which were really *quite* white. My hesitation evaporated—I wasn't going to let them down.

And I didn't! Honestly, I hardly remember the climb, other

than the fact that whenever my hand found a jug or I reached a bolt, I thanked the climbing gods and sagged with relief. *5.6 my ass.* It probably took me 20 minutes to do the whole route, given frequent small bouts of panic and nonstop pump. I downclimbed and asked for tension often, but I eventually did make it to the top, 55 feet above, and successfully lowered off the anchor.

The only thing that got me through some of those sections was the knowledge that so many others had done it before me, in their own unique ways. I just had to be patient, and look and feel around; nature would always provide. And when I wasn't patient enough to figure out what nature wanted of me, Lina or Cassie were there to give me some beta.

They gave me beta on a lot of things, that weekend. They gave each other beta, too. Cassie and Lina had warmed to each other like they were dear bosom buddies from the third grade. Maybe it was a climber thing, or maybe it was just Cassie. Either way, through real conversations about love and loss, and through nonstop badassery, they quickly came to love each other...and of course, me too. We'd formed an awesome crew of lady crushers. And after that weekend, I was healed, whole, *light*. All because of those two wonderful women.

Well, maybe it was because of the climbing, too. I'd faced and conquered my fear, over and over, and gotten through some tough sections of rock that seemed almost impossible at times.

But nothing's impossible when you've got great friends, *biatch*.

* * *

"So would you do this again?" asked Cassie on our Sunday night drive back to New York City.

I snorted. "Are you kidding me? This was the best weekend of my life."

Cassie tittered. "Better than that non-stop sex buffet you had with Ian that one time?"

I grinned, though my chest tightened. *"Way better.* Chicks before dicks!"

Cassie laughed and chimed in, "Sisters before misters!"

"Uhh...girlfriends before...burlfriends?" said Lina. We all cackled.

"I think *we're* burlfriends. The three of us, not the guys," suggested Cassie.

"I like that," I said. "We're burlfriends. And we should do this every year, an annual burlfriend reunion!"

"YES!" they both shrieked in unison. And then we all howled with laughter and excitement, chatting about where we wanted to go the next year.

It really was the best weekend of my life, spent with two women who were more like family to me than any biological family had ever felt. I was so incredibly grateful for them, and by extension, to Ian, for being the one to introduce me to Lina—and to this world of climbing—and for helping me understand a little bit better, what it meant to grow mentally and physically stronger. I understood him a little bit better, too...and with understanding came respect.

And maybe a bit of love.

* * *

After the revelations of that weekend, I threw myself into my playlists with boundless enthusiasm. I filled them with hope, renewal, and growth, with every wonderful emotion that was bursting in my chest. And my writing was inspired, varied, full of feeling.

I was *not* broken. I was whole and strong, and growing ever stronger.

And one day, a month later, I was invited (INVITED! I hadn't even reached out!) to write a sample piece for Moonslick Mirror, one of the biggest and most famous music news sites. They were well-known for their raw tone and brutally honest reporting, which was 100% my style, and they asked me to write about my favorite band and submit a post by the end of the month.

It'd been a long time since I'd last seen them live, so I checked The Llama People's tour schedule and saw that their next show was in two weeks, in San Francisco. I told Cassie the exciting news and asked if I could crash on her couch. She nearly blew my eardrums with her squealing through the phone.

I thought about texting Ian, but...maybe that was asking for too much.

Everything else was looking up.

Chapter 24

-Ian-

I never thought that I'd be working next to my mom and aunt, selling desserts out of a food truck. But I also never would've thought that the fusion *jiandui* were going to be as popular as they were.

People loved them.

And they loved the story behind my truck name, *Tiantian Desserts*. *Tiantian* could mean multiple things in Mandarin, depending on the tones. Two first tones meant *everyday*; Everyday Desserts. Two second tones meant *sweet*; Sweet Desserts. And one tian, first tone, meant *heaven*. I hoped my dad could taste my creations from there.

But I think people liked the unofficial English street name better: *Ian's Tasty Balls*.

The line for the food truck was often at least three times as long as the truck itself. People lined up, not just for our *jiandui*, but also for the Chinese-inspired flavors of ice cream that we made, including honey pomelo, ginseng, and lychee.

If I hadn't gotten back into climbing, I'm sure I would've gone soft from all of the experimenting that I was doing at

252

home. In fact, my cousin had started to gain weight from being one of my guinea pigs, but he didn't seem to mind—he was all too happy to keep trying my new creations.

My mom and aunt were so much more excited at the idea than I'd thought they'd be. I'd been expecting a lecture on keeping a good job in tech, about needing insurance and a steady income. Instead, they'd given me tips on how to cut costs. They had friends in the restaurant business and knew wholesalers who could help me out. They helped me tweak my recipes until the entire family approved.

I'd been so grateful and relieved to find support and not judgment.

And not only support, but labor. They worked in the truck with me, joking with customers in broken English as they collected money or fried balls. I think they enjoyed coming out of retirement and working part-time. My mom and aunt split shifts so that neither of them had to stand on their feet for a full day, but I was there from 11am till 9pm almost everyday. My customers were insatiable.

On weekends, I parked the van near touristy places: Golden Gate Park on Saturdays and Dolores Park on Sundays. During the week, I stopped around office buildings. I knew well that tech workers loved going on walking meetings and ice cream runs, and I was always there to serve them, to help brighten their days a little. And on Fridays, I parked close to the Stumpstash office, and Cassie always brought a contingent of coworkers out to visit the truck.

At first, I was embarrassed, having gone from technical lead to *tasty balls guy*. But after seeing their delighted faces and hearing their praise, and even their envy, soon all I felt was pride.

In my new role, my former coworkers opened up to me way more than they ever had when I was a tech lead. I learned about their secret fantasies of becoming authors, or of opening their own coffee shops or bars. Even Rich, when he visited once, grudgingly told me that my balls were delicious. We'd had a laugh together about it. Then he told me about his grandfather's cannoli, and how he'd always wished he could sell *those*. I told him to give me a call if he ever wanted tips on how to start his own food truck, though I knew he probably wouldn't need any. Stumpstash was in the business of helping small businesses—all Stumpstashers knew a little bit about how to raise money for our dreams.

My dream? I guess I really liked sharing what I loved with people. There was no better feeling than loving something, being proud of it, and having people discover that they loved it too. Each and every day, I got to spark joy in people and experience that feeling of wonder and appreciation over and over again.

It made me think of Anna, and of the joy she derived from discovering and sharing new music. I understood a little bit more about her decisions, about the tradeoffs she'd made in pursuing a career in music journalism. Reading her posts and listening to her playlists after going through my own career transition...her passion came through more than ever. Her writing had objectively gotten better, too, to the point where I'd felt compelled to send a link to her blog to one of the biggest music news sites out there. They'd thanked me for the tip, but I hadn't heard anything from them after that.

I was genuinely happy that she seemed to be doing so well. I never asked about her, but Cassie gave me occasional updates about her anyway. For example, they'd gone climbing together in the Dacks, along with Lina, and Anna had been brave enough to try leading a 5.6 face-climb. The last time I'd climbed with her, she'd still been too scared to jump down from the top of the bouldering wall! I was glad to hear that she was well on her way to becoming a total crusher.

Cassie also told me that Anna had found her own little place in Jackson Heights. The way she described it made it sound like a closet, but it was *her* closet. She'd finally made it on her own, after all.

Cassie never mentioned anything about Anna's love life, though. I guess she thought that I didn't want to know about it.

She was right.

* * *

"I'll take two Baba specials, please, dark chocolate and lychee!"

"You know I appreciate your business, but you're going to get diabetes if you keep supporting me this much," I told Cassie as I handed her two dark chocolate *jiandui* and two lychee ice creams.

"Worth it!" She dipped a *jiandui* into the ice cream and took a bite, then closed her eyes, licking and smacking her lips. "Ah! So good."

I shook my head and took the next person's order. But Cassie didn't leave, merely stepped to the side of the window.

"What's up, Cass?" I asked as I handed the next customer their coconut *jiandui*.

"You're a big fan of The Llama People, right?"

I glanced over at her. "Yeah? So?" After I'd started listening to Anna's playlists more, I'd actually become a pretty big fan.

255

Drops of Thistle Milk was one of my favorite songs.

"They're going to be in town tomorrow! And I bought two tickets because I was going to go with Michael, but he had a work thing come up." She took another bite of her *jiandui*. "Want to come with me?"

"Really? What time and where? I don't get done till 9pm."

"That's totally fine. I'll text you the details and transfer the ticket to you. Yay!" She carefully balanced the desserts in her hands, then walked back into the building. "See you tomorrow!"

I smiled, excited. In many ways, the food truck business was fun, but usually it was tedious and boring, and I'd been working *a lot* recently. I looked forward to going out and letting loose to some awesome music.

I considered texting Anna about it, for old times sake, but decided against it. There was no reason to message her—nothing would come of it.

Besides, I was going to the show for me. Not for her.

* * *

After closing up the truck, I drove home and took a quick shower—standing in the truck all day near a vat of oil usually didn't leave me smelling the freshest. Then I dressed quickly and ordered a rideshare to the venue. It wasn't too far from my home, but I wasn't sure how trashed Cassie planned to get that evening, and I wanted to be able to keep up.

When I arrived, there was no one waiting in line. It was already almost 11, but as headliner, The Llama People wouldn't be on until at least midnight. Cassie had texted me earlier, telling me to just go inside, so I handed over my ticket to the attendant, stepped inside, and looked around. The venue appeared to be a large gallery, with two stages on either end, connected by a bright, art-lined corridor. Two very different openers played at each stage, the dissonant sounds reverberating down the hall to clash in the middle, breaking out into an open-air area on the side where vendors were selling food and merch.

Though there hadn't been a line, there were quite a few people already dancing or milling about inside. I glanced around the first stage area and didn't see her, so I walked through the art corridor, stopping periodically to examine the paintings on either side. There were Pollock-esque paintings with complex swirls and splatters, optical illusions that played with color and perception, and psychedelic portraits of animals and naked women on mountaintops or in trees. I stopped to look at one of these latter paintings, a closeup of a blonde woman's face. Where her eyes would normally be were golden slits of light. Only the third eye on her forehead had a brilliant blue iris and deep black pupil.

"That one kinda looks like Cassie."

"D'you think—" I paused, recognizing the voice. I turned around to find a woman standing behind me.

"Anna?" She looked...different. Her hair was now a natural black, and shoulder length, much shorter than before. She'd replaced her sapphire nose stud with a thin rose-gold nose ring, and her skin was a gorgeous tan instead of her previous creamy white. She wore a simple black shift dress with thin straps that displayed her now-muscular shoulders to full-effect, and black combat boots. There was something else different though, and I couldn't quite put my finger on it. Whatever it was, it was definitely a good thing.

She smiled and came in for a hug. "Hey, Ian."

I stood stunned while she leaned in and wrapped her arms around my waist. I quickly unfroze and pulled her close, burying my nose in her hair and fighting the urge to inhale deeply. "Are you here for The Llama People?" *Did Cassie arrange this?*

She pulled away, and I reluctantly let her go. "Yeah, I am. I'm writing a piece about them for Moonslick Mirror."

"Hey, congrats! I'm glad they reached out to you."

She cocked her head, puzzled (and cute). "How'd you know they reached out to me?"

I smirked. "It was only a matter of time before they did."

She narrowed her eyes and crossed her arms. "Did you...?"

I dropped the smirk and raised my eyebrows. "Hmm?"

After a quick scan of my face, she shook her head, then said, "Nevermind. How've things been for you?"

Heh, fooled her. "They're actually pretty good. I opened a food truck."

"Yeah, I visited the Stumpstash office today for lunch and Cassie got a chocolate *jiandui* and some lychee ice cream for me. Your balls are so delicious!" So Cassie *hadn't* been looking to get diabetes after all.

"Thanks. I'm glad you licked it. Liked it."

She laughed and winked at me. "I did lick it."

Whoa. She was flirting with me. Blatantly.

So *that* was what was different. The way she carried herself, her playfulness...she was more *confident*. She wasn't even touching me, but the realization brought me to half-mast. I willed it to go away, not wanting to lower myself in the eyes of this new, intimidating, Anna.

Overwhelmed with the need to touch her, I poked her

shoulder. "I see that you've been climbing a lot."

She nodded, then poked my abs and said, "I see that you've been eating a lot."

I put a hand to my stomach. "Hey, I still have day-old challah in there. It's just a little fluffier now." She laughed, and I warmed at the familiar, vibrant sound. The beautiful twinkle in her eyes.

"Have you been here long? Is Cassie here?" I asked. We both turned to look down and around the corridor.

"You know, she said she was coming but I haven't seen her yet." She met my eyes. "We might've just been *Cassied*."

I chuckled and shook my head. *Classic Cassie*. "That's a good way to put it."

"Do you want to walk around and look at more of the art? Or maybe get a drink?" she asked.

"A drink sounds good. It's been a long day, and it'd be good to be served by someone else for a change." We walked towards the bar across from the far stage.

"How do you like the food truck business?" she asked.

"I actually like it a lot more than I thought I would. I get creative license over what I make. I meet and serve customers of different ages and backgrounds and get to see their joy and satisfaction with my product as they eat it." I chuckled. "It's very different from software engineering."

She regarded me curiously. "Are you glad you made the switch?"

"Yeah, I am. It's hard work, but I really like being able to share something that I'm proud of with other people." I glanced sideways at her. "Maybe it's a little bit like what you've been trying to do with music writing. Wanting to share your joy with others, doing it in a way that's creative and fun."

She smiled to herself and nodded. "Yeah, I think so, too."

We arrived at the bar and I ordered a whiskey-ginger. Anna asked for the same.

"So what about you? How are things in New York?"

"They're great, actually. Stumpstash is still fun. I've got my own place. And Lina's now *my* climbing partner."

"Yeah, I heard that you guys went to the Adirondacks together with Cassie. How was that?"

"It was...thrilling. Terrifying. Inspiring. I'm so glad that Cassie invited me and Lina. We're going to go on a climbing trip together every year from now on."

"That's great! You've really gotten into it."

She smiled at me and tapped me on the chest. "Thanks to you!"

I shrugged, grinning. "You can lead a girl to a wall, but you can't make her lead a climb."

She chuckled and playfully slapped my arm. "You totally *made me* top rope that first time, though."

I guess I had. "Well—"

"$20." The bartender placed our drinks in front of us.

"I've got it," said Anna, reaching for her wallet.

"Nope, I've got it. You're a guest." I pulled out my credit card and handed it to the bartender.

She smiled, uncharacteristically chill about letting me pay. She picked up the glass and raised it towards me before taking a sip. "Thanks, babe."

Babe? It was a simple, friendly endearment, but my penis twitched again at her confident delivery. I carefully leaned into the bar and slowly signed the credit card slip.

We picked up our drinks and walked back towards the art corridor to keep talking. "So then it sounds like things are really looking up for you. I'm really excited that you're writing for Moonslick Mirror, too."

"You know, it was definitely surprising to me that they just kinda reached out." She narrowed her eyes at me. "I get the feeling that *someone* might've told them about me."

I looked up at the rafters, whistling tunelessly. She slapped my arm and exclaimed, "I knew it!"

I chuckled. "I was just speeding things up."

She stopped walking, turned, and met my eyes. "I really appreciate it, Ian. I appreciate... everything you've done for me."

I shrugged. "I just emailed them. You're the one who did all of the hard work and wrote such amazing pieces."

She shook her head and looked down at her drink. "I mean, more than that...back when we were together. I...you were good to me."

I lifted her chin until we locked eyes once more, then apologized the way I should have, months ago. "No, I was the biggest jerk to you, a complete asshole. You shared so much with me and I...I used it against you. I'm so sorry."

She lifted her hand as if to cup my face, but casually dropped it to my shoulder instead. "That's—I know you were just angry because I was being immature. I said some terrible things, too. You obviously have your own dreams and desires, just like I do. And I'm sure your family must be great, to have produced someone like you."

"I mean, my family *is* pretty great. But that doesn't excuse the things I said to you. You're...you deserve better."

Her eyes were wide, earnest and searching...her pink glossy lips only inches away.

If only she hadn't left my apartment. If only my dad hadn't

passed away. If only I hadn't moved. If only...

But she was there before me, in the flesh. In the moment.

I let out a slow, shaky breath, whispering her name and tracing her lips with my thumb. Her eyelids gradually lowered as I brought my face closer to hers.

Then the crowd erupted, and people began streaming towards the bigger stage, jostling us in their haste.

The Llama People had begun their set.

I slowly straightened and dropped my hand, taking a step away and shooting her a friendly smile. "Let's go get a good spot."

She glanced at me sideways, but didn't say anything, just took the hand I offered and followed me into the crowd.

I didn't want to push my luck with Anna. It was clear that we'd both changed over the months, both grown humbler and more mature. More into ourselves.

It was great that we were here, together, and on good terms again. For now, that was enough.

Chapter 25

-Anna-

My heart was pounding. Why hadn't he kissed me? I nearly stood up on my toes to finish the job, but he'd taken my hand and pulled me into the huge crowd of people. An exquisite, comforting warmth blossomed in my chest at the familiar feel of his rough, callused hand, fingers interlaced with mine. I held on tight and refused to let go, even as we slipped between tightly-packed clusters of people, until we finally stopped just a few feet in front of the stage.

The Llama People opened their set with a fast-paced song (*We Come in Fleece*) and people were jumping up and down and side-to-side to the beat. We joined in with everyone else, joyfully bouncing, waving our arms and shaking our hips. The Llama People were masterful performers, and their live shows were always incredible. Letting loose and dancing my cares away to their music never failed to rejuvenate me.

They always started out with their most upbeat songs to get your heart racing, to trick you—maybe your heart is beating so fast from love, or lust, or joy. Maybe anger. All you know is that your blood is pumping, your lungs are pulling in air, and you're more than a little alive.

And once you've broken a sweat, worked up a lather, they bring it down a notch. You've been launched into the air like a feather, but your descent back to earth is gradual, easy sailing, whimsical. A slow, satisfying exhale.

And when you finally touch the earth again, you settle into the ground...and sensations awaken, the caress of grass and soft dirt against your skin, the beautiful brush of existence. You are where you belong.

My body hummed with energy, infused by the band and the excitement of the crowd. I inhaled the ambient marijuana smoke, then breathed out fully and slowly, willing all conscious thoughts to leave my mind. And I danced, and I *moved*, only occasionally aware of Ian next to me when we brushed against each other. Mostly, I ignored him, and he thankfully left me alone. It was good to see him again, but I'd come to the show for me, not for him.

I closed my eyes and experienced the show to the fullest.

But when the music finally began to slow, I glanced over at Ian...and was surprised. He was losing himself as much as I was. He wasn't staring at me or looking bored, like I was afraid of, and he hadn't tried to get my attention or break my flow. His eyes were focused on the band, and he was smiling and dancing with feeling.

He was there for himself, too.

I placed my hand on his arm and smiled warmly at him. He grinned back, his expression one of pure, unadulterated joy. A perfect reflection of my own.

He'd found passion. And I'd found strength. We'd completed ourselves, and in some ways, each other.

Here was someone who could understand me, support me

and push me, and whom I could support and push in return. Someone who could be part of the family that I'd only just begun to form.

Maybe there was a chance for us after all.

My heart soared with gladness, lightened by all of these thoughts...

...and then it dove headlong, straight into lust.

I wanted, needed the resonance between us to go deeper.

The song slowed. An electronic piano began to play, sensual and shimmering, and a gut-deep bassline threaded through the chords. Bodies paired off and swaying couples emerged from among the crowd. I met Ian's eyes and watched his eyelids slowly lower as I positioned myself in front of him.

And instead of dancing for myself, I danced for him.

I swayed my hips from side to side, then threw him a sultry look over my shoulder, pushing my hair over the other shoulder to expose my back and neck. I raised my arms above my head like twin serpents, then slid my hands back down my chest, past the curves of my breasts, until they rested on my thighs. Keeping my knees bent, I twirled my hips in little circles, forming one bigger circle, inviting him to touch me. After a long moment, he accepted the invitation and melded his body to mine, following my ass with his hips, pressing tight against me. I could feel him growing hard, and my body vibrated at the contact. I slipped my hands up behind his neck and into his hair, holding him close as he slid his hands down my thighs until he reached my bare legs, then back up to cup my breasts. Breathing shallow, I shivered with pleasure, wanting so much more.

I turned my head up to meet his eyes. "Bathroom time?"

He laughed, louder and with more mirth than I'd ever heard

him laugh before. Then he kissed me, oh so deeply, squeezing one breast with his hand and pinching my nipple through my dress, trailing his other hand down, down, then up to stroke my wetness with a finger. *Oh*! I broke away and took his hand, conscious of many eyes upon us, then pulled him through the crowd.

We had to wait in line for a minute because there were only a few single-stall bathrooms in the venue, but eventually, it was our turn. Ian ushered me in and locked the door behind him.

Ah, the bathroom. It was definitely a live-music-show-after-midnight kind of bathroom, not a private apartment bathroom or a wedding venue bathroom. A public-ass bathroom, with empty toilet paper rolls and graffiti everywhere, and all the wet and nasty smells that you can imagine.

But we didn't care. As soon as he'd locked the door and turned around, I threw myself into his arms and kissed him as fiercely as I could. He leaned against the door and lifted me up by my ass until I could wrap my legs around his hips. Even after rushing through the crowd and waiting in line, he was still rock-hard for me. I squirmed against his chest and pushed my hips against his jeans, seeking friction, any friction.

He broke off the kiss, breathing hard. "You're not wearing panties again."

I giggled, then trailed my tongue down his warm, thick neck. "Make love to me, Ian."

He lowered me until my feet were on the floor again, then turned to lean me against the door. He sank to one knee and slid my dress up my to my waist, then lifted my left leg up over his shoulder.

And then he went to *work*.

I breathily whispered his name and held his head as he dipped his tongue inside me. His hands cupped my ass as he savored me, licking me up like the most delicious bowl of melted ice cream. He twirled his tongue on the cherry on top and pulled it into his mouth, nibbling and sucking gently. And his facial hair...*oh god*, how I'd missed his facial hair. It was almost too much.

Still swirling and twirling his tongue, he trailed his fingers up my leg and tentatively slipped a finger inside, just to the first knuckle, making me clench against him and beg for more. He added a second finger, then slipped them in deeper this time, all the way in. "Fuck, *Ian*." I almost came then and there.

But I held back. I wanted him to come with me.

I gently pushed his head away and lowered my leg, then took his hand and pulled him up so that he was standing in front of me. I lifted my leg and placed it on his arm, pulling him tight against me. "You know the drill."

He chuckled, putting one hand on my hip and one hand against the door. "Am I pulling out or buying you Plan B?"

"Neither, you're buying me *dinner*."

His breathy laugh tickled my cheek as he unzipped his pants and sank into me.

I nearly came at the sensation of being filled by him again. My leg was shaking so badly, I could barely stand. I guess he could tell, because he lifted my other leg too and held me against the door, supporting me as he thrust in and out, in and out, slowly at first, then harder and more frantically as I felt myself coming more and more undone. I cupped both sides of his face with my hands, our foreheads nearly touching, our panted breaths mingled and shared. We stared into each other's eyes, every thrust so deep and fulfilling, the intensity multiplied by the knowledge that our pleasure was fully mutual. I wanted him to see how he made me feel, to watch my face as he unraveled me. And I wanted the same from him.

Never before had fucking in a bathroom felt so intimate.

Just as The Llama People ended their song *Drops of Thistle Milk*, and right before the crowd erupted, I screamed with violent pleasure as Ian spilled himself inside of me. He kissed me then, swallowing my cries, our tongues joining like our bodies below.

I came so hard that my ears rang and my head felt light. I'd never before felt so wholly sated, physically, emotionally, and spiritually.

I fucking *loved* The Llama People that night.

* * *

I ended up going back to Ian's place and not sleeping on Cassie's couch. I texted her to let her know, and all she texted back was the sweat droplets emoji. *Oh, Cassie.*

As per our MO, we made love at least twice more that night, until it was well into morning and not night anymore.

I woke up wrapped in his arms, feeling happier and more relaxed than I had in a long time. Well...since we'd last done the same. He was already awake, leisurely running his fingers through my hair.

"Good morning," he said, brushing his lips against my forehead.

"Good morning," I replied, kissing his pecs. *Mmm*, pecs.

We held each other for a moment, willing the haziness of

sleep to remain...not wanting to deal with reality.

Finally, Ian said, "I guess I'm not going to work today."

I glanced at the clock. It was noon. "You can still make it."

He rolled onto his back and pulled me onto him. "I don't think so. I already texted my mom and aunt and told them that I wasn't going to open the truck today."

"What a lazy guy." I kissed the tip of his nose, then pushed myself up and off of his chest. "When do you have off?"

"Mondays. Though I usually only work until 5 PM on Sundays."

I slipped my feet off the bed and stood. "Then let's go."

"Where to? You don't want to just stay in bed all day?" He sat up to watch me, pouting a little.

I rolled my eyes and pulled on his hand. "No, come on, let's go. You're taking *me* to work today."

He raised an eyebrow at me, but finally started to get out of bed. "Do you know how to make *jiandui*?"

"My dad's was better than yours, that's for sure."

"Oh ho ho...now we'll have to see," he said, catching me and kissing me tenderly on the lips. I beamed up at him, then let him go to bend down and pick up my clothes.

We hurriedly got dressed and drove the truck to his Sunday parking spot, not far from Dolores Park. A crowd had already gathered there, and people cheered as the truck pulled up.

"Sorry about that, everyone!" he said out the window. "I'm a bit short-staffed today, so I had to pick up some help. Everyone, this is Anna."

I stuck my head out the window and waved. "Hello!"

Several people said, "Hi, Anna!" and waved back.

Then Ian *actually* got to work, and so did I.

* * *

"Wow, you can make a killing on desserts."

Ian nodded while slurping up his ramen. "Yup. I did the math. If sales keep going like this, I'll be making close to what I was making as a tech lead."

"That's...that's crazy! Why can't music journalism be like that?" I bit into my hard-boiled egg, then followed it up with a spoonful of miso broth. Ian had driven the van back home and we'd walked over to a nearby ramen food truck.

"Well, the pay is great, but I have to stand in that hot truck for hours each day, soaking up oil and chatting up customers. And I spend my free time trying new recipes, working on marketing, replying to online reviews. It's a lot, but it's worth it." As he spoke, his last slice of chashu pork slipped out of his chopsticks and fell onto the pavement. His sad little frown tugged on my heartstrings, and on the corners of my lips.

"How'd you get the idea?" I asked, placing a slice of my chashu in his bowl.

Ian's eyebrows shot up at me, giving me a *Really?* look before he broke into a huge grin and devoured the pork. "Cassie and Michael gave me some shrooms."

I nearly choked on my ramen. I drank some water to try to wash it down, then coughed even more as Ian patted my back. "Seriously?"

He nodded, contemplating my face. "Yeah. It gave me some perspective about the things in life that have really brought me joy. Definitely wasn't building apps." His eyes bore into mine before lowering back to his bowl. "I thought a lot about my past, my family...my dad. Boston cream donuts were my his favorite, so they're really nostalgic for me. But I wanted to make desserts that were uniquely mine. Thus, the balls were born."

"Definitely sounds like you've done some shrooms," I replied, smiling at the passion in his words.

He shoveled the last of his ramen noodles into his mouth, then placed his bowl and chopsticks down. We sat in silence for a moment, but it was sweet and companionable. Like old times.

Until Ian blurted,"You're only here for the weekend...right?"

"Yeah," I answered softly. "I was just here to see the show."

"I see." He took my hands in both of his, brought them to his lips, and planted a soft kiss on each. "I'm really glad I got to see you." His smile was bittersweet.

"Me too." I blinked away my tears and smiled back, then slowly withdrew my hands and stood up. "I should probably go. My flight is really early tomorrow morning, and I want to start working on my writeup while the show is still fresh in my mind."

He nodded and stood up. "Okay."

We brought our bowls back to the ramen guy and thanked him for the meal, then walked back to Ian's place and got into his car. He drove me to Cassie's house, silently holding my hand for the entire ride, gently kneading it with his thumb. When we arrived in front of Cassie's, he parked the car and got out, then came around to open the door for me. I stepped out and leaned into his arms, and we held each other for an all-too-brief moment, just long enough for me to breathe in his scent, the old familiar smell of him mixed with the aroma of oil and pastries, and imprint this new Ian's scent in my memories. Then he stepped back and kissed me again, oh so sweetly, one last time.

"Goodbye, Anna," he whispered.

"Goodbye, Ian."

He let me go, his sad little smile mirroring my own. I reluctantly took a step back.

The front door to the house opened and Cassie stepped out.

"Hey, guys! What's going on?"

"Hey, Cass. I'm leaving," Ian said, walking back around to the driver's side.

She stepped further down the stairs. "Hey, wha—I MADE MARGARITAS—"

Ian waved at us both as he drove away.

I looked up at Cassie and smiled, tears rolling down my nose. "Thanks, Cassie."

She flew down the stairs and engulfed me in her arms.

Chapter 26

-Ian-

Monday was my day off, so I went to visit my mom and aunt. As soon as I walked through the door, though, I could tell that something was wrong.

My mom was smiling too much. Much too much.

"Ian, how was yesterday?" she asked. She took my arm and led me to the backyard, where she and my aunt were cracking sunflower seeds and eating the kernels of meat.

"It was fine." I decided not to say more than that, just sat and reached for a seed from my aunt's pile. She slapped my hand away.

"Your *Ayi* and I walked past the park yesterday and saw the truck there." She studied my face, smiling coyly. "Why were you working?"

I narrowed my eyes. "*Ma*. Were you spying on me?"

"Me? Nooooo." She adamantly waved her hand back and forth.

"*Ma*. Did you see her?"

My mom leveled a look at me, then turned her attention back at her pile of seeds. "Is she your girlfriend?"

My aunt playfully elbowed me in the ribs. "She was *very pretty.*"

"No, she's an old friend from New York." I reached for a seed from my mom's pile, but she slapped my hand away, too. "*Ow.* She was just visiting for the weekend."

"Just for the weekend?" my mom asked. She paused in her eating to study my face. I took the opportunity to snatch a seed.

"Yeah. She's probably back in New York by now." I cracked my seed open, only to find that it was empty. I sighed and threw it in the pile of husks.

My mom was silent for a moment. "Was she the one that you told your *Ba* about? You had coffee together, you lived together...that one?"

I nodded wryly, unsurprised that my mom's memory issues weren't an issue at all when it came to potential brides.

My mom simpered. "I knew she'd be good for you." At my puzzled expression, she unhelpfully clarified, "*Her face.* I told you she had a good face. You two are good together."

I shook my head. I'd never understand my mom's mysterious ways. "But it's over now. We're just friends."

My aunt snorted and cracked another sunflower seed between her teeth. "Liar."

"What? It's true."

My mom and aunt both tittered and shook their heads before my mom continued, "We saw how you two looked at each other. How you made jokes together even as you worked side by side. She couldn't stop looking at you and burned herself with hot oil, *twice.*"

My aunt added, "It didn't look like it was over *to me.*"

Such romantics. I sighed again and rubbed my face. "*Ma,*

274

Ayi, she's back in New York now, and I'm here."

They exchanged a look, then turned their eyes back to me. "*So?*" they asked in unison.

"There's something called a *phone*, Ian," said my mom. "You can call people with it."

Well no wonder I hadn't wanted to date Lina.

* * *

I paced back and forth in my room, smacking my phone against my hand with each step.

Should I call her?

Would she even want to talk to me?

What would I say?

More importantly, what was the *point*? We were living on two different coasts. And she was different now...stronger, more intimidating. Independent. Would she even want to hear from me?

It felt a little like I was psyching up for a big move on the bouldering wall. *Don't overthink it.* Just do it.

Before I could chicken out, I tapped on the phone icon under her name.

And then I chickened out and promptly hung up. Shit.

I texted Anna an excuse. *Hey, sorry about that. I just accidentally called you. I was trying to call my Ayi and your name is above hers.*

A few minutes later, she texted back, *No worries.*

I waited...but there was nothing else.

Sighing, I put my phone down and went to make dinner.

* * *

275

A few days later, I was surprised to find an email from Anna.

Hey Ian,

I'm sending you a draft of my writeup. I can't post it to my own blog yet because it's for Moonslick Mirror, but I wanted to share it with you before it's published (if it's ever published). Thanks so much for reaching out to them on my behalf. And thanks again for the weekend—it was wonderful to see you.

Cheers,

Anna

I opened the draft and read the following:

The Llama People: Not Your Mama's Alpacas Tour is their most spiritual and dominant yet

By: Anna Tang

The Llama People (TLP) have been around for years. They've been lurking in your fields, munching on your grass, and spitting on your children since 2006.

I, hipster that I was, first discovered TLP that very year in high school. Of course, it was love at first listen. I was a DJ for the school radio station, and I nearly got fired for playing two of their earliest and raunchiest hits, Your Ass is Grass *and* Shear Me Out. *It was gratifying to hear the principal tell me that I wasn't allowed to play music with such sexually gratuitous lyrics, then ask me for the artist's name to "make sure that no one else played their music." I caught her humming the tune to* Camelid Toe *a week later.*

Back then, their sound was raw and outrageous,

brutally erotic, and perfect for those early years of adulthood.

Their sound has since gone through epochs of evolution.

In 2009's Llama Kush, they introduced stronger elements of Latin American polyrhythms and syncopation into their sound, and their songs soon invaded salsa clubs around the city. One could not escape Bachata Night without hearing Como Se Llama at least once. But their most popular track off of this album, the slow and haunting Dam and Her Cria, truly allowed singer Maria Lopez to shine, with her soothing vocals and poignant humming. The song inspired any number of mugs, t-shirts, and Mother's Day cards, and no doubt induced millions of people to call their mothers that Sunday.

With Nuzzle My Fuzzle (2011), TLP reassured fans everywhere that sex was still on the menu. But unlike the wanton, provocative lyrics and sounds from their early years, the music was sensual and intimate, and Lopez's voice caressed deep into our ears and left us yearning for more, especially with their track, 30 Minutes on Top.

Then in 2014, TLP devastated fans everywhere with the Pack it Up tour. Fans were dually disappointed with the uninspired pop lyrics and catchy, but basic, melodies and beats. TLP announced that it would be their last album, and fans were both glad and disappointed that Lopez and TLP's keyboard guru, John Matthews, were headed into early retirement so that they could start a family together.

They spent five years in relative privacy, only occasionally spotted holding hands with their adorable daughter, Mia, and their son, Milo, as well as on date nights at romantic nooks around New York City.

But after five quiet years...they're back. And they've brought Drops of Thistle Milk.

Not Your Mama's Alpacas is more playful and energized than any of their previous albums, bringing in more synths, percussion instruments, and strings than ever before. Matthews introduces us to a unique orgling sound, which mingles with Lopez' otherworldly vocals to transport us to the terraformed hills of Mars, where the grass is plentiful and the llamas are looking to fuck.

This album is the magnum opus that fans have been waiting for.

Bottle-fed hearkens back to Dam and her Cria, but the Cria is all grown up with a cria of her own, and the lyrics are even more maternal and heartrending than before. No doubt there was another major spike in their merch sales in May.

Fiber of My Being tackles existential dread and loneliness, but the exquisite harmony between Lopez and Matthews belies the desolation of the lyrics. The essence of the song is perfectly captured in Lopez' last line: In your hands, my fleece is spun to lustrous threads, and though I lie bare, I smile at your warmth.

Drops of Thistle Milk is the most sensual, arousing track on the album, and very likely of all time. Full stop. The crisp percussion sounds build and overlay thick, warm synths, and Lopez dissolves panties with her intimate purring. The beat builds slowly until it crescendos into a climax of epic proportions, then drops *back, slowly fading, shimmering in an afterglow of sound. My skin prickles every time I hear it.*

But while the digital album is amazing, it merely hints at the profound experiences that await you at their live show. I cannot emphasize it enough—the enchantment of their music needs to be experienced live.

I literally orgasmed at their show after Drops of Thistle Milk *finished.* Literally. *Not a fakegasm, not even an eargasm. A real, mind-shattering orgasm. As in,* my labia twitched uncontrollably as a wonderful, lovely man filled me up with his baby juice.

And it was the most beautiful and gratifying moment of my life.

I'd grown up listening to TLP's sexually explicit lyrics and their stimulating beats, but never had I truly understood the magic that their music carried until I'd experienced it in this way, in the way that they'd surely intended.

The things they sing about—love, lust, loss, and family—it really is everything.

So I urge you to go. Go to their show and bring someone you cherish. Someone you want to make magic with. Someone you'll regret not making love to, just one more time.

And fuck him or her (or them!) in the bathroom as Lopez and Matthews croon and work their spell.

It will heal you.

I reread the last several lines again. Had she really just submitted a piece urging people to have sex at a show?

Was our brief encounter in the bathroom as miraculous and

touching for her as she'd so poetically described?

Did she feel the same way about me that I felt about her?

Chapter 27

-Anna-

For a full day after I hit send, I compulsively checked my email every ten minutes.

After 24 hours, with still no response, I reduced the frequency of checking to within a normal range—once every *twenty* minutes.

After two entire days of radio silence, I stopped checking. Instead, I cut and pasted over my favorite photo of us so that it was actually a llama man with fluffy white tufts of hair, long ears, killer lashes, and big square teeth who had escorted me to Cassie's wedding ceremony.

Ass.

On Saturday morning, unable to deal with his total lack of response any longer, I picked up my phone to text him.

At just that moment, my phone vibrated with a text from you-know-whom. *Are you at home right now?*

My pride disintegrated and my fingers flew across the screen to immediately text back, *Yes what's up did you read my piece?*

As soon as I hit send, there was a quiet *knock-knock-knock* at my door.

I lifted my head and stared down the short hallway to the door. *No way.*

Heart racing, I tossed my phone to the bed, then jumped up and ran to the door.

With one quick glance through the peephole to verify what, in my heart, I already knew, I unbolted the door with shaky fingers and threw open the door.

Ian picked me up in his arms and pushed me against the wall, crushing his mouth to mine. I did my best facehugger impression and wrapped my arms around his neck, my legs around his hips, and kicked the door closed behind him.

He'd come for me.

* * *

Ian was fast asleep, his head on my lap, his warm, naked body curled up around my legs. I trailed my fingers along the tips of his ears, watching his chest rise and fall as he evenly inhaled and exhaled.

I thought back to months ago, about that fight where everything had fallen apart.

It had seemed so intractable at the time...all of the pain that we held, the anger, the fear, had seemed like too much for either one of us to handle.

Stroking his warm, bristly cheeks, it didn't seem so impossible for us now. We were more sure of ourselves, and of each other. Of our dreams.

I smiled and kissed Ian's forehead.

He slowly stirred, then opened his eyes and looked up at me. I smiled and kissed his forehead again.

"Hi, sleepyhead."

"Anna," he mumbled, stretching and yawning. "Should I go get you some Plan B?" He sleepily smirked.

"Hah. Actually, I got an IUD a couple months back so that I could stop stuffing pills in my face." It helped that Stumpstash's insurance policies were so good.

He stopped stretching—that woke him up real fast. It woke *Mini Ian* up real fast, too. "So now...I can come inside you all I want?" He turned his head and kissed my thigh.

I giggled. "Only if I let you."

He pulled me down to the bed and we playfully wrestled, our laughter echoing in the tiny room. His full weight settled on top of me, pinning me against the bed. I wriggled my ass against his growing erection and sighed.

We needed to talk before we got too distracted. "Ian."

"Yes, Anna?" he replied, kissing my neck.

"Can we talk for a sec?"

He kissed my neck once more, then drew back and simply held me. "Sure. What's up?"

I'd been the one to ask him to talk, but I hesitated for a moment before whispering, "What are you doing here?"

He brushed his fingers along my thigh. "I came to see you."

I turned in his arms so that I could study his face. "Why?"

He stroked my jaw with his fingers, the tender feeling in his eyes unmistakable. "Because I want to be with you."

I inhaled sharply. "Be with me? In New York?"

He kissed my shoulder and trailed his fingers up my abs to circle my breast. "Yes, be with you, in New York."

I grabbed his hand—we needed to focus. "But you live in San Francisco."

"So? I can sell *jiandui* anywhere. Or get a different job." He

283

shrugged.

"But your family is there."

"They have each other. And I can always go visit."

"But that's...silly. You can't just move here for me." *Right?*

"Why not? I don't really care where I am, I care about who I'm with." He kissed my forehead. "And I want to be with you."

"You don't want to try long-distance first? Like...calling and stuff?"

He rolled his eyes and chuckled softly. "Wow, you're all the same. I *am* aware of how phones work, if that's what you're about to tell me. But no, I'd rather do in-person, if you're okay with it." His thumb gently stroked my cheek. "We've been through enough together for me to know that you're worth it. *More* than worth it."

Tears sprang to my eyes as I scanned his face. "Why?" I whispered, finally allowing hope to seep in.

He smiled and kissed my left eyelid. "Because you're beautiful."

My right eyelid. "Because you're fierce."

The tip of my nose. "Because you're hilarious."

Finally, my lips. "Because you're *my* Chinese-American dream."

Tears slipped out of the corners of my eyes, and he lovingly wiped them away with his thumbs. He smiled and kissed me again, sweetly, tenderly, and I arched up into him, holding his head, trying my best to devour him.

But after a moment, he broke our kiss to finish his thought. "A lot has changed during these past few months. I think we've both grown a little more into ourselves, and I would love to spend some time getting to know the new you, the old you...all of you. I want to do things the right way this time, to make things last. Will you let me?"

I nearly cracked my head on his chin with how vigorously I nodded. We both laughed, and he pulled me against him and held me as I cried into his chest. He stroked my hair and whispered soothing sounds as tension drained out of me, replaced by excitement for the future. Hope.

I abruptly pushed away from him and sat up. "Nope, I'm moving to San Francisco."

"What? Why?" He pushed himself up on his elbow to look at me.

I wiped my tears away, determined. "I'm done with New York. It's been over eight years, it's time for me to try someplace new. There's nothing keeping me here, and I basically live in a closet, for goodness sake." I stroked his jaw and added, "Besides, then I can see Cassie more often, and maybe...maybe meet your family."

He studied my face, then asked the safer question first. "What about your job? Stumpstash? Will it affect your music writing at all?"

"I mean, maybe. It's hard to tell how things will change. But like you, I can find another job, and I'm pretty sure that I can write about music from anywhere. And I'll have fresh material when I discover local bands and stuff. I could use a change of scenery." San Francisco had been really fun when I'd last visited, and the prospect of exploring a new place filled me with excitement, not sadness.

Then he tackled the real question. "Are you...sure you want to deal with my family? I have a big family."

I smiled and nodded. "If they're your family, and you tell me that they're great, then I...I trust you." If he loved his family, then I was sure I could learn to do so, too.

He held my hand. "You sure about this?"

I settled back down into his arms, sighing contentedly. It felt right. "I'm sure."

* * *

So we packed up my shit and I moved to San Francisco a month later.

Saying goodbye to New York hadn't been that hard. I organized one big going away party for my friends and acquaintances in the music biz, which Asher helped with. He even DJed, and the thoughtfulness of his set nearly brought me to tears. I was nervous when Ian said he'd come, but they shook hands without breaking each others fingers, and Ian even danced and asked Asher about his music. Thank goodness.

Saying goodbye to Lina was another story. I convinced her to continue the tradition that I'd had with Cassie, of Sunday night Google Hangouts calls. Besides, we'd promised to do at least one outdoor climbing trip together each year, and I meant to hold us to it—I was super stoked for Burlfriendfest II. But even with that to look forward to, Lina was annoyed at Ian for depriving her of yet another climbing partner. She was incredibly hot and amazing at climbing, though, so I was confident that she'd have a replacement for me in no time. Based on how she and Asher had traded stares during the party, I not-so-secretly hoped it would be him.

I had to quit my job at Stumpstash. Ian had been able to transfer offices as an engineer, but as an office admin, I couldn't just transfer to the other office if they didn't have an opening for me. They didn't, so I quit. My coworkers were sad to see me go, but they promised to follow along on my music writing career, and to stop by Ian's food truck when they were in San Francisco.

I still planned on finding another job in San Francisco, but in the meantime, Moonslick Mirror ended up buying my piece (they'd called it "utterly charming and deeply reflective of [my] soulful connection to the band") and had asked me to become a regular contributor. I'd definitely be okay without another job for a few months.

And I found an apartment with some roommates that wasn't too far from Ian's place. The rent was no better or worse than in New York, but it felt good to take care of myself and have breathing room while still having him close by. I liked my new roommates, too, and was unsurprised to find that they were all climbers.

And Ian and I got to know each other at the slow and leisurely pace that he'd promised. We'd started out all wrong before, but now I could sense that we'd have a long time to learn everything about each other. I was in no rush, and neither was he.

But even so, I knew that, sooner or later, I'd have to meet his family.

The thought still scared me a little.

* * *

It happened a few months later.

"How do I look?"

"Like a little skank."

I playfully slapped Ian's arm, then asked him again, "How do I *look*?"

He kissed my temple, eyes laughing. "Beautiful, as usual."

I smoothed my sundress and stared at the house before me. We were at Ian's aunt's house in Dolores Heights, and it was huge, daunting, and likely full of Chinese people, given that it was his mom's birthday party.

He took my hand and gently pulled me up the steps. "C'mon. You'll do great. They're all basically me, just older or younger or more feminine."

"Not more masculine?" I joked.

He cocked an eyebrow at me. "Is it even possible to get manlier than this?" he said, alternately flexing his pecs at me.

I shook my head, chortling, then followed him up the steps and through the door.

"Ayi?" he called. "*Ma?*"

We stepped into the house, took off our shoes, and looked around.

The walls were a simple white, the floors and furnishings hardwood, all matching golden oak. The floor by the entryway was littered with dozens of pairs of shoes, the hooks on the walls overloaded with colorful sweaters and jackets. I swallowed a flash of panic at the thought of meeting that many people.

They were just people. *Ian's* people.

I took a deep breath and walked further in.

There were voices coming from outside, from the backdoor in the kitchen. It sounded like everyone was in the backyard. At the familiar sounds of loud Mandarin, the savory smells of grilled meat, soy and garlic...my stomach clenched. I needed a moment to collect myself. "Hey, I'm going to use the bathroom first," I said.

"Do you want me to wait here for you?" Ian asked, concerned.

I faked a little smile. "No, it's okay. You should go greet your family. I'll come out in a bit."

He hesitated, then nodded. "Okay. Bathroom's down the hall and on the left." He walked towards the backdoor. "If you want me to come back in or anything, just text or call."

"Thanks, babe." I silently crept into the bathroom and closed the door.

Unlike the rest of the house, the bathroom was papered with little yellow flowers. A plain, grassy green shower curtain enclosed the tub, and the toilet had a matching green chenille lid cover. There were several toothbrushes and sets of toiletries by the sink—more reminders of how many people awaited me outside.

I lifted the toilet lid, peed, then sat for a few minutes, trying to prepare myself for all of the questions and judgment that were likely to come. I didn't want to face—

The door opened, and Ian's mom stepped in, froze. Our eyes met for one agonizing moment.

Then she slowly backed out and silently closed the door.

I stared at the closed door and tried not to panic. His mom. She'd just caught me on the toilet. With my panties around my ankles. Then backed out without saying anything, like Homer into the bushes.

I focused on breathing as I hurriedly got up and wiped, then tried to flush the toilet. But to my utter horror, it only dribbled and got slightly fuller.

There was a knock at the door. "Anna, *na matong huai le.*" It was still Ian's mom, and she was speaking Mandarin to me. Surprisingly, that part of my brain wasn't as rusted over and full of cobwebs as I'd thought. I easily understood her to say,

"Anna, that toilet is broken."

"Really?!" Shit.

"If you open the door, I can help you."

"Ah, it's okay, *Ayi*, I'll try to fix it." While she wasn't my aunt, I remembered that it was what I was supposed to call her in Mandarin.

I lifted the toilet tank cover to see if there was anything wrong. The tank had water and the fill-valve-flapper thingy seemed to be working just fine. It was probably just a clog in the toilet then, but I didn't see a plunger anywhere. Damn.

My first time interacting with Ian's family and I'd clogged their toilet? I hadn't even met them yet and already I was humiliating myself. No doubt I'd be a complete laughingstock for years to come, known to them only as Ian's weird girlfriend who didn't know how to use a toilet. A tiny part of me knew that it was ridiculous to think so, but I couldn't stop the tears from pooling in my eyes as I struggled to stem the flow of negative thoughts.

Another knock on the door, then Ian's mom's voice again. "Anna, let me help you."

I knew I couldn't do anything about the clog. So I blinked away my tears, squared my shoulders, and threw open the door to find Ian's mom still standing there. She was a full head shorter than me, with kindly eyes and beautiful laugh-lines in the corners, and her hair was shorter and grayer than in the picture I'd seen in Ian's old condo. With a purplish-blue button-down shirt and black silk pants under her pink apron, and pure white house slippers on her feet, she was the picture-perfect Asian mom.

She was utterly intimidating. And somewhat familiar.

"*Ayi*. The toilet is clogged." I met her eyes, then looked

down, ashamed.

She stepped past me and glanced at the toilet, then nodded, as if this were a common occurrence. I was so glad that I hadn't taken a shit. "I'm going to get the plunger."

"Xiexie, Ayi." Thanks, auntie.

I waited by my toilet of shame, hoping that no one else would come by, until she came back a minute later with a plunger. I reached to take it from her, but she continued into the bathroom.

"Wo lai ba, Ayi," I said. *Let me do it.*

She shook her head and said, "I've got it, I've got it. Go sit outside with everyone else."

I refused to leave, and I didn't want to get into a game of tug-of-war, so I had to watch helplessly as Ian's mom stuck the plunger into the toilet and began to plunge in earnest. Within a minute, the clog cleared and the toilet was flushable again.

"Yes!" Ian's mom said in English, then lifted her hand up to me, as if seeking a high-five. *Wait, really?* I wonderingly gave her one, and both of us laughed, relieving the pressure in my chest.

"Xiexie, Ayi." I gave her a genuine smile of relief.

She smiled back, then reached towards the sink to wash her hands. After, I belatedly washed my hands too.

"Anna, *ni zhende hao piaoliang." You're really beautiful,* she said. "I knew you'd be a good woman for Ian when I saw you in the Japanese restaurant. You have such an auspicious face."

The Japanese restaurant? I hadn't eaten at a Japanese restaurant since—OH. Oh.

THE Japanese restaurant.

Ian was the one who'd footed the bill at that fancy restaurant so long ago? The naggy son? He and his parents had witnessed that horrible moment? And Ian's mom thought that I had an *auspicious face*? What did that even mean? Was she really superstitious? Did she just—

She smiled, and her eyes were so lovely, large and expressive. So like Ian's. I smiled softly in return as my doubts evaporated. "I'm lucky to have Ian," I told her. "You have a very good son."

She took my hand and kneaded it, just as Ian did sometimes. "Tell me, do you love my son?"

I was surprised at the question, but didn't hesitate. "Yes. Very much." A tear slipped down my cheek.

She wiped it away and her smile grew brighter, more genuine. "That's good, that's good. Come on, come meet the family." She gently led me out to the backyard.

* * *

"I think my mom likes you better than she likes me," said Ian.

We'd just gotten back to his place from his aunt's place. I'd had too much to eat and drink, so I'd taken a nap on the car ride home. We were only just now getting around to the debrief.

"She's a really sweet lady. So funny." I smiled at Ian. "Your family members really *are* kinda like you."

Besides his mom, I'd met three of his uncles, two aunts, and six cousins, and they all really were like Ian in some way—lively, loving, and full of ridiculously corny jokes. They'd asked the usual questions, like how old I was, what I did for a living, when we would get married, when we would have kids...but Ian and I faced them together, hand-in-hand, and while we were met with some teasing (there would always be some), my answers didn't set off any avalanches.

Conversation, warm and easy, continued on, and by the end, I knew I'd be just fine seeing them again.

Especially for the food—his family could *cook*.

They were what a family should have been, what I'd always wished for, growing up. No families were perfect, and his certainly wasn't...but they were a good one, and they'd readily accepted me as one of their own.

He wrapped his arms around me and kissed my forehead. "Well..if they're like me, then you must love them."

I leaned back and laughed. "Uh huh."

"*Uh huh*. Does that mean that you love me, too?"

I nuzzled his chin with my nose. "Yes, as I've told you many times now."

Ah, that look on his face. The one he'd been giving me since the beginning.

He got down on one knee and took my left hand in both of his.

Oh shit. Tears sprang to my eyes and I covered my mouth with my other hand, the sudden rush of emotion nearly bringing me to my knees before him. He pressed my hand to his lips and gazed up at me with soft eyes, so tender and earnest. *The look*.

"Anna, we've been through a lot together. Heh, sometimes, it feels like we've had to free climb El Cap to get to where we are, you know? But the view from where we are now, together, is breathtaking. I can see the edge of the world with you, and every day feels like we're waking up on a clear, brisk morning, cozy in our sleeping bags, to that gorgeous sunrise, that perfect world of possibility. It's honestly so much better than anything I could have imagined."

He paused, cleared his throat, then continued. "But there's

one thing that could make it better. I know it's been less than a year, but even when I first met you, I already started asking this question in my head. Will you…"

I drew in a deep breath.

"…let me put it in your butt?"

"IAN! What the hell?" I pulled my hand out of his and slapped his shoulder.

He stood up and laughed in my face, then pulled me close and kissed me again. "I'm just kidding. I love you, too. So much." He buried his face in my hair and coiled his arms tightly around my waist, like an apologetic child.

Coward. How dare he make me the *butt* of a proposal joke? I'd been on the verge of tears from his speech, had filled my lungs with air to give him the biggest, most resounding *yes!* in the history of proposals. But it was all a joke.

Ass.

Then again…

That look in his eyes, that purest of emotions that I saw…his heartfelt speech. It really hadn't *seemed* like he was joking. The sentiment behind the gesture was surely real. Why hadn't he followed through?

Perhaps it *was* a bit soon. Or maybe he'd changed his mind at the last second, afraid of what I'd say. Maybe he'd actually listened to me when I said that I didn't plan on getting married, or thought that I'd react with horror and doubt, as I'd done once before to Asher.

But my actual reaction told me so much.

I knew that I would never tire of his kisses. His humor. His love. I would never tire of *him*.

And we were so strong as individuals. We'd only be stronger together, as partners.

294

Plus, tax benefits.

So I leaned back and gazed lovingly at him, pulling the next words *out* of my ass.

"Ian, I know that we haven't known each other for that long. But I get the feeling that, no matter how long we spend together, it will never be enough. Each and every day brings new revelations about your strength, your courage, your willingness to grow...and with each step we take together, mine as well. I've never been so in sync with someone, nor so attracted. Like, seriously, I can't stop staring at or touching your sexy-ass back muscles." He laughed as I stroked the muscles in question, pleased at their meaty firmness.

Then I got down on *my* knee, and gazed lovingly up at *him*. His eyes widened as I took his left hand in both of mine and pressed his hand to my lips, just as he'd done to me. But unlike him, I wasn't a coward. "I have a really big crush *on* you, and I want to spend forever crushing *alongside* you. Will you marry me?"

For a moment, he simply stood there, staring down at me, uncomprehending. When he finally understood that I was serious, his face crumpled, silent tears spilling over his cheeks as he got down onto his knees to plant sweet, wet kisses all over my face. Then he crushed me in his arms and I crushed him back, both of us joyfully embracing our future together.

Voice thick, he whispered in my ear, "Only if you get me a big diamond ring."

I laughed and wiped away my tears. "Then we might have to wait a little while." A long engagement suited me just fine, anyway. It would give me time to get used to the idea. Besides, then I could plan a totally unique wedding. Maybe one with llamas or climbing.

Ian gently lowered me to the ground and kissed my brow, then my nose. My lips. "For you…" He kissed my neck. "…I'd wait forever." He continued his slow trail of kisses, all the way down.

And then we had epic, magical, emotionally-fulfilling sex in a place that was *not* a bathroom.

Afterword

In September 2019, I quit my job in tech. I didn't have anything lined up after, and it was stressful to not know what was next, to not be in total control of my life. And I felt a little bit like a failure, because when I do something, I treat it like a climbing project—I always give 110%. Yet this time, despite my best efforts, I hadn't sent it. My job had broken me.

But after a lot of reflection, I realized that some things aren't worth giving 110% to.

But also, some things are.

This book was one of them.

After I quit my job, I didn't know what to do with myself. I cooked, I climbed, I watched stuff. I half-heartedly applied to other jobs. And I vegetated.

But boy did I *read*. A lot.

I've always found comfort in the written word, and this time was no exception. I gobbled up books for breakfast, lunch, and dinner, and I literally lost some weight as a result. But like most readers (I assume), I've always wondered what it would be like to be on the other side, to be the person weaving the story instead of the one waiting to see what happens. And with all of the free time that I had, it seemed like a good time to try.

So in October 2019, with the blessing and loving support of my husband, I wrote this book. It took me two months, start-to-finish, to publish something that was longer than my PhD dissertation. This is the kind of output that I'm capable of, when I give 110% to something that I *really* want to do. I mostly enjoyed my time in academia, and I mostly enjoyed my time in tech, but writing this book was *necessary* for me, an utter addiction.

I've lovingly filled these pages with every ounce of my being—my affection for my family, my appreciation for my friends, and my joy of life. So if you enjoyed this book, then I'm sure that we could be good friends (feel free to drop me a line!). And as my friend, I'd like to ask for your help. Please help keep my dream alive, and write a review for this book. Tell me what you think, and spread the word. I've got some great ideas for what happens in the next two books...but sometimes reality is hard, and all we can do is watch Asian dramas.

I'm thankful for the opportunity that I had to write this book, but I hope it's not the last. And with your help, it won't be.

Thank you, dear reader!

Acknowledgments

"Nothing's impossible when you've got great friends, *biatch*."

I have so many people to thank for helping with this book.

Lillian Ly and Leslie Huang, whose support and kind words helped convince me that I was not alone in my Chinese-American experiences, especially with respect to family. Special thanks to Lillian's sister Carol Ly (carollydesign.com) for providing guidance on the cover (your covers are amazing!) and to Leslie's friend, Andrew Chou, for providing the SF-NY-climber-tech-guy view.

Lan Nguyen and Mariana Barthelemy de Brito, for pointing out the weaknesses in the beginning and the end. It's so much more *butt*oned up now! #buttjokes But really, you guys helped me punch up the feelings so that the funny bits landed even better.

Erica Frohnhoefer, my most wonderfully critical editor, who soldiered through the book despite it being decidedly *not* her genre of choice. Your comments really helped to enhance the credibility of Ian's character so that he wasn't just a convenient asshole, as well as believability about life in New York.

Climber / tech buddy Brice Pollock (bricepollock.com) and real-life lady crusher Sadie Skiles. Because of Brice, Ian is so much better than a douchey tech-bro, and both of you helped me clean up my climbing scenes until it actually sounded like

I knew what I was talking about (shoutout to lady crusher Leslie here, too).

Jessie Booth and Matt Barackman, for reading it together as a couple and giving me great feedback on readability and flow...and for helping me boost my poor ego!

Rachel David, Lili Ehrlich, and Xin Gao, for lending their perspectives and helping with the realness of several key aspects of the story, and Jean Dahlquist, for taking time away from her own romance writing journey to help with mine. Check out her book when it's ready!

It's amazing how much trash gets collected when so many people work together to clean something up, and how much more beautiful it is in the end. This book would not be what it is without you. My deepest, heartfelt thanks.

Last, but not least, my husband, Jia Liu. He's never read a romance novel in his life (until now), but as a designer (jialiulabs.com), he's wonderfully intuitive and great at getting into people's heads. He was my sounding board, my life boat, my cover designer, my final reader, and of course, my muse. I'm so grateful for the opportunity to share with all of you just a fraction of the joy and happiness that I experience with this man every single day. Thanks, bub.

Made in the USA
San Bernardino, CA
11 December 2019

61246887R00190